ONCE UPON A MURDER

S.I. Gudger

Ampersand Press * Los Angeles

ONCE UPON A MURDER

A Polly Sloan Mystery
Published by Ampersand Press

Edited by: Wendy Allyson

Copyright ©1995 by S.I. Gudger
Printed in the United States of America

All rights reserved. No part of this book may be
reproduced or transmitted in any form or by any means,
including information storage and retrieval systems,
without the written permission of the author, except for
brief quotations to be used in a review.

Library of Congress Catalog Card Number: 95-96074

ISBN 0-9650224-7-1

First Printing November 1995

10 9 8 7 6 5 4 3 2 1

For my two nonfiction works

Wendy and Todd

DISCLAIMER

This is a work of fiction. All names, places, characters, and incidents are the author's invention and any resemblance to persons, living or dead, or actual events is entirely coincidental. The setting is fictitious and suggests with any actual name only a locale indicative of the one in this novel. The only purpose of this book is to entertain and the words used are solely for character and plot definition. No mode of behavior in this novel is held up as a standard for the reader and neither responsibility nor liability is accepted by Ampersand Press or the author for any personal interpretation of the text.

ACKNOWLEDGMENTS

Even though the exhaustive pace of meeting deadlines, dealing with unforeseen obstacles, making critical decisions on no sleep, and frantic last minute telephone conferences may have created the impression once or twice that this novel was a one-person production; it was not.

Sincere thanks go to my family for their early and favorable reviews; to George Mendoza for his technical expertise to an author who is computer illiterate; to Noel Jason Scott of Grand Graphics, Covina, for his artistic interpretation of a cover drawing by Steven Aragon; and to Fran Jessee for her encouragement and guidance above and beyond the scope of her job as Account Executive for Griffin Printing, Gendale, California.

*Finding web of spider does not prove
which spider spin web.*

Quotations from Charlie Chan
copyright © 1968: Warner Bros. - Seven Arts, Inc.
Based on a character created by
EARL DERR BIGGERS

ONE

"I'm absolutely consumed with curiosity. I have to ask. Ma'am, why is the word *PISS* on your suitcase?"

As Polly looked directly at the airline ticket agent she answered once again the familiar question.

"When I purchased the bag three years ago from an exclusive leather shop in New York, the girl who waited on me was the daughter of the store's owner. This fact was enough to have gotten her hired, but unfortunately not enough to have instilled in her an adequate presence of mind regarding the handling of even the simplest of tasks. I purchased this case in spite of her attempts to dissuade me from what I wanted to what some rapid-fire sales training course had assured her that I had to have. This case has an excellent warranty which was dated and registered

Once Upon a Murder

at the time of the sale as an added courtesy to the buyer. I was asked to fill out the warranty card with my complete name and address and I complied. The girl took the case and the warranty card into the back room and returned shortly with the case and the warranty receipt, concluding the transaction satisfactorily--I thought. I could see that she was pleased with herself about something and I realized what it was when she handed me the bag and showed me the extra touch she had taken it upon herself to add without my permission. The salesgirl explained that fourteen karat gold initials were included with each purchase and she had imprinted them on the suitcase from the name on the warranty card. My complete name is Pollidora Isabelle Stanford-Sloan. The clerk had even used her own initiative to give me the extra letter since only three were usually provided per customer."

Polly paused in her story hoping she had sufficiently explained, but the look on the ticket agent's face was similar to the one on the salesgirls so she continued.

"I politely tried to tell her I would prefer not to have my initials on the case as I had not requested it to be done and didn't care whether there was a charge for the service or not. The clerk told me it was impossible to remove the initials as the process the store used required burning them into the leather. I could see by this

Once Upon a Murder

time that the girl was becoming overwrought at my audacity and would soon break into tears if I didn't take the case the way she had altered it. I finally agreed to take the bag when, after asking her to look at the letters several times in the hope that a light might go on somewhere, she still did not realize what the initials spelled. Either she couldn't spell or she was completely ignorant of her own bodily functions and I hadn't decided at that point which of the two choices I believed suited her best. I walked out of the store mumbling to myself about the incompetence and general lack of service provided by people in service-oriented positions. I have long since forgiven the girl and rather enjoy the case as a conversation piece. Since I'm not a particularly pretentious person I find it amusing the interest and misplaced embarrassment people assume on my behalf."

Polly's last remark had silenced the ticket agent and he busied himself attaching the luggage tag to her suitcase. He directed her to the boarding gate and wished her a pleasant trip. Polly thanked the agent and started walking toward the gate to board her flight. She tried to get caught up in the excitement of other vacationing passengers around her who, like herself, labored all year for a short burst of freedom and happiness away from home. She automatically offered her boarding

Once Upon a Murder

pass at the gate and prepared to settle herself for the hours on the plane that would deliver her into the sunny seclusion she richly deserved after the hectic pace of last semester at Clairhaven University.

The mere thought of her last semester made her cringe. Why she had taken on an additional class to add to her already overloaded schedule could only be explained as sheer lunacy. She had been at the English Department Meeting just like all the other professors and none of them had volunteered for hazardous duty by agreeing to take Dr. Florens' Beginning Comp. Class. The Department Chair had singled her out with his desperate eyes when he had pleaded for help and she found herself responding rather than let the two week old class be canceled.

Unfortunately all of the students in this particular class needed serious help of one kind or another. She had posted extended conference hours and even agreed to take a few students to her office after class for individual tutoring . To these few students she had given her home phone number so meeting times could be adjusted if necessary. With all the calls she had received at home last semester about everything that even bordered on English, someone must have added her name and telephone number to the graffiti in the rest room. She could visualize it now in large

Once Upon a Murder

letters scrawled over the toilet paper dispenser--*Dr. Sloan gives great*, and in very small letters, *advice to students*. As she smiled to herself about the ingenuity of the students in all of her classes, she couldn't help being mildly pleased and enormously relieved that she had been successful in helping them squeak by with satisfactory grades even if she wouldn't dare guess all the hours of work it had cost her. She couldn't remember when she had been through a rougher semester and that was why she was especially looking forward to this vacation.

Over the years Polly and her friend Sara had developed a sort of pre-vacation noncommunication policy several weeks before they would meet. Neither one wanted to intrude prematurely on the pleasure of those first days of sharing stories from their independent experiences during the semester. This year that policy had been easier to keep with Polly's heavy schedule and with Sara giving a series of Art History Lectures on top of her regular university classes. Even so, Polly had picked up the phone to call Sara dozens of times before inevitably talking herself out of it. Strangely, it had been Sara that had broken the silence with a late night call Monday evening. Sara had sounded as if under a strain and, while her anticipation of their meeting was genuine, there seemed to be a reticence on

Once Upon a Murder

Sara's part to confide the cause of her uneasiness to Polly. Sara finally admitted that some things had happened recently which had made her uncomfortable being alone in her apartment, but that she would explain completely when Polly arrived in Florida. Sara said that she was sending something to Polly in the mail and hoped it was received before Polly left Minneapolis.

Polly had been puzzled by the way her friend had left her hanging with only part of the story and became even more puzzled by the letter she received from Sara a few days later. Taking out the much read sheets of paper Sara had sent her, Polly read first the short paragraph from Sara's computer:

Dear Poll--Here is the letter I spoke to you about over the phone. I thought it a harmless prank one of my students might have devised and I ignored it, besides you know how I detest writing anything and leave all my letters of any kind for my assistant at the University. I received the letter about five days ago and had completely forgotten about it and, maybe there is no connection, but yesterday I took a rather peculiar fall on the stairs in my building. Nothing serious, but nevertheless I send the enclosed to you for your opinion as well as your usual bizarre interpretation. Can't wait to see you. Love Sara

Polly unfolded the second sheet of paper and read:

CHAIN LETTER

Through the innocent to the guilty
                where will this letter stop?
If you're innocent send it on;
                if you're guilty let it drop.

You can not afford to ignore this letter. Follow the instructions below carefully and return this letter to the first name on the list within five days or you will receive a more insistent message. Your participation is a lifetime guarantee.

Polly had tried to call Sara after she had received and read the letter but had been unable to reach her; Sara's answering machine only spewed out a list of engagements and commitments she would be fulfilling over the next month--this week she was lecturing out of town up until the day of Polly's arrival.

What could the letter mean? As the plane touched ground, taxied, and then deplaned its passengers Polly tried to read between the lines. What kind of person would send such a letter and with what ultimate intentions in mind? Was it the author's purpose to generate fear and to have control over the recipient or had the letter been sent just for general malicious principles? Was it from a student who hadn't received the desired grade in one of Sara's classes? What kind of fall did Sara have and what were the circumstances surrounding it that would make the most unsuspecting of natures like hers suspect something malevolent?

Polly was entering the baggage claim area so she quickly folded and put the two sheets of paper back in the envelope hoping that she had worried without cause. She had pleaded emergency travel changes to the airline and had been able to arrange an earlier departure date which made her feel somewhat better but no closer to finding out what was going on at her destination.

If only baggage claim were as easy as the name implied! Polly searched the overhead signs for the flight number below which her luggage would eventually swing into view on the circular rotating belt. Finding flight 201 to be on the sign over the middle carousel of the three in this area she went to position herself not where the luggage would emerge from the interior belt that was hidden from view by a rubber flap, but almost completely around to the far side of the belt where no crowd had as yet gathered.

Once Upon a Murder

Polly had boarded the plane in Minneapolis wearing a full-length lined raincoat which she had no need for here so she slipped it under the handle of her large open-topped canvas carry on bag which held her necessary personal items. She always traveled with this bag since her fiasco five years ago when she had temporarily lost her checked luggage including a similar raincoat by relying on airline expertise to reunite her with her belongings at the end of her flight. The promise of returning her luggage within two days had turned into ten and when she finally took possession of her luggage she found that it had been opened and ransacked for valuables by persons unknown. The bags' exterior surface displayed the trauma of its travel and she was intrigued about the route it had taken since one bag had advertisements about a special tour to Buckingham Palace while the other bore several *Welcome to Warsaw* stickers on it.

Polly could see the first of the bags from flight 201 begin to appear on the luggage belt about five to ten feet apart. These were the bags of the last minute boarders and inconsiderate travelers who held up the flight because they refused to show up thirty minutes before departure time as requested by the airline. Somehow it seemed unfair that at baggage claim these same people should be rewarded by seeing their luggage parade first in this three-ringed baggage circus. Perhaps knowing

Once Upon a Murder

the last on first off positioning of luggage had become too widely known among regular flyers because, to Polly, over the years these travelers made up an ever increasing breed of stragglers on her flights.

Passengers that she recognized from flight 201 were starting to fill out the space around the adjacent carousels as well as the central one because every seat on her plane had been sold and the area was too crowded nearest to their baggage claim belt to accommodate the large number of travelers. As more and more people filtered into the area it became even hotter and noisier than before. She was intent on maintaining her original position by refusing to be jostled away from it by more aggressive and later arriving travelers. She was determined to stand fast to her spot when her attention was distracted by an insistent tug on her arm.

Polly's concentration was being interrupted by a short elderly lady who was leaning with one hand upon a wooden cane while with the other she had been applying constant and increasing pressure on Polly's arm. Now that Polly's awareness was brought down to focus on the lady she apologized for her inattention and asked what she could do for her. The lady introduced herself only as a senior citizen who had come to Florida with a group of women from New York. The lady was distressed because she couldn't attract the attention of any of the overburdened porters to help her and the other ladies remove their luggage from the carousel. None of them were quick enough to extract their bags in time without severe strain or possible injury to their fragile frames.

Standing around Polly were ten or more women aged she guessed to be between sixty-five and eighty. Of course, she reassured the women she would be glad to help them, but as she looked up and around her to take in the larger area of the three conveyor belts she saw chaos. The third flight had come in during her distraction and now all around the room were groups of milling lost souls like those in the limbo of Milton's *Paradise Lost*. Polly could see that the carousel for flight 228 had broken down and there were several sweaty baggage handlers carrying baggage out from carts just beyond the passengers' view. The handlers were working as fast as they could to set the bags on the impotent conveyor belt where passengers were eagerly pawing over them in hopes of finding theirs first.

Polly couldn't find anyone to help her with the almost hysterical seniors so she volunteered to remove their bags from the belt and then secure porters to escort them from the baggage claim area. She had successfully removed two bags from the belt when its speed suddenly increased, the reason for which she could not immediately understand. It might have had something to do with the controls for the other belt which were being repaired, but at the moment she was too busy to speculate as to why the belt with luggage from her flight had picked up speed. The lady-with-the-cane's friend standing nearby, who had been addressed as Astrid, was gesturing as a plaid belted suitcase wheeled into view. The lady-with-the-cane said, "Oh please get that one. It belongs to Astrid."

Polly leaned out ahead of her position on the circular perimeter of the belt to put her hand on the bag's handle at the first opportunity. As she grasped it at the full extension of her balance several things happened at once. The excited woman with the cane, stamping it nervously over and over again while moving closer to the belt near Polly, unknowingly brought the rubber tipped foot of the cane down on the toe of Polly's stable front foot which was supporting the majority of her weight. At the same time Polly was jostled from behind by an enraged group of passengers who were trying to get out of the maelstrom of overheated bodies. Polly could only turn her head quickly to yell to her newly found friend to move her cane for fear she would cause the woman to go sprawling without its support as Polly toppled gracelessly onto the belt. She fell on her side atop

Once Upon a Murder

a bilious blue two-suiter, a shapeless flowered magenta satchel and a hard brown businessman's attache case.

No one seemed dismayed about her condition as she righted herself just in time to prevent her skirt, which was caught in a crevice of the belt, from being dragged over her head as she revolved in the opposite direction. She was now not anywhere near her group of ladies as she continued on her way around the belt. Anguished faces begged for her help. She became like a *Joan of Arc* from the Ages; she was St. Polly--patron saint of luggage. All around her shouts of help welled up until they formed one helpless cry. She couldn't resist coming to the aid of the people behind the voices. Pushing up the sleeves on her yellow blouse she hefted first one and then another bag over the rubber rail to waiting and eagerly thankful hands.

As she came around to the lady-with-the-cane she was glad to see that her own fall had not caused the lady any injury. She yelled out to stand back as she carefully lifted the plaid troublemaker to put it on the floor in front of her little group of senior citizens. As she grabbed the handle with her left hand the buckle from one of the bag's belts caught in her left stocking leg. She had no time to disengage the one from the other so she simply pulled the bag free and placed it on the floor where she herself had stood only moments before. Her left leg now bore its battle wound proudly as a large oddly shaped hole exposed her flesh to the world while several major runs took off for parts unknown.

She labored tirelessly around the belt helping first this passenger then that one until she was noticed by the passengers from the doomed-belt flight as well as the passengers from the New York flight which had been the last of the three to arrive. The shouting of cheers began and applause as people saw her as the one functioning human among a mechanized catastrophe. She continued to off-load bags until the crowd around her had thinned and almost completely dispersed.

The belt she was on began to slow and then stopped as two uniformed security guards approached her position and carefully lifted her off the belt and set her on the floor. Their uniforms were no longer dry as the broken air conditioning system in baggage claim had merged the sweat patterns of their shirts into one. They explained to her that what she had done was against Airport Regulations . When she tried to explain her plight as accidental they halted her story, stating only that it was too hot for the paperwork she would cause them to report her and they would let her go with a warning.

Once Upon a Murder

She noticed that whereas before on the rotating belt she had been a heroine, on the floor she was stared at and avoided as a kook or an eccentric of some sort. She looked around to find that the lady-with-the-cane and her traveling companions had gone. Polly refused to let her enthusiasm be daunted by Airport Security, the heat, the ungrateful passengers, or the state of her appearance. She rolled her blouse sleeves down, buttoned them, and straightened her skirt which had been twisted until the side zipper appeared in front. There were several black stains along the bottom of her skirt and in one place the hem had been torn loose. Her stockings were laughable and the nails she had carefully nurtured for months in preparation for a relatively inactive vacation were once again broken and ugly nubs.

The belt from flight 201 had been restarted and her suitcase was easily removed as it came within her reach. Her carry on bag had fallen over and been trampled on spilling some of the contents on the floor. As she picked up the letter Sara had sent her Polly felt a vague darkness block the Florida sun glaring in from outside. The letter only brought back the uneasiness Polly had sensed in Sara's last communication. Polly finished shoving her belongings back into the bag, keeping out the baggage claim ticket that the agent had stapled to her ticket wallet in Minneapolis, and walked over to join the other passengers filing out of the baggage claim area.

TWO

Temperature 106 degrees humidity 90 percent. Tomorrow's high expected to reach over 110 with a slight rise in the humidity as records for June in our city are surpassed daily. This is Myron Boggs for KKOX where we only promise the music and the DJ will be cool, not the weather.

Polly tried to tune out the radio announcer's proverbial patter and settle into the rhythmic lunge and halt of the cab. She was being badly racked over the lumpy back seat and was just barely resisting the urge to yell again to the driver, Juan Capistrano, to slow down. Her previous attempts to reason with the man had resulted in Juan telling her, "You be O.K., lady, I best taximan in city."

The humidity was unbearable for Polly since she usually dealt with two known weather conditions only: cold and beyond freezing cold.

Once Upon a Murder

She was thankful that she had discreetly wriggled out of her damaged pantyhose in the back seat of the cab and had stuffed them in her bag. Now at least her legs could breathe. The silk material of her blouse was soaked through and prevented her upper body from getting any air, not to mention the adhesive fit of the fabric Juan kept staring at through his rearview mirror. Moisture was running steadily now down her neck, between her breasts, and under her arms.

Trying to take her mind off the heat and the lurching cab she looked around the back seat where passengers sat who were ferried twenty-four hours a day by the A-1 Cab Company. At the prices charged each tenth of a mile it certainly was an expensive and unglamorous way to commute. She wondered but really didn't want to know who had been here before her sitting where she sat now. What else had been done in this seat aside from the obvious vandalism of the seatbelt being ripped from its moorings? What kind of woman had written the name Phyllis and a telephone number on the armrest? What person had taken the time and felt the need to scratch the names of betting entrepreneurs on the metal door frame just for a little free advertising? Polly could understand after a ride like this why anyone would take revenge on the cab company, but she decided defacing property wasn't a satisfactory recourse for her.

"Lady, we almost there. I make good time. Juan knows many short cuts."

With a sharp left turn he careened onto Woodley Court and suddenly slammed on his brakes at the curb.

"Holy shit, lady, look at the cops! This a convention or somethin'? I never seen so many cars flashing lights even on them TV cop shows."

Polly stared speechlessly at the scene in front of her. Don't panic she told herself. There's a perfectly simple explanation for a few police cars to be here--someone had a heart attack; there was a burglary. Just a few police cars...seven, ten, eleven police cars and an ambulance. Oh God, an ambulance!

Blocking the street around the pink stuccoed Meadow Oaks Apartments vehicles were wedged into every conceivable opening. Five or six police cars formed a periphery of protection as a Special Forces van and two ambulances lined up on the lawn. A strip of yellow provided a barrier between the apartments and the onlookers two and three deep trying to see what was being hidden from them. Just then a man in a drenched dress shirt jumped on the van bumper and yelled in his bullhorn for the crowd to disperse. He also announced that all residents from the surrounding apartments and houses would be questioned individually during the process of the investigation.

Sweeping her eyes incredulously across the scene preventing her entrance to Sara's building, Polly's subconscious read the words in yellow on the police banner--**Crime Scene Do Not Cross.** The taste of pure and strong stomach acid slowly backed its way down her throat as the full impact of Sara's vaguely expressed fear passed into Polly's consciousness. Not fully roused from her shock at the scene, yet realizing instinctively that some action was expected from her, she pushed open the taxi door and started to walk away. Before she had gone more than a few steps Juan thrust a suitcase into her left hand and took as payment for his services the first single bill she could pull from her wallet. She had no idea the denomination of the bill, but the smile that reached her through her haze signaled the welcomed end to the transaction for both of them.

Feeling light-headed and confused she moved toward a small group of people starting to leave the area. As they passed her she heard snatches of conversation, words unconnected, members of the group talking over each other without waiting to see if anyone was listening. "Another violent crime." "Who was it?" "Why here in our neighborhood?" "Mostly senior citizens...who would want to kill them?" "Murdered in their beds." "Nothing exciting ever happens on my block." But why?" The words brought Polly up sharply into awareness again and the last of her fog wore off leaving her shaken yet determined to find out in any way she could what had happened inside the apartment building. She wouldn't let herself reason beyond the fact that this craziness had nothing at all to do with Professor Sara Jean Cornwall.

She tentatively approached an elderly couple standing a short distance from the barrier. The man was holding and gently rocking a petite gray-haired woman while the officer who had been speaking with the couple was coming directly toward Polly.

"Officer, please, can you tell me what's happened here?"

"Ma'am, I can't answer any of your questions so please stand back and away from the barrier so we can do our job."

"But someone said there was a murder. Who? Who was murdered?"

"Ma'am, I can't tell you anything. Go home"

"I won't. I mean I can't. This *is* where I'm staying . That is if I can get in. I just flew here to visit someone who lives in these apartments. Please tell me she's not involved."

Once Upon a Murder

The officer made a slight pause, reconsidering his words and lowering his voice and his attitude a little.

"Ma'am, I'm really sorry, but that would be against regulations until the next of kin has been notified."

A cry escaped before she could stop it.

"Then someone has been murdered?"

"Two someones, I can tell you that much," the officer said as he hurriedly walked away to step inside the yellow-bordered street scene and mingle with the other uniformed officers.

She understood that he was only parroting police procedure, but this was one story she wouldn't wait to read about in tomorrow's newspaper. And then what would she know? Need to know basis. Need to know. She damn well needed to know and right now. Everything she would have to do would be justified by her right to do it. In the absence of Sara's next of kin, she thought this in the abstractest of ways, Polly was going to act on behalf of the family Cornwall. Under normal circumstances she wouldn't have dared contemplate interfering with a murder investigation, but this was Sara and that meant anything goes.

She had only been standing there on the grass of the apartment building for a short time but she felt exhausted and dragged down somehow physically as well as emotionally. The weight of the suitcase she had been hanging onto since leaving the cab had numbed the fingers in her hand. When she tried to shift the bag and regrasp the handle her numbed fingers refused to respond. She let go and the bag fell. She was forcing herself to think of some way to get inside while she massaged her hand and coaxed the circulation to return. She needed one hundred percent cooperation from her body and her mind and she needed it now.

There was a small private alcove over to the side of the building for two apartments, 1A and 1B, these were two of the units built after the original apartment construction. Polly remembered Sara telling her about these and a few others which had private entrances at the rear near the garages. The original units, including Saras, were all accessed through a central patio enclosed by a wrought iron gate. The gate was the center of the police activity and there was no way she could get through as an unauthorized observer.

The privacy of the alcove gave her a chance to regroup while taking her away from the scrutiny of the law enforcement officers. She dropped her bag on the concrete porch and paced the small area trying to formulate a way to get inside. She couldn't do that for more than a few minutes before worry and fear supplanted the space in her mind she needed to build a plan of action. She looked back beyond the yellow tape and saw that more cars were being allowed to enter the restricted area. One of them was a TV Station van followed by two regular vehicles. Judging from the equipment being unloaded from the cars she guessed they must be affiliated with the news media in some way too.

Suddenly there was a commotion. One of the men holding a minicam had snuck under the yellow tape and was running toward the front gate. She used it. Polly quickly reached in her bag pulled out her camera and put it around her neck. She snapped a professional looking extender lens on the camera and several rolls of film on the strap. She threw her carry on back into the alcove, grabbed her purse, and started to mix with the others carrying equipment. Looking for a natural way to establish herself as one of the party, she went to the open trunk of a 1992 white Honda where she could see a man taking cases and equipment out and putting it on the curb. Polly stepped up and started helping him unload the trunk.

The man who stood up and challenged her with his eyes was short, chubby, and she decided immediately, inherently irritable. He was puffing from the exertion and wheezing through his nose from a long neglected deviated septum. To add to

Once Upon a Murder

his distressed breathing he coughed several times, and as if on cue, drew another unfiltered cigarette from his pocket and lit up.

"So you're the new junior photog back-up they sent me. A little old for a junior anything, aren't you? I heard it was a woman, not that I mind working with a woman, just so she knows it's me that gives the orders. This your first murder? I thought so. Well I've seen lots. I'll show ya how to get the most mileage out of your shots and how to make the other rags take notice when I pick the shot that hits the street in the morning. What's your name?"

"Polly Sl---"

"Polly's good enough. I like it. I'm the trainer; you're the bird. You got nice legs for a bird. Pretty funny ain't I to come up with lines like that without even thinking or anything? O.K. let's go. I wanna be ready when they let us in. Wait a minute. Hold on there. What'reya tryin' to pull?"

Polly was dumbfounded at having been discovered. She knew it hadn't been the best opening, but it had been the soonest. She'd just apologize and pretend she made a mistake and was looking for...

"Where's your press badge? They didn't give ya one, did they? *Stupid ass newspaper brass*. That's what I always say. They don't know anything about how important a badge is. Without one you can't get in. Here, I always carry extras. Clip this on that nice looking wet blouse and let's go. Remember, you take the general shots for background: furnishings, objects d'art and like that . Sometimes I need them to think out my angle. I do the people shots. Freeze frames of pain I call 'em. What you'll hear in there...take notes. I don't. It's all up here. Once I hear it, ya understand...?"

She nodded as he continued to make his final point by thumping his forehead with four fingers until she could feel his headache developing.

"Name's Hecht, Milo Hecht. Let's go Polly."

THREE

"Hey Milo, how's that old fart you work for?"

"Still better than the turd at that toilet-paper you work for. Push in there Polly, over to the left against the wall. Good angle, not too crowded, and I can smoke without some asshole saying 'it's too close in here for smoking.' Want one?"

"No thanks, I don't ..."

"Yeah, yeah, I should have known."

"Who's he, the man with the black hair who looks like he hasn't slept in days?" Polly ventured, at once recognizing him as the man who had made the announcement to the crowd outside.

"That's Savitch. This case is his I'll bet. And by the way he's yellin' at his gofer, Detective Burch, things ain't being handled to his pussy-assed satisfaction. A good cop. Our misfortune's that he hates the press. He's coming over to give his little spiel. We won't get much with him at the scene, but maybe you could get him to give ya a personal statement ...?"

"I'm sure he'll give us what information he can, what he's allowed to tell us that is. He seems nice enough, maybe just tired and upset about what's in there." She nodded toward the bedroom of apartment nine, across the courtyard and up the stairs from Sara's number five. The location of the murdered victims had allowed her heart to return to its regular pumping rate. She was shamefully glad the murders were in this apartment and not anywhere close to Sara. Though the victims' names had not been mentioned, she had overheard them referred to as *the couple* and she was all but sure one of the two was not her friend.

"Him upset about what's in there. You must be daft. He's seen it all. It's routine for him and for me--we're professionals--and after tonight it'll be routine for you too old girl."

She doubted that. But the man who was talking to her and the group from the press had lapsed into what she suspected was a standard no disclosure speech which she hoped would preface the basic factual information she was waiting to hear. After that she would simply dump this sexist cretin Milo with some ruse about getting out of the apartment for a little air. As she was dragged into hearing what she had only been half-heartedly listening to, she decided that Sgt. Savitch couldn't really feel as matter-of-fact about death as his manner implied. As his monotone droned on from the standard material to the particulars of this case his voice changed to a singsong rhythm that would have been an interesting linguistic challenge to analyze if things had been different. She was listening intently now.

"...Jacobson, Harriet A. and Stephen T., 66 and 68 respectively. No time of death yet and wouldn't give it to you if I had it. I don't want anybody planning their alibis before I tell them they need one. The heat hasn't helped either. I imagine Herb's going to take a little while with this one. But since they aren't too aromatic yet it can't have been more than...well let's just say we have a witness who saw them recently and will help us to narrow the time field. I will let you hear a general statement from the coroner and then, since we're done in there, I will allow five minutes--don't beg--five minutes only for pictures as the bodies are brought through here. If any one of you breaks the rules or goes beyond the officers to get a particularly artsy shot you'll all have to leave. Got it? Herb, over here.

"This is Herb Nettleman, coroner for the county. Just tell them a little Herb. We don't want them to know more than is necessary to meet their deadlines. They don't have to solve this crime and we certainly wouldn't want them to try. With such

Once Upon a Murder

minds as these on the track of a killer they would no doubt put us both out of work posthaste."

Savitch, finding that sardonically hysterical, sent up a tension releasing chuckle as he stepped over to confer with several officers waiting for instructions.

"Cause of death strangulation for the woman; a clunk on the head for the old guy. Maybe he wasn't supposed to be home. I say that because her death was prolonged and took our murderer a little time. I would say premeditated because there are signs it was a culmination of something, a long awaited event between the two of them. Her husband met a quick death. Afterwards the killer hung around for a while--playing, ridiculing, defining--you put a name to it. You'll see when the victims are uncovered. Don't know anything specific except that the killer touched the victims a lot, specifically the woman, seemed to be arranging them according to his memory of something from the past. That's all."

"Did ya hear that? We got a real psycho here. Probably a serial killer. Maybe this is the beginning of somethin' big for Milo. Four or five murders like this is good for months, could even be a year. Good material like this stays on the first couplea pages before it moves on to be a back page item. And sister do I ever know how to milk it."

Once Upon a Murder

Polly strained to ignore the callousness of Milo's declaration. He fed on the maudlin for his livelihood. It wasn't hard to see why the sergeant hadn't welcomed the press. He must see them here now as she did, all of them relishing the goriest detail--hyped with anticipation over viewing the corpses. She only felt like an intruder, an intruder into the private world of the Jacobsons. Looking around, she put away the pad she had scratched the facts on for Milo and began to take a few shots of the room just to stop the insistent nudging of an elbow that belonged to Milo the Magnificent, *journaliste extraordinaire*.

Leave now she thought. She slowly pivoted around while taking a few shots of a comfortable living room grouping where the Jacobsons had probably started their evening watching the five o'clock news. Backing up, trying to exit casually from the rapidly flashing camera-fest, she suddenly found herself sandwiched between them on all sides and literally propelled to the forefront by an older journalist who gracefully nodded as he said, "ladies first." A fine time to play the gentleman! She was stuck. Milo sidled in next to her and congratulated her for pushing in front of everyone else.

Two stretchers were being wheeled out by three men and a woman dressed in medical coveralls. Under Savitch's direction the stretchers were placed side by side with the feet not eighteen inches from where she stood. Before Polly had time to prepare herself the sheets were pulled back and flashes brightened and dimmed in unison over her head and around her from both sides. She focused on the feet of the victims in front of her and quickly drew her camera to her eyes to prevent her uncontrollable peripheral vision from seeing upward to their faces. Through the camera it was unreal, an historic moment, a distant image far from reality; yet the expletives that hit her ears were like drugs to her mind enticing her to look at what they had seen. Theirs were excited voices. The voracious and insatiable voices of the press were clamoring for more information about the faces. She had to look. Inching her camera up from the feet she focused on the bright blue print of a summer housedress. She was up to the neck and hadn't seen any blood--of course not--the woman had been strangled. But she still expected to see blood and was preparing herself for it. Slowly the chin, the mouth, the cheeks and nose, and the eyes...they hadn't closed the eyes. Her slick fingers lost hold of the camera when she saw those eyes and out from behind her Nikon shield she found herself staring openly at the dead woman's face.

She had to swallow frequently as she continued to stare; nausea was approached and overcome repeatedly at the impersonalized way this couple's death was being received around the room. The light and almost jovial banter of the crime team was epitomized by the two officers near the stretchers talking about an upcoming baseball game. Next to her Milo was stretching and reaching for just the right angle on his shot, staying barely within the rules they had been given. What was the right angle on the reality of death? There was only one angle she could see, straight forward and head-on. There was nothing curved or rounded about these violent deaths. They were one-dimensional, flat and ugly. Two people had been drained of life and essence and the dignity of self, and the right not to be viewed like this had been taken from them. There was no blood. More than once she looked for it, needed it, as if dying meant to let go unwillingly of the red fluid that had been consciously trapped and hoarded by its owner. No wonder those around her talked of other things: perspective, objectivity, sanity made them do it. She didn't envy the investigating unit the morbid and tireless task of finding out who had done this.

And why, when the killer had finished the Jacobsons' lives, had he not left? Why had he stayed to do the other? Looking from her face to his face and back again Polly tried to interpret what she was seeing, unable to release herself from

Once Upon a Murder

the coldly analytical turn her mind had fashioned on. The killer had painted the faces, not carefully or well, but nevertheless with some perverse logic in his own mind. He had done it on the man as well as the woman, making on each a second face: eyebrows above eyebrows, exaggerated eyelashes on the lids and on the high bones beneath the eyes. And around the mouth a second set of lips, a simple outline on his face, a smile on hers--the effect on both was identical--nothing could enliven the unbending stillness of the mute victims.

Looking at them made her think of the crayon drawings her own daughter had brought her proudly from kindergarten. Thinking and feeling released her forced enchantment with death and she was overcome by a wave of nausea she couldn't swallow as she backed out quickly through the open door, running down the stairs she knew would take her to the side of the building and away from the two dead faces.

FOUR

"You didn't. You couldn't have. You, who can't even force yourself to step on a spider, forced your way onto the scene of a violent crime!" Sara rolled her eyes and shook her head in disbelief from her firmly ensconced position deep in the cushions of her buttery-soft sofa.

"I did. I had to. I didn't do it for some perverse pleasure or because I preferred those surroundings over any other on the first day of my vacation. I was terrified that somehow the violence might have been done to you. After all, your letter was dangerously cryptic and you are s-o-o-o-o helpless."

As if to make her point Polly poured the contents from a hot kettle into the foot soaker in front of Sara.

"You should have known I wouldn't be so inconsiderate as to get myself murdered on the first day of your vacation. How could I even contemplate such a thing anyway? If I were dead I'd miss visualizing another momentous expression and the galvanization into action that always follows."

Once Upon a Murder

"...and it shouldn't really surprise you that once again I refused to do as I was told by authority figures, in this case the police, and remain where I was told. Just mention the words *it's not allowed* or *you can't possibly do that* and that's exactly where I'll be and what I'll be doing to prove otherwise. It's such a fine line between compliance and rebellion--you need very special shoes to walk it--and I have mine custom-made."

"How did you get in and how did you get out again without Milo in tow?"

The question asked, she was doing it again; she was quickly going over in her mind what she would have done if their situations had been reversed and it had been she instead of Polly waiting for news outside the apartment building. She had to do it now. Actions didn't always come to her when she needed them. She had to hammer out a rough plan in her head while she was thinking about the probability that she might need it someday. She could retrieve it from her mind's menu just like she could access files from her computer under.....under what? MURDER.PLANS, ESCAPE.IDEAS, TACTICS.POLICE. Too many letters. Too many letters for the computer, dummy, not to remember when you need them.

Sara's mind veered off the specific subject and onto the general area of differences between herself and Polly. They both knew she had her own brand of spunk and outrageousness. It was just that she hadn't had as many fallen idols in her life as Polly so she was more reserved and practiced propriety with an outsider, she was more believing in people as she saw them. Sara had never liked having to force herself to fit into uncomfortable people situations. She would usually back off; Polly would invade. Where Polly being Polly could impose herself anywhere without recriminations; Sara being Sara would rationalize that it wasn't worth the effort. Sara would have been at the murder scene pressing the officers, screaming and demanding and maybe even crying as part of her repertoire until she had made a spectacle of herself, then she would have been told what she wanted to know just to get rid of her. She wondered again how two so different temperaments had withstood so many years of friendship and, yes, appreciation of each other.

"Yo, are you listening? It was really pretty easy since I was determined to find out if anything had happened to you no matter what I had to do. Standing on the curb with that obnoxiously crude toad Milo I think I would have had no compunction about shoving him in his own trunk and doing his job alone if it had been necessary."

It was as if Sara's thoughts had been transferred into Polly's voice. Do something.

Take action. If something or somebody was in the way use the bulldozer effect. To Polly over and over again it seemed to be the right decision at the time. It never occurred to Sara until it had been done by Polly. It was a funny kind of compatibility but it worked, and the unimportant differences between them fell into the background.

"I see your judgment of men has softened." Sara knew Polly liked men, that is, given the necessity for another sex.

"You noticed. But he was so stereotypical. 'Watja doin tanite babee?' You know Homo sapiens, genus Homo for man without the sapiens part from sapere--to be wise. I just don't think Descartes would have appreciated his basic philosophical premise being changed in this day and age to the deep and complex male viewpoint: *I fuck, therefore I am.* Milo is another perfect anatomical specimen; his brain is in his jockstrap."

"Polly, you have to be exposed to a lot of basic types before you can appreciate a gem when you meet him. The average working man is not going to inquire into your knowledge of opera; not going to know that you're rarely without a classic of literature in your purse, and certainly not be aware that the purse is precariously perched on your shoulder by an almost imperceptible wood chip. The average man at heart and in reality is a fruit sampler in the produce stand of life. He's anxious to squeeze a couple more melons and rate them against others he's picked from the market."

"Ah, now I know why I have such an aversion to produce men in markets. Thank you for explaining it to me." Polly was always amused by Sara's fruit analogies. Sara never questioned the man/woman attraction, it was simply there and Sara fell readily into her role when the occasion presented itself.

"Enough, enough. Tell me how they were murdered, but try to tone it down for me would you?"

As Sara prepared for the interpretation of facts, for that was surely what she would get, her foot and ankle wouldn't let her completely relax. Torn and twisted inside she had refused to have it immobilized by the doctor. She had chosen the longer and more tedious method to cure her injury. She was also refusing to take the pain killers prescribed unless she absolutely couldn't sleep and she guessed this would be one of those nights.

"I can be somewhat objective now but seeing them, forcing myself to see them if only for you, brought back stronger than ever my inability to deal with death, to accept the death of anyone or anything. Their deaths were premature and sadly unnecessary, and the way they were displayed was degrading. I felt it as a human being, wanting to cover them as a friend who knew it wasn't right for

Once Upon a Murder

them to be gawked at in their own home. It was a lesson to me. I'll try not to be murdered. And if I die while you're around don't let anyone do that to me. This experience has convinced me that there is a lot to be said for being blown to bits. At least then I wouldn't have to suffer the indignity of being given the once over by unfamiliar eyes after I'm dead." She knew her statement was ridiculous and practically impossible but being on display in death seemed totally unfair to her, and she believed in being fair almost above everything else.

"Always the extreme reaction, the subjective one. Polly could you just try and remember what was said? Why were they killed? Do the police have any clues, weapons, suspects? Why did someone murder here in this building? The Jacobsons were quiet people. The most excitement they had was working the Sunday Crossword Puzzle together. Why them?"

Sara knew the answers before she asked the questions. It was too early for answers. It was just that the whole situation, knowing that Polly was talking to the police and the press inside the apartment, should have provided Sara with some privileged inside information.

Polly took Sara's edgy diatribe about the Jacobsons in stride. Sara was astute, smart and clever; but hidden motives and relationships with undercurrents weren't within her realm of understanding. Polly always delved beyond the obvious, almost resisted it. She was certain in her mind that most people were not as represented. To Sara people were always as represented. Sara, in spite of excellent preparation, was forever being surprised by people and by life.

"Any children?" Polly asked, trying to mellow into the format of questions expected of her.

"I don't think so. She might have mentioned children to me before. I'm not sure. But she wasn't a grandmother or a mother who talked about it all the time. And I never saw any young visitors. It seemed like they only had each other. I don't think either one of them would have fared well without the other. They were inseparable, not madly in love, just like a complementary set of people. He had his things to take care of and she had hers and together that totaled up their completeness as a couple."

"I'm trying to imagine visiting crime scenes for a living. Not knowing how bad the crime really is until you see what's been done to the victims. And then the forced objectivity that must follow. How do they know when they can react to people, to what happens to themselves? Maybe that's why there are so many divorces for enforcement officers. Maybe the need's too strong for survival to let emotion reach below a safe plateau."

Once Upon a Murder

"Is there someone's emotion you would want to go beyond safe limits?"

"Whatever could have made you ask that? Just because Sgt. Savitch made me want to frolic through the local produce market with a sign reading *melons* on my chest, that's no reason for you to imply anything unseemly for a professor of my mature years. Not to change the subject but you haven't mentioned the chain letter. Why not?"

"I'm convinced it's only a student's prank. Why should I make myself look ridiculous by implying some connection between the dreadful murders of two harmless innocents and a cruel and childish chain letter warning?"

"Because the murderer acted out the warning. He was both cruel and in a way childish, painting the faces like that."

"Are you going to interject some of your seat-of-the-pants-psychology into this murder?"

"There are demons driving us all if you would only admit it to yourself. Yours are just harmless unrecognizable beings politely dispensing lowfat yogurt. I'll know if there's a connection between the letters and the murders once I canvass the tenants here about...."

"Oh no! The people here think I'm a perfectly nice professor who minds her own business and has normal friends. And you're not going to screw up that impression. Knowing you and your

Once Upon a Murder

approach the tenants would be alienated against me after your first sentence. About the letter. I casually brought the subject up to a couple of my colleagues recently to see if they had received similar letters."

"And?"

"None of the professors I asked or the staff of the department had heard anything about a chain letter, and they all volunteered the info that they would never respond if they got one."

"That's a pretty universal feeling about the damned things. But why did this particular sender think he would get a positive response? And why was he so brazen as to demand one and threaten the letter's receiver?"

"How the hell would I know? You're the one who wants to play detective. I've lost interest in it without any more definite information."

Polly hadn't. As always her friend's interest waned long before her own so she slumped down and pretended to muse to herself while looking at what Sara had done to the apartment since the last time Polly had seen it. The look as always was functional comfort achieved by sparsely decorating with no color or style sense to the arrangement. Actually there was no arrangement. The furniture was just there approximately where you would expect it to be. As a visitor you weren't catered to but rather allowed to enter and find some comfort

Once Upon a Murder

zone of your own. It was called *democratic decorating* and it hadn't caught on yet. And if the purchase tags were still dangling from a much used piece of the decor it was merely an oversight.

"Well, I've had enough for tonight and I've soaked this foot until it looks like a lobster. Help me wrap it so I can get the swelling down. I hate wearing tennis shoes with polyester."

"I'm waiting for you to hate the polyester too. I'll wrap if you tell me exactly how you fell down the stairs. Don't leave out anything."

"I told you. I was upstairs visiting Mrs. Sotheby and her dog. I was only there for ten or fifteen minutes. I brought the dog a bone and some mints for her. I wasn't paying attention to the stairs and I tripped, stepped on something that gave under my weight and sent me sprawling to the foot of the stairs. My foot and ankle got twisted and beat up from hitting that huge terra cotta planter on the landing. The strangest thing is not that I fell, I'm clumsy enough for that, but that when I finally stood up and looked back up the stairs they were empty, clear of any obstacle. Then what did I trip on?"

"Maybe you just wrong-footed yourself and tripped over your own shoe?" Polly offered unconvincingly.

"No. There was something there all right or someone and.....the light was out. The light was

Once Upon a Murder

out! Now I remember. It was dark when I left her apartment and walked down the hall to the stairs. The light at the top of the stairs was out. It was on when I went up. Thanks, Poll, now you've let me get myself worried again. Life here at *the Oaks* has just become a little too fucking weird for me."

"As always you can't see the challenge we have here. After your injury you should have been led away from the student's prank idea being responsible for the chain letter. We need, O.K. I need, another letter just one more sent to someone here. Someone like the Jacobsons. That would substantiate my theory. The pictures I took! There were some notes and papers on a board....oh....but they might have sent the letter back. No they had to have kept it to make this valid. Would she've, would Harriet A. have sent it back? Sorry, a rhetorical. The pictures could be good enough, they might show--something."

"Small chance. You don't even know what you have on film. Given your technical expertise you probably had the lens covered. You were too shook-up to have taken good pictures, if that's even possible for you. You were clicking shots on reflex."

"If there's even a corner of paper on one shot I'll have it enlarged first thing tomorrow. Better yet tonight. There must be an all night foto place around here. Isn't this vacationland? Where's your telephone directory?"

"I know it's pointless to offer logic and common sense and plead fatigue and unusual circumstances.....? I thought so. You're like a runaway express train when you're like this. There's a place two blocks away. The keys to my car are on a table somewhere."

"Ohhhhh no. Friends who follow a challenge together stay alive together. I'll be glad to help you hobble to the car, O gimpèd one."

FIVE

"Please everyone. I'll try to answer all your questions and address your concerns about safety, but you must sit down and be patient." Savitch to the room after repeated efforts to speak to one person at a time had failed.

"I'm going to my sisters in Indianapolis and I'm not coming back until this whole thing is over." Heard from an agitated female voice close to the sergeant.

"I'm afraid I can't let you do that Mrs. Whittsted, leave at this time I mean." Sgt. Savitch's automatic response to the comment.

"You would stop an old lady from visiting her sister?" A disbelieving Mrs. Whittsted.

"Yes ma'am. I have the authority to do just that, to prevent you or anyone else in this room from leaving the state. All of you are involved in a murder investigation. Please. Please sit down so

Once Upon a Murder

we can get this over with as quickly as possible and then you can all go back to your apartments." This last statement makes more of an impression than the others and people move away from the sergeant and go to find a place to accommodate his request.

"Mrs. Goldman, I don't quite understand the numbering of the apartments. Exactly how many are there and how many tenants live here? The list you gave me shows eighteen tenants, excluding the Jacobsons, and you said four are on vacation? Then why are there fifteen people here?" Savitch doubted seriously whether he could make any sense of the landlady's computations, having realized when he stepped into the room that he was on his own and would have to dig for any lucid response from this group.

"I can explain that, Sergeant" A gutsy confession from Polly under the circumstances.

"I know you. You were here last night in the Jacobson apartment. Aren't you with the press? Lady, this is a closed meeting. How did you get in? Detective Burch remove this woman."

"Wait! You're right. I'm not a tenant, but I will be staying here with Corny--sorry--Sara Cornwall since we were supposed to be flying to Bermuda today to catch a cruise ship tomorrow and your office won't let Sara leave as planned. About my appearance as a member of the press, well, it was a case of mistaken identity and I can explain more fully later."

"O.K. you can stay. Detective Burch interview her with her friend and find out about this press business and report back to me"

"Yessir." Burch's assent halfhearted at best.

"Now continue Mrs. Goldman and please try to be uh brief."

"There are fifteen apartments; five were added about ten years ago. These newer ones all have private entrances outside the courtyard and have letters after their numbers. I have owned this building since 1975 when there were only ten apartments. About nine or ten years ago my nephew, he's a wonderful architect in California, showed me how I could convert my building with a minimum of construction and expense to include five more units. We talked about it quite a bit. I wasn't sure you know. The cost for a lady my age, it was all I had, and I couldn't decide if I should take my nest egg and put it into more apartments. How would I know if I could rent them? Then a lady at the market heard me talking about enlarging my place and wanted to rent one of the new ones that hadn't even been built yet so I started to take the idea of adding on seriously."

"So you added five more units?" He cut to the chase for her.

Once Upon a Murder

"Yes. But I didn't want to add five new numbers to the apartments so I got an idea to just add letters to some of the numbers I already had. You see I had preprinted receipt books made for all of the apartments even my number one; I thought at one time I might like to move upstairs and let one of the other tenants have number one. It was easier to add a letter to five of the receipt books than to order five new ones and pay that man at office supply to make five new masters that he would of course overcharge me for. My apartment is number one and around the corner on the outside in front are 1A and 1B. Upstairs and across the courtyard is number ten and 10A, 10B and 10C were added just below and on the outside facing the parking garages."

Mrs. Goldman finally took a breath having just related the tale of the construction coup of the century.

"Which of the apartments is empty?" Savitch hoped by keeping the question short and direct he might this once get the same kind of answer.

"Apartments #2, 10A, and 10B. Larry Stone in number two is in Hawaii. Chrystal Langford is a retired professional dancer--vaudeville of course-- and went to a reunion in New York City. And the Kearneys took their R.V. up north to visit their children and grandchildren. Miss Langford is 10A and Tom and Ruth are 10B."

Once Upon a Murder

Savitch couldn't believe his good fortune. After having been forced to listen to a series of circuitous stories and embellishments he was finally going to be able to start the individual questioning he had hoped for almost two hours ago. False starts on his part due to delays in getting his detectives away from commitments in the office and false starts in trying to get direct information from Mrs. Goldman without first having to listen to mounds of extraneous detail that she refused to omit had all but foundered his attempt at a speedy witness processing.

"Okay, this is what I want to do. Detective Burch, you start with Cornwall and the press friend in #5, then talk to Mrs. Sherman in #4 and the Browns in #6 and finish with Mrs. Sotheby in #7. Detective Koslovsky, take tenants from #8,10, and 10C. I'm going to continue my *conversation* with the manager, then speak with Mrs. Whittsted and the tenants from apartments 1A and 1B."

*   *   *   *

Sargeant Savitch tried for the third or fourth time to keep Mrs. Goldman on the subject of the Jacobson murders, but as she once again drifted he found himself hypnotized by the single fantailed fish in a small tank on the table behind Frieda Goldman.   *Mitzi* the fish moved like an aged stripper working with one slow fan, mesmerizing him with her movement as the monotone of Frieda's voice completed the mental paralysis.

"Thank you, Mrs. Goldman. I'm sure that I will need to call on your recollections from time to time during the investigation. Do you think we could have some coffee? The other officers and myself have been up most of the night on this case and would appreciate some coffee that didn't come from a machine." He wanted to be free to ask his questions for a while anyway without her well-meaning intervention.

"You poor boys. Let me go and make coffee for everyone and something else maybe? I almost forgot in the excitement that I have a special Danish that I bought which will feed us all. Oh, such a Danish that melts in the mouth. In only a few minutes you can taste it for yourself."

*   *   *   *

Sgt. Savitch turned to face off with Mrs. Whittsted, a wiry gray-haired lady in her early seventies who was somehow still expecting him to excuse her to go visit the sister in Indianapolis. The sister, he later found out, was a twin and Jerrie in Indianapolis and Carrie in Florida had never gotten over their separation from each other which occurred when the sister in Indianapolis married for the first time at the tender age of sixty-six.

"Now Mrs. Whittsted, you're in number three right?"

"Yes. It's the largest apartment with the best view from the bedroom." She offered this possessive declaration as if it had some bearing on the matter at hand.

"That's nice."

Always acknowledge seemingly meaningless information volunteered by a witness to let them establish a free flowing pattern of conversation on their own--basic enforcement manual technique lingo.

"Last night where were you from about six o'clock to eight-thirty?"

"Why in my apartment of course. Where else would a woman who lives a quiet and private life be at that time in the evening?"

"You were alone?"

"Yes!"

"How well did you know the Jacobsons?"

"They were already living here when I moved in. I was polite and said hello when I saw them but..."

"But what...?"

"Stephen Jacobson was a flirt. There I've said it. Ill of the dead and all be damned. The day he first winked those beady blue eyes at me on the

Once Upon a Murder

stairs, that was the day I stopped being polite to him and started to feel sorry for his wife. He was a chaser you know."

* * * *

"I don't know how the Sarge's going to take the news about you sneaking in with the press last night." A very uncomfortable Burch settled down to what promised to be an interview full of information he just didn't want to hear and wouldn't want to retell.

"I didn't do it to break the law or to be privy to information that I wasn't entitled to or to intrude on the murder scene for any disruptive purpose. I did it, I had to do it because the officers on the scene wouldn't answer a simple question about whether or not Sara was dead."

Polly glanced at Sara because she knew the blunt and cold way she had blurted the statement out had caused a mental ghost to walk across Sara's mortality, and sure enough the look that reflected the thought was there.

"They couldn't, it's their job to..."

"I know Detective Burch. I understand. But last night you have to understand that I wasn't going to remain a passive spectator. Not me. Things weren't happening fast enough, answers promised to come too slowly to appease my

Once Upon a Murder

anxiety. Why don't you just tell Savitch I was the helpless victim of PMS?"

"I doubt that he knows what that is or that he would consider it reason enough to cross the lines of a closed crime scene, but I'll do what I can to defend you and your hormones." The tongue-in-cheek remark was obviously a departure from routine for him and he quickly returned to business.

"Sara, you are so much different from the other tenants here. Why here and not some singles apartment building or a place along the water? You and your friend here have to be at least twenty or more years younger than the youngest of the people I've seen here at Mrs. Goldmans. If you ask me this is more like a retirement home than an apartment complex."

"I genuinely like it here. I like the privacy I get here. I teach Art History at a small private university and when I'm not teaching I'm reading or doing research for an ongoing series of articles I have been commissioned to write. I spend hours at my computer terminal inputting notes and storing my research to prepare these articles which are a combination of art, history, and the political influences that change the tastes of famous collectors. I have very little tolerance for children or teenagers and this place seemed ideal when I moved in and it suits me and my semi-reclusive life

Once Upon a Murder

style even more now. I confess that I don't know my neighbors very well, but when I want to get caught up on the latest I go visit Frieda Goldman and she gives me a capsulized version of what's been happening. She loves to do it and she's an incredible character when she relates her stories. Here she comes now with one of those huge Danishes from Sterns Bakery." Sara's reasons for living at *the Oaks* were wordlessly culminated by the entrance once again of Frieda bearing a delectable food offering for them all.

* * * *

"What kind of a name is Koslovsky, Detective?"

"Polish, Mrs. Turnbull."

"Ohhhh. I never knew any Polish people before."

"They're just like anyone else, Mrs. Turnbull, and if they happen to be Polish and detectives like me they love to talk to principals in a murder investigation quickly and send them on their way."

"The way you say it makes it sound official and demanding. I don't know that I care for your manner of rushing me either. After all I'm not a suspect, am I?"

"I certainly don't want you to become alarmed at the thought, but I do have to ask you, like everyone else, some questions about last night and about the Jacobsons."

"You think I could be a suspect, don't you?" Mrs. Turnbull adjusted her position on the couch as if to unloosen the defenses that surfaced in her attitude.

"Let me explain why I may seem to you a little abrupt and impatient and perhaps why I haven't the time to either try and make you feel completely comfortable talking to me or to insure you that you are definitely not a suspect. Last night two relatively seclusive and happily married senior citizens were cruelly murdered. I arrived on the scene at 8:00P.M. and didn't leave until 5:00A.M. this morning. It took all that time to go over the apartment and examine the decedents' personal items and to confer with the Medical Examiner and the Evidence Team. We have no real clues yet as to who murdered the couple or why. They belong to a social club of local seniors, about forty members, and were parishioners at a church with a large congregation. After we speak to all of the tenants here, Detective Burch and I have to go to the church for a list of members and to the seniors club for a roster--guessing I would say close to 200 people total. Most of those people will be crossed off the list after one interview, but there will be others we will investigate further or who will give us additional

Once Upon a Murder

names to follow up on. As you can see there are a lot of hours of work involved in a criminal investigation and anything you or I can do to get to only the pertinent facts in the quickest way possible must be done to speed to an end this unpleasant situation. Don't you agree?"

"Yes, I agree. What do you want to know?" Mrs. Turnbull had taken his speech to mean that the other tenants wouldn't be capable of responding as quickly or concisely as she could. She meant to show him her alertness and intelligence by her responses to his personally directed plea.

"You live in apartment eight. The Jacobsons were murdered next door to you. Did you hear anything unusual or observe anything strange in or around their apartment, in the courtyard, in the hall or on the stairs last night? Anything at all?"

"Not that I recall, except the sound of the television long after the Jacobsons usually retired. That was what I told Frieda last night. It was I who alerted her to call the police when the unfortunate couple didn't answer the phone when I called to complain about the television being too loud."

"Why don't you summarize what you did and heard last night from about 6:00 P.M.?"

"Very well. I take my walk every evening promptly at six. Three miles a day. I used to be a

Once Upon a Murder

physical education teacher, grades four through six at Hershfield Elementary, and I like to keep up my stamina. At my age stopping regular exercise can be deadly. On the way home, the last mile, I slow down and go through the park. I watch the kids and sometimes I break my diet and get an ice-cream cone. Usually I'm back here by 7:30-7:45. At this time of the year I'm home before it gets dark. I remember putting my key in the lock and hearing the television quite loudly coming from the Jacobsons' apartment so they must have been home. It's impossible to see through the drapes in their living room so I couldn't see who was inside. I came in, showered, and had a bowl of cereal for dinner. I switched on the TV and caught the last of a quiz show that started at eight. I guess I fell asleep in my chair. The next thing I knew I was being awakened by a TV program I could hear on the set next door, not from my own television. Well, it was too late to go over and complain so I called Frieda, after all she is the manager and that's her job. Before I had finished getting ready for bed there were sirens and all kinds of racket from the front yard and the street. Almost immediately Frieda came to tell me they were dead and to stay inside my apartment, so I did. Much later an officer knocked and told me to stay in my apartment until I was told otherwise and here I am as requested."

"Thank you. That was very thorough. We found information about the husband, Stephen Jacobson, in the apartment but nothing about her. What can you tell me?"

"I don't think there was any other family on that side. All dead I believe and, no, she didn't have any children. I thought that was odd because her husband loved children. Once I saw her with some kids in front of the building, saw how uncomfortable she was with them, almost afraid of them. And then I thought maybe she was better off childless. I adore kids. I have two boys living in New York and four grandchildren. It makes me sad to think of anyone disliking children, almost avoiding them like she did."

*   *   *   *

The clashing patterns of Herbert Norwich's shirt and slacks when looked at without blinking formed an optical illusion. It made the viewer imagine he was seeing large insects fly south and get trapped in a maze of cages; in actuality there were very stationary bees and butterflies on Herbert's shirt and large open checks on his slacks. Yes, he had known Stephen Jacobson pretty well. They had each spent their childhood in Kansas and enjoyed reminiscing about the slow-paced life on their rural farms. He didn't socialize with Stephen

Once Upon a Murder

outside of *the Oaks* because Herbert quite simply preferred the company of women. Evidently he was quite comfortable living here where most of the tenants were single women. He had been paying court to both of the tenants in apartment 1B, two sisters named Lilly and Lorraine Stangely. He took them out, never letting on which one he was interested in but playing the perfect escort to both of them, forwarding his intentions individually with each one without ever making a declaration or commitment. It was his intention to encourage both women equally into finding him an indispensable companion. He verified that the Jacobsons seemed to be happily married. No, he hadn't noticed anything different about them lately except that Mrs. Jacobson appeared a little edgy, nervous, and preoccupied the last couple of times he had seen her. Yes, Mr. Jacobson had family, a brother in Kansas who maintained the family farm.

* * * *

As Burch soon discovered, the Browns, Miles and Olivia, had a social eating problem. They were both about five feet two or three inches tall and weighed about 250 pounds each. He had been talking with them for about fifteen minutes and during that time Mrs. Brown had taken from her large suitcase-style bag sandwiches and chips for

Once Upon a Murder

both of them followed by a bag of cookies. They were currently devouring the last two pieces of the Danish that Mrs. Goldman had put on the coffee table. Between bites they managed to tell him that Mrs. Jacobson was a good cook, an important observation for two such able carnivores, and that the few times they had all been together nothing unusual was noticed about the Jacobsons' actions or their relationship. Mrs. Brown had seen Mr. Jacobson take some kind of medicine once and believed it was for high blood pressure. The detective left them happily digging in Mrs. Brown's bag. Looking for what? Maybe a small ham....?

* * * *

"Lilly, I saw you talking to Herbert earlier...." was as much of a response as Burch got from his questions before the sisters started their territorial battle over the skinny, nattily dressed tenant of apartment 1A.

"Detective Burch, isn't he marvelous? Funny and smart and cute too." Lilly offered barely able to contain a swoon.

"I'm sure that the detective isn't interested in Mr. Norwich's obvious good looks and wonderful personality. He wants us to give him information about the Jacobsons, isn't that right officer?"

Once Upon a Murder

Lorraine appeared very comfortable taking the upper hand over her sister in this as, he assumed, she must try to in everything between the two of them.

Lilly and Lorraine Stangely were carbon copies of each other. Lilly a little taller than Lorraine; Lorraine a little heavier than Lilly. Both were dressed for living in the sixties. The maintenance alone of the two coiffured blonde heads must have set back the sisters quite a bit each month and he couldn't help but wonder how they slept on so many piled curls without needing to be redone each morning. They had on layers of eye makeup so that when they smiled the puffiness around their eyes together with the heavy makeup created one continuous black line where an orifice should have been below each brow. Their dresses had starched full skirts and he was tempted to lift up a hem to see if the full underskirt that he suspected was there was actually there. His other option of course was to have them do a twirl for him, something he was sure they did quite frequently in their ballroom dance class.

Both sisters were completely mortified by the deaths and yet were able to maintain a distance and aloofness when they spoke about the crimes that even had the detective believing the murders must have happened in another building. The sisters had been reasonably friendly with the couple, but confessed to tension between Mrs. Jacobson and themselves, excusing it as jealousy because they were two attractive single women who had caught Stephen Jacobson's fancy.

* * * *

Detective Koslovsky was pleasantly surprised by the tenant in apartment #10C. Maria Montoya was a quiet and self-contained Spanish lady who sat erect in her chair while her fingers rhythmically inserted and then pulled the thread through garment after garment as they talked. There was a certain determination and pride in the way she held her head that was reflected in the immaculate and solid manner in which her grayed hair was neatly pulled back in an oversized bun behind her ears. She spoke slowly and spent a lot of effort on each word, trying to minimize a heavy accent that pervaded her speech when she quickened her words.

"I have lived here only three years. I came here after the death of my husband. I couldn't stay in our house; too many memories, too many things of my husband in every room. His records, his paintings--the ones he did for only my eyes--and outside too his tools and in the yard his beautiful flowers. The hours he spent in his garden. It was impossible for me even to take pleasure in his flowers after he was gone. They needed care and it hurt me to go outside and see them needing him and suffering without him just as I was. So I came here. My children convinced me to retire from the business my husband and I had begun so many years ago. We started with one small laundromat and cleaners. Both of us working twelve, fifteen hours a day to do everything ourselves. Within three years we had opened up two more shops and eventually stopped at six business locations in Southern Florida which made us quite comfortable financially after our six children had graduated from school."

She pointed to the mending in her lap and explained that she continued to do alterations for the shops her daughter and son-in-law now managed simply because her hands couldn't be idle after so many years of hard work.

Looking at her hands, Koslovsky couldn't help thinking how deftly she would be at murder. The strength he saw in her fingers and the determination he saw in her face and carriage made him believe her capable of carrying out any purpose she chose. But his mind-wandering speculation was soon put to rest when she provided him with an alibi that surrounded her with family and friends at the time of the murders.

* * * *

Once Upon a Murder

"Mrs. Sherman, when did you say you saw the Jacobsons last?"

"No, dear boy, you're still talking too fast. Now what is it you want to ask me?"

Detective Burch tried not to look as exasperated as he felt. Dorie Sherman, the tenant in the number four apartment, had a severe hearing problem. She had excused herself three times already to adjust the volume control on her hearing aid. She had to leave the room because she still insisted on wearing one of the heavy volume controls hidden beneath her dress front with a white wire emanating from the neckline of her purple paisley print up to her right ear. She was leaning practically in his face now while pushing the ear piece of the aid into her head with one hand while lifting the microphone out through her dress with the other. To no avail. He couldn't possibly consider her a suspect and thought it ludicrous to continue questioning her further.

The only notes he took from their interview were *send Mrs. Sherman literature on high tech hearing devices--anonymously.*

*   *   *   *

Once Upon a Murder

"The moon and the planets know who killed them. We could tell you but we need to make the astrological charts for both of the victims and the charts for all of the suspects. And then. The rest is easy for Momma and me. Isn't that right Momma?"

"But of course. From the charts it is simple deduction. You waste your time sitting here listening to their lies. The planets don't lie. The moon, the sun, the stars don't lie. Only people lie; but no one lies to Flo Gotjcik. I see everything. I study astrology for twenty-five years. I tried tea leaves. I tried Tarot. I tried the crystal ball. But the best way to find the truth is to ask your questions of the universe. The sky throughout history has always provided answers. It will this time. Try me. I will be one of your detectives. You will see how easy a crime can be solved!"

"Momma is right, Detective Koslovsky, whenever I can't make a decision or there is a problem between us we take out our charts and compare them to the daily position of the bodies in the universe and we have our answer. I came late in life to astrology; I am a novice compared to Momma. She had the calling even from childhood to follow the stars. Go ahead, Momma, tell him the dream you had after your aunt gave you the blue dress with the silver stars on it for your seventh birthday."

Once Upon a Murder

"It was an omen, a...."

"Mrs. Gotjcik, I'm sure it is a memorable story and perhaps some other time I will be able to enjoy it completely and appreciate its meaning fully, but for now I need the answers to some questions. I apologize for not using charts or astrology in any way and I must rely only on my own instincts to evaluate the answers. You see, I believe most people tell the truth. If there is trust from the person who asks the questions, there will be truth from the person who answers them. If my instincts detect a liar, well, let's just say I can be a very rough person to lie to."

As he said the last words, Momma Gotjcik did it again. She grabbed a large astrological medallion hanging around her neck and mumbled some words, perhaps a curse on his whole family, and made a sign with her hands invoking the astrological gods to spit on him at their convenience. She had periodically grabbed for the medallion before, but this time it was with malevolent purpose against him. He was a disbeliever, an astrological infidel, and even though he didn't believe her hocus pocus he was going to be very careful for a few days just in case. He told himself to downplay the effectiveness of her influence and try to get the answers from the daughter. As he turned to question the younger Gotjcik the mother began to facially hex him by

68

slowly closing one eye completely while the other one stayed wide open. Then she switched eyes and did the same thing again. Obviously her right side was stronger as her left lid drooped ineffectually when it was that eye's turn to be all-seeing.

Sonia Gotjcik was a walking astrological chart. In one ear extending from the top to the lobe were six holes and from each one dangled a gold symbol for one of the signs of the horoscope. In the other ear were six studs with mini replicas of the remaining signs. Her face glistened with cream or olive oil or cosmic fluid and she had three graduated stars tattooed at the corner of her left eye. Her appearance alone was a statement of her faith, her belief in the absorbing realism and power of her mother's teaching. He was talking to an astrological cult of two and, in spite of his skeptical nature, he couldn't help feeling that he might need deprogramming after he was done with the Gotjciks.

"Mrs. Jacobson was a disbeliever like you, Detective, but she liked my earrings. She was a Taurus and admired my sign earring. I offered to order a pair for her but she never brought it up again and seemed to forget that we even had such a conversation."

"I warned her about the positions of her moons this week." Flo taking the floor from her daughter and beginning to sway a little in semitrance to elucidate her retrospective predictions. "I all but predicted her death. I can do that you know. Astrology gives me ESP as well. I see things that will happen and I try to advise people how to avoid evil until the moons change. She came to me only two days before her death. We had tea. I saw it first in her leaves, but she laughed it off. Then I did Tarot and she herself saw me turn the death card--not once--but twice! Then the chart, the chart for her time of birth was in violent disarray with the one I had done for this week. The friendly moons were obliterated by her arrangement of planets, and I had never seen the universe in such chaos as the charts revealed. I warned her. I told her she should let me go further into my new planetary arrangement theory and the overlapping of random moons, but alas, she refused and now she is dead. Do I need to say more? Flo Gotjcik had spoken directly with the heavens on those charts and Harriet Jacobson refused to heed me. Now she is spinning out there somewhere with those same unfriendly moons."

Detective Koslovsky was mentally considering possibilities. He wondered if he could just look in the yellow pages under deprogramming, it might not be a long list but...certainly worth a try.

*   *   *   *

Once Upon a Murder

Detective Burch couldn't help but feel comfortable with Helen Sotheby. She was the lady down the block who had given him cookies on his way home from school at a time when a kid knew he could accept cookies from a stranger and get only the wholesome and harmless treat offered. She was a grandmother figure not unlike his own who had died five years ago. She looked the epitome of a content senior citizen, warm and friendly, and eager to make those around her happy. She oozed kindly enthusiasm and thoughtfulness, a woman truly enjoying her golden years and it showed. As he gave back her wallet he once again mentioned how proud she must be of the two grandchildren standing with her daughter in front of the house in Oregon beneath the scratched plastic photograph window in her wallet.

"You must come to my apartment and see the others, pictures I mean. Suzanne is almost a woman now and Sean is only interested in baseball; and their mother, my daughter SueAnn, works so hard to care for them. She was my only child you know. I don't know what I would have done without her after my James died."

"Mrs. Sotheby, I promise I will stop by your apartment and see the other pictures."

"...and to see Snowball too don't forget."

Once Upon a Murder

"Yes, Mrs. Sotheby, and to see your little dog as well. But first let's finish with the talk we were having about what you can remember in the last few days. During the last week or so has anything unusual happened? Have any strangers come to your door? Did you see the Jacobsons at all?"

"Well, on Saturday I took Snowball to the doctor for a shot. The nasty nurse held her so tight while the doctor gave her the shot that she snapped at the woman. It would have served her right if Snow had nipped one of her mean hands. I told the doctor twice now to get rid of that nurse. She makes Snow so nervous; she's just not an animal person."

"What about the rest of the week?"

"Well, Sunday I called my daughter and we had a long chat. I call her every Sunday or she calls me, whichever one of us can't wait any longer calls the other you see. Monday I was home all day until that nice young lady from apartment five came over. Snow and I enjoy her visits so. She always brings something good to eat for both of us. Usually a bone for Snowball and some sweets for me. It happened on the stairway down from my apartment after she left to go home, but I didn't find out about it until the next day."

"What happened on the stairs?"

"She fell, poor dear."

Once Upon a Murder

"Apartment number five, you mean Sara Cornwall? She doesn't appear to be hurt."

"Oh but she bruised her foot terribly and I feel so guilty about it. She came to see me out of kindness and got only pain for her trouble. I don't see how I can ever make it up to her."

"I'm sure she doesn't blame you. How could she? It must have been just an unfortunate accident."

"Yes. I'm sure it was, yet she hasn't come back to visit me since and I'm almost out of mints and I'm sure Snowball could use another bone."

"Maybe her foot is bothering her and she can't get up the stairs to your apartment without a lot of pain." Detective Burch's comment was meant to explain away the tenant's building anxiety, but it was completely ignored as Mrs. Sotheby continued to reason aloud.

"She has been such a dear to me and Snow. I guess we will have to be patient and wait until she is ready to visit us again, but it really was a regular thing with us. She would come once a week bringing goodies for me and Snowball. Now I suppose that is to stop all because of a wicked accident. Three of us have to suffer because of one little accident. It doesn't seem fair, does it? I'm sure I don't know how I'm going to explain it to Snowball. It has been five days since Sara's last visit and Snow is getting anxious, afraid she won't come back again next week. Snow does take notice of the smallest detail, the slightest change in her schedule. What excuse will I use when she has no new bone for the week?"

* * * *

Sgt. Savitch thanked the tenants for their help and handed each a card with the Department's telephone number on it as they filed out of Mrs. Goldman's apartment. As the last one departed he was anxious to exchange and compile the information that he and the two detectives had received from the tenants. It was critical to do it now while it was still fresh in their memories; now while they could add their impressions of voice tone and body language to the gut feelings each officer had mentally noted about the individual tenants he had interviewed. Without making any final judgments they could still kick around any potentials who looked good for the two homicides. Most of all Savitch wanted to see if they could build a composite sketch among the three of them of the Jacobsons' character, habits and lifestyle.

Frieda was soon finished saying her good-byes at the door and Savitch wanted to take his detectives away from *the Oaks* to somewhere she

Once Upon a Murder

would not be a welcome interloper for the discussion he had in mind.

"What a night. I haven't had all of my tenants together like this since Christmas four no five years ago. And to think it took two murders to bring us together again. More coffee?"

"Thanks for the offer but it's late and after the excitement and the sadness of your loss I'm sure you could use some rest. It's been almost twenty-four hours since the murders and we have a lot to do yet before we can go home. By tomorrow, Sunday, we have to go over the Coroner's Report, examine all the evidence from the crime scene, compile everything you and your tenants have told us, and begin the interviews with the parishioners of the Church of Three Crosses. Time is extremely important in a murder investigation. Every day that goes by puts distance between the murderer and the crime; and every day that goes by makes the clarity of possible clues more remote to us. People's memory of details fades with time and the sharpness of my men on an investigation dulls, even though I hate to admit it. We need to share our ideas and opinions now and decide how the investigation will be divided, and then get to work. Good night now and thanks again for your hospitality and the great coffee."

As Mrs. Goldman started into the kitchen with her hands full of Danish crumb- laden plates,

Once Upon a Murder

Hart Savitch and the two detectives simultaneously gulped the last of their now cold coffee and headed for the door.

"Well guys, do you wanna go over the information now or start fresh tomorrow morning around 7:00A.M.?"

"On Sunday?"

"I want backgrounds started first thing Monday morning. I can have Hill and Freeman start the records check and make a lot of calls if we can get the information compiled from the little chats we had from this evening. Besides, Koslovsky you have to be up early tomorrow anyway because you're going to church. And tomorrow night the two of you are going stag to a senior citizens' mixer. They'll love you. I hear those things never have enough single men. Wear your dancing shoes"

"I can hardly wait!"

"Since you have us booked for tomorrow that means we have to sort out our notes and prospects for most likely tonight, right?" Burch clarified the sergeant's own conclusion with his question.

"That's why you're one of my best investigators, you never overlook the obvious."

SIX

"Just an average cross section of Geriatric Americana." This from the visiting cynic.

"Quite a group aren't they?" This from the resident stoic.

"Just like spending an evening at Madame Tussaud's Wax Works."

"They're really very nice people, but not at their best under the circumstances."

".....and when are they at their best? Certainly not when awake. I can only imagine them pleasantly harmless and tolerable with their nightcapped heads peeking out from under a fifty-pound comforter."

"Polly, I will admit that in all the time I've lived here that was the most exposure I've had to most of them and, I'm sorry to say, the most I ever want to have. I want to go back to my arrangement of quiet detachment from the tenants

Once Upon a Murder

and intense involvement in my research. I find my computer more responsive and communicative than most of the people who live here."

"It certainly was a night to remember for me, Corny. I've never seen so much captive senility dressed so spiffily in one room before."

"You're not going to go off on a scathing observational tangent again are you?"

"Who me? Yes I feel it coming on and I must submit or it will fester in my brain and come out at the most unpropitious of times as I'm sure you may recall from other visits."

"Hold it in for just another minute. I'll go get us a couple of soft drinks and a cigarette for me and be right back."

Polly let her shoes drop as they dangled from her feet with only the tips of her toes inside. She put her legs over the arm of the couch and slumped down on the cushion, stuffing a limp couch pillow doubled up under her head. She closed her eyes for the time it took Sara to get the sodas. On the inside of her eyelids she saw the room at Frieda's apartment as though she were still there. Each face and voice was as vivid as the image of the Jacobsons' bodies which threatened to supplant the much happier scene from Frieda's living room."

"O.K. Polly, let 'er rip."

Once Upon a Murder

"I hesitate to do the full shtick because I know you will get indignant about my mistreatment of people, but can I help it if my mind takes a first impression and runs with it? I have to get it out of my system and then I can put those instant perceptions into the background and forget about them and relate to the people normally--for me that is.

"Let me preface this by saying that every age group sees the one ahead of it as out of touch and too old to enjoy life. Each age group in retrospect is more tolerant of the younger times gone before and less anxious to approach the older times to come. To me, even though this is an unrealistic appraisal of senior citizens in general, it is still unrelentingly what my human nature dictates that I feel. I don't want to get old. I don't want to lose my credibility; my value as a person involved in and contributing to life. I don't want to become a peripheral observer looking into the mainstream of life from a distance as these people appear to be. And yet every day when I look in the mirror I don't grouse about new wrinkles, but instead at the fact that I am all too quickly approaching the reflection that is my mother--a woman from their generation. This to me is very scary, and I get the same eerie feeling looking at the people here.

"These people are the bizarre imaginings of a new type of artist, a Geriatricist: a kind of artist that goes one step beyond mere caricature and all the way to replicating individuals that live the trait each represents.

"Let's start with the most obvious--the Gotjciks--a walking horrorscope. For them any day is a bad day to be born. Facing their predictions you don't feel glad about the sign you were born under, but come away looking for a rock to hide under for the rest of your astrological life. I think they were thrown off a caravan to the stars and landed on their heads. If I believed in alien beings, they're what the aliens would look like. Enough said. They provide too much material and I'm sure it's all been used before.

"And those Stangely sisters, completely believable participants in a time warp. I didn't think it was possible for the skin of the face to support that many layers of makeup without forming relief craters for run-off. And those eyebrows. When I was a preteen I knew a girl who did her eyebrows just like they do. I hated it then and I hate it now. I know how it's done though because all those years ago I made the mistake of asking. At first my friend, Janie Goodrich, would pluck her whole natural eyebrows(after a while it took less time to just shave them off). Then she took a black eyeliner pencil, spit on the end to make it soft, and then proceeded to color in a large bubble where her brows should start. She arched the brow straight from there and made it come down in the shape of a boomerang. I was a tomboy and used to catch frogs and tadpoles in the stream when she first started to do this to her eyebrows; it made her so mad when I told her she looked like she had two tadpoles above her eyes instead of eyebrows. It confused me a little at the stream too; I didn't know if I was looking for tadpoles or eyebrows. I think the two sisters are vain enough to have killed Mr. J. if they thought he had spurned them collectively or individually, but it would be more likely that they would have revenged themselves on each other by sabotaging a beauty product or two since the only thing they care about besides men is their own appearance.

".....and our little *Lady of Spain*, Maria Montoya, is a very strong woman of purpose, and if her purpose were murder I have no doubt that she would be properly very good at it. But she has no conceivable motive. She is an anachronism in this group and has no link whatsoever to the Jacobsons."

"The guy with the atrocious wardrobe.....?"

"Herbert Norwich."

"Yeah, Herbie. He could have gotten into it with Mr. J. about the sisters, but I can't see him as violent. He would more likely have gone to Mrs. J. and complained about her husband if he felt competition from him romantically. He would have let Mrs. J. punish Mr. J. Herbie wouldn't have done it himself.

"Frieda, of course, has nothing to gain from killing a tenant although she could have played an innocent and unknowing part in the crime. Maybe she passed on a piece of gossip to the wrong person, retold a story told to her in confidence, or perhaps she somehow incited one of them to take action where they had previously been content to let things stand.

"Dorie, too childishly senile and physically weak to have posed a threat to anyone. Although I can see someone wanting to kill her if forced to communicate through her antiquated hearing aid for long periods of time. I'm not even sure she knew who the Jacobsons were and that they lived in this building. She has been *out of touch* since she lost her natural hearing or maybe she just prefers not to know what's going on around her. Don't eliminate her too quickly, she could be keeping a secret and really be smarter than anyone thinks and uses her hearing impairment as a clever protection against suspicion.

"Carrie Whittsted doesn't seem to have the ability to care about anything or anyone very much. She's totally self-absorbed and reclusive. If she were to murder anyone she would have to invite them over so her personal inconvenience would be minimalized. And then everything would have to be perfect: the atmosphere, the opportunity, the means. If even the slightest defect in plan required her effort to correct it she would have called off the crime.

"Mrs. Sotheby is too restricted physically, too awkward to have murdered two people she would have had to overpower and surprise with her movements. She could have used her walker as a weapon I suppose, but it does seem unlikely that she could murder by surprise the way it seemed to have been done. It would be difficult to sneak up on anyone using a walker and, even without it, she is too weak and ineffectual as a serious murder suspect. Since she takes that dog of hers everywhere with her there would have been unplanned and unappreciated barking and probably several aborted attempts until the dog got it right.

"That Turnbull lady has the presence of a murderess. She's tall with a strong upper body and generally very athletic for her age. She's paranoid and guards her privacy. If she felt threatened physically or emotionally I have no doubt that she could react quickly and carry out any action she started to its completion efficiently. She lived next door to the victims. Maybe she had been forced to put up with some kind of behavior or indignity that Mr. and Mrs. Jacobson had been guilty of in the past. Clare strikes me as a person on her own internal clock, pacing the input from the outside carefully, absorbing only so much and then demanding an immediate halt to any kind of unpleasant behavior or else. I definitely feel she doles out justice in a rational way according to preset standards. She certainly has an overdeveloped sense of right and wrong and, when it comes to being just, she would always make sure the tally balanced in her favor. But that's a personality supposition and not valid evidence, just a feeling I get about what goes on behind those eyes.

"The Browns are perfectly content being passive observers where the other tenants are concerned. The only active thing they do is eat. They couldn't murder anyone; they have to stop too frequently for food fixes. Remember, I was at the crime scene and there were no food scraps around the bodies, no telltale crumbs that would signal a Brown had been there. I find it hard to believe that he is a retired naval officer. The only water image I can associate either one of them with is a vision of his and her flotillas: a sea full of very low-riding ships with heavily stocked larders. They certainly are capable of murder since they function almost as one individual. Everything they do is in tandem. They don't even need a murder weapon; they could just fall on the victims and cause concussions, contusions, and crushed bones.

Once Upon a Murder

Or better yet they could make a unique victim sandwich, the idea of which would be totally to their liking I'm sure. But I digress. I've gone over the top again and am being too hard on them, especially Mr. Brown. It's just that he reinforces my observational theory on a heavy man's lack of sexual display."

"Whatever are you talking about?" Sara queried after having taken the rest of the soliloquy in stride.

"I tried not to notice, honestly, and I am very indifferently concerned, but well...."

"Well what!"

"Okay. I'll tell you. I'm sure we talked about this before on a plane or a train where we might have seen men sitting down before." Polly offered with certainty, but was equally sure Sara would not remember.

"Now I'm thoroughly confused."

"I'll just say it. When a heavy man or a man with a large low stomach sits down and inadvertently sits with his legs apart, the way men do, where in the hell does their male stuff go?"

"What!!!"

"Their male stuff. The *triumvirate*. The three traveling companions in Hanes or Jockey; briefs or boxer longees. Where on earth do they go? A heavy man it seems has three choices: he must either sit on them, have them hidden in a roll of fat forward of the normal position, or they must simply retract. I'm open to any additional suggestions, but I assure you I have considered and dismissed all other options within my *off the wall* reasoning ability."

"When did this bizarre notion pop into that sickly pragmatic yet malignantly creative mind of yours?"

"Well, of course it started right after I knew what there was to disappear and I have faithfully updated the data until I have become convinced that it is a trait peculiar to overweight men. The options available are the ones I laid out for you and nothing short of a full investigation by an unbiased party will convince me of any other possibilities."

"Polly, where do you get these ideas anyway? The last thing I would be looking at on a plane or a train would be an obese man who couldn't keep his legs closed in order to hide the disappearance of his 'male stuff'. Thanks to you I will probably never feel comfortable again in the presence of an overweight man for fear the intimacy you have made me privy to will show embarrassingly on my face."

"Forget it, Corny, you had to be there. We'll take this subject out again and go over it when you have some data to contribute, and you will you know. I have just made it impossible for you to ignore my observations simply by having introduced them to you."

"Bitch."

"Spokeswoman for the group at large and trendsetter in my own right."

"Let's get back to the murders, shall we?"

"If you insist. I think I've covered all the suspects here except you."

"Thanks."

"Even if you had motive, opportunity, and weapon and were told no one would ever find out you did it, you still couldn't do it. Your Catholic upbringing would never allow it. Oh yes, you have the temper to conceive the crime and the just punishment. But the punishment to you in your own mind would be brutal and cruel and torturous; your psyche would never go along with carrying out your mind's desire. So you're innocent."

"Thanks again, I think. You just vindicated me from committing a murder by telling me I'm a closet psychopath without the strength of my convictions. Thank you, Polly Sloan....." Sara's comments were cut short by the ringing of her phone. "No, stay there and dream up another reason why I couldn't have committed the crimes, one that I can tell to the police in my own defense and not one that might have me wearing a very restrictive white jacket. It's times like these when we really get close."

Once Upon a Murder

"Hello. Yes Fred. No, it's not *that* late...well...I don't think...no I won't be taking the trip I planned but that doesn't mean I'm not going to use the time coming to me, well-deserved time I might add, for a local vacation with my fr...I know all about responsibility and obligation Dean Zinnman, but I don't think Sgt. Savitch will let me go anyway. You did...he did...when would I have to leave? Tomorrow! Can't Dr. Ogelby go or Andrews? Either one would represent the University in...how long?...four days! Where is the seminar?...New Orleans!...sorry, I seem to be making a pattern of extreme reactions. Can't Dr. Hillyard go and conduct the seminar, after all it was only a broken leg? Ohhhh... in traction at least a week. Don't push Fred; I'm considering it. I'll call you back...yes... within the hour."

"Sounds like one of us is about to take a trip and I blew my quota coming here to visit you."

"You could come too..."

"Realistically, how much time would we have together doing vacation-type things?"

"Realistically? It's more than just a four-day seminar. There will be lectures during the day and in the evening I would be responsible for entertaining some of the professors visiting from out of the United States. I would be back on.....damn this whole miserable situation. I promised Frieda, well never mind what I promised Frieda."

"What does Mrs. Goldman have to do with you going to New Orleans?"

"She took me aside earlier tonight and begged me to come for coffee tomorrow morning. She has something to tell me about Mrs. J. Wants to confide in me. Wants my opinion. Wants to know if I think the police should know what she knows."

"And that is?"

"How the hell do I know? Mrs. Goldman is an expert at drawing out a secret she has every intention of eventually revealing. I'm sure its nothing, just her imagination. After all what could she know?"

"I don't know and I don't drink coffee but I'll be there tomorrow morning and she will reveal all to me as soon as I produce one of her favorite coffee cakes from Sterns, a very large one just for the two of us. A sugary masterpiece guaranteed to extract every little detail from even the most stalwart of secret keepers."

SEVEN

"Good morning, Mrs. Goldman."

"Good morning, dear. You must forgive me for being a little surprised at seeing you at the door. I was expecting Sara. Is she coming down soon?"

"I'm afraid not. She was called away on University business for several days. She is sorry for not being able to be here this morning after she promised, but her arrangements to leave town were made very late last night. It was much too late to call and inconvenience you after the upsetting day you had yesterday on top of the sadness and grief you must be feeling at the loss of your tenants in this way. Won't I do? I assure you I'm just as good a confidante as Sara and it will be a shame if this raspberry Danish I picked up from Sterns isn't devoured with every bit of

Once Upon a Murder

conspiratorial fervor that you and I can give it. Raspberry was a good choice, I hope...?"

"Raspberry is my favorite and those hoggish Browns ate the remainder of last night's Danish that I had intended for my breakfast. I know that wasn't very kind of me to say, but sometimes even my family of tenants here can get on an old woman's nerves."

After offering a few understanding words in response to Frieda's ingenuous comment Polly stepped inside the cluttered room, negotiating her way between the shelves of inexpensive knickknacks that lined the entry to the living room. She had given the bakery box to Frieda who was bustling around in the kitchen getting ready for the presentation of the sacrificial pastry. Polly tried to pick out the best setting for her purpose, tried to guess where Frieda would sit, where the comfort and atmosphere would be most conducive to eliciting information both she and Mrs. Goldman knew she was not entitled to as a stranger at *the Oaks*. Polly spied a well-worn chair with a neatly folded lap blanket on the arm. The chair had a matching ottoman across the room. Obviously it had been used as an extra seat for one of the many tenants who had been here last night. Polly dragged it back to its rightful place near the matching chair and then placed a wooden rocker for herself facing Frieda's chair and ottoman just as

Once Upon a Murder

the apartment manager emerged from the kitchen with a tray.

"Why thank you, dear. That was very thoughtful of you to bring my footrest back where it belongs for me. I'm afraid my back problems and my arthritis limit my ability to move or carry anything heavy. As you can see everything is just as it was left last night. All of the chairs that were taken from the kitchen and the rest of the apartment have not been returned to their proper places. I simply can't do it myself. I should have asked that nice sergeant and his detectives before they left, but my mind was in such a dither over the murders and then finding out I would have no Danish with my coffee, well, I forgot all about how I was going to get the furniture back where it belonged."

"I'll be glad to move it for you, Mrs. Goldman, if you'll just tell me where everything goes."

"How kind of you.....but please not now. Let's talk for a while and please do call me Frieda."

The landlady was slowly sawing through the crust of the Danish with a regular stainless dinner knife. She seemed to be debating with herself, pausing with the pressure on the knife as she shook her head and mumbled unintelligibly to herself. She appeared to make a decision, nodded, and then pressed through with the knife to make a complete cut. She did this twice before the haltingly sliced coffee cake was ready to be placed on the small glass plates from the tray. Polly tried to take this annoying procedure in stride as she sat outwardly calm in the rocker waiting for Frieda to divulge her secret in her own time and in her own way.

"My dear, I have decided to confide in you just as I would have confided in Sara had she been able to be here this morning. I wasn't sure until a few minutes ago that I had the right to tell something that was told to me in confidence and with a fear of exposure, but Mrs. Jacobson is dead now and something she told me and shared with me might help find her murderer. She really only wanted me to keep it from her husband anyway and he's dead too, poor man, so he'll never know the secret after all. Now eat up and drink your tea before it gets cold and I'll be right back."

Polly watched as Frieda disappeared down the hall toward the rear of the apartment. She had no interest in eating the sweet and fruity delicacy on her plate, preferring instead a bowl of cold cereal and some juice which she would have later. If only Mrs. Goldman had a dog or a cat Polly could feed the pastry bites to it, but a fish? Polly settled on a rather devious and wasteful tactic to rid herself of the unwanted breakfast item. She cut her slice of Danish into pieces and pushed them

Once Upon a Murder

around on the plate to simulate partial consumption. When she was satisfied that her plate looked convincing, she drank half of her tea and sat back in the rocker nervously anticipating Frieda's return. She was rewarded almost immediately when Frieda appeared carrying an oversized shoe box under her arm. She sat down ceremoniously and slowly pulled a pair of reading glasses out of a crocheted case she held in one hand.

"When I first heard about the Jacobsons being killed I thought immediately about the afternoons Harriet Jacobson had spent here in this room talking with me, sharing a part of her life with me that she couldn't share with Stephen. She needed those afternoons to free herself from the burden she carried around in her head and her heart all those years. Did you know that she and her husband were my very first tenants?"

Polly only shook her head not wanting to delay the revelation that was to come.

"Yes, they had been married only a short time when they moved in. They were middle aged newlyweds just happy being in love and together. The afternoons started about six months after they moved in. I could tell she was troubled when she stood outside my screen door making small talk with me all the while begging with her eyes to be let in. And so one day when I opened the screen and invited her in she accepted. She was relieved and yet apprehensive as she moved to the sofa that first time. I knew she had something on her mind. I suspected marital problems or maybe some female complaint she wanted to share with another woman, but never in a million years would I have guessed the story she told me that day about her and Marilyn."

"Marilyn?" Damn. Polly had not meant to respond and interrupt the story but it just slipped out.

"Marilyn Jacobson or rather Marilyn Henry as she eventually came to be known. She never would have been called Jacobson unless Stephen agreed to adopt her. But then how could he? He never knew about her. That was Harriet's decision; a decision I tried to talk her into reversing. 'Your husband will accept your daughter and understand what you did just give him a chance.' I told her that many times and just when she was weakening he would show his awful temper to her and his unwillingness to accept any change in their lives. Then she would defend him and her reasons for silence. She explained how Stephen was absolutely sure about everything he did and in the way that he did it and that he had taken over making decisions for her as well. She said he knew what was best for him and for her and their life together. He planned everything

Once Upon a Murder

right down to where every dollar would be spent up until he retired and then how they would spend their time and money after that. She repeated these same thoughts to me many times almost word for word as if he had written them down for her to remember and coached her to repeat them. But that's over now. Let me show you the collection of mementos from her daughter."

Frieda opened the shoe box to reveal rows of pictures, letters, and assorted papers neatly wedged inside.

"You see even though she kept her daughter a secret from her husband, she came to me to share Marilyn's youth with her. She couldn't forget her daughter or lose track of her so on that first day when she came to me and confessed her secret we made a pact. The woman who adopted Marilyn when the child was a few years old agreed to write to Harriet and keep her informed as to what was happening in Marilyn's life in exchange for a promise from Harriet never to try and see her daughter. My part was simple. I allowed Mrs. Henry to write to Harriet using my address. I got the letters about Marilyn and Harriet would read them here, add them to the collection in this box, and then write a letter back which I would later mail.

When Marilyn was fifteen her adopted mother died. Harriet nearly went out of her mind. We

Once Upon a Murder

hadn't received a letter in three months. You see Mrs. Henry would write one letter a month and when none came after three months Harriet was frantic. She threatened to go to her daughter and reveal herself as the birth mother, but as frightened as she was of going through with the threat she would have done it if the thought of Stephen finding out about Marilyn hadn't been worse. She cried and begged me to do something to help her. I made a call to the Henry home posing as a magazine saleslady and discovered that Mrs. Henry had died. That wasn't enough for Harriet. She had to know how the girl was doing. She wanted that monthly letter again. She needed it or she told me she would do something desperate. I finally agreed to go and visit Mr. Henry and Marilyn pretending to be an old friend who had just heard about the death of Mrs. Henry.

"Marilyn was a lovely girl and I couldn't help thinking what a waste it had been that Mrs. Jacobson couldn't have known her. Marilyn and I struck up a friendship and closeness from just that one visit. She asked me to tell her things I knew about her mother, Mrs. Henry, but instead I told her what her real mother was like slipping in the comments Harriet had told me about her joy in watching Marilyn grow up through the pictures she had been sent. I told Marilyn how her mother had remembered the beautiful red dress Marilyn had worn on her eighth birthday; how proud she'd been when Marilyn won first prize in the talent contest for her elementary school; and how scared she'd been when Marilyn fell off her bike and broke her arm; and most of all what a mature and sensible and wonderful girl she had become almost on her own with hardly any help from her mother. Of course this last statement Marilyn disagreed with, saying 'my mother never interfered with my decisions, but she was always there supporting me and letting me know that it was all right to be me.'

"Marilyn had only good memories of Mrs. Henry and had accepted her death maturely with those memories to comfort her. I had thought to tell her about Harriet but it would have been cruel to throw Marilyn into emotional turmoil when she was handling her loss so well. Instead I went to Mr. Henry and pulled a bluff. You know I have quite a poker face when I need it. I told him who I was and that Harriet was ready to step in and fill Mrs. Henry's role with Marilyn. He was furious and threatened to move where she would never find him and Marilyn. He knew about the arrangement his wife had made with Harriet and had let it continue even though he disapproved of any contact with Marilyn's natural mother. I offered a compromise. I asked him to write to Harriet once a month just as his wife had done. He reluctantly agreed to do it to keep Mrs.

Once Upon a Murder

Jacobson away from Marilyn. He begged me to persuade Harriet not to push for anything more for Marilyn's sake. I told him the same arrangement would be satisfactory and so the letters continued until Harriet Jacobson was killed. Now I am the one who must return a letter to Mr. Henry and explain about Harriet. I'm sure he will be relieved and maybe even glad. I know that's unkind to say but I can't help but think it. I'm sure he couldn't have had anything to do with her death."

"Why did Mrs. Jacobson give up her child for adoption? What happened to her first husband?"

Polly felt the revelation had ended and it was safe to start asking the questions that had been popping up in her head since the story had begun.

"Mr. Jacobson was her first husband."

Frieda began searching the rows of papers for something and pulled out a yellowed envelope and handed it to Polly. Inside the envelope were two newspaper clippings. Polly unfolded one that was from a newspaper in Pennsylvania. The article described the rape of a local woman by a man who had kidnapped her from a football game. The second article related the shooting and wounding of the same kidnapper and rapist by another victim's father. The father had been an off duty police officer who had caught the man trying to rape his daughter in the parking lot of her high school after a basketball game.

"The rapist was Marilyn's father?"

"Yes. The way Harriet explained it to herself and to me it seemed to make sense. She never believed in abortion and didn't want one unnatural act to correct another. She had been brutally forced into sex by the man, her body had been violated and she swore it would not be again and so she refused her doctor's offer to perform a therapeutic abortion. She had a terrible pregnancy with periodic hemorrhaging and confinement to bed, and when the child had to be delivered by cesarean the doctor took the liberty of tying her tubes having convinced himself that her uterus could not carry another child. Back then these decisions were out of our hands. She had to stay in the hospital two weeks recovering from the ordeal. In spite of her good intentions in having the child she couldn't force herself to care for the baby. She suffered from postpartum depression and after almost two years of sharing her daughter's care with a neighbor, Harriet was persuaded to sign papers to give up her child to an agency. She never forgave herself and blamed her mental condition for her inability to keep the child. Her guilt was so deep she didn't think she had the right to a second chance and that's why she never tried to get the child back."

"That was a lot for her to keep from her husband all those years."

"It was even more difficult later when she discovered what her doctor had done to her after the delivery. You see that doctor had refused to add to her depression after Marilyn was born by telling Harriet about the surgery. When Mrs. Jacobson finally went to find out why she hadn't gotten pregnant with Stephen, her old doctor, Dr. Blaine, had died of a heart attack. She came to me and I recommended Dr. Morse, the doctor who treated us before Dr. Spellman, and he revealed the news to her. She was horrified. She thought to make up for Marilyn by having a legitimate child with her husband, but that was not to be. She offered him a divorce when she found out that by choosing not to abort her baby she had unknowingly prevented herself from conceiving again. Of course she and Dr. Morse agreed that the reason was to be their little secret   Mr. Jacobson said to her that they would close off that part of their lives that dealt with having children. He made the decision for both of them and that was that. So how could she think of suggesting the possibility of bringing an illegitimate child from rape, the only child she would ever have, into their home?"

"What a painful turn of events it must have been for her. At least she had the letters, the pictures, and the memories as Marilyn grew up.

Did she let you read the letters Mrs. Henry sent her?"

"She read them to me and then we imagined and recreated as we talked together how Marilyn had acted, looked, and talked during the incidents contained in the letters. I shared everything sent to her by Mrs. Henry."

Polly flipped through the letters in the box pulling out each successive photo and then replacing it. Occasionally she unfolded a copy of a report card or a test paper with an *A* on it. When she had gone through almost all of the neatly organized papers she pulled out a recently dated envelope that didn't match the others. It contained one sheet of paper. Polly opened the single page and began to read the familiar words. They were the same words that had been printed on the sheet of paper Sara had sent to her in Minneapolis. Harriet's last piece of treasured correspondence was a duplicate of the threatening chain letter.

EIGHT

It didn't matter that the weatherman had been correct about today, after all statistics showed they were accurate in this part of the South up to seventy-five percent of the time. It didn't matter that the humidity had reasonably abated and that there was a slight breeze that could only have come from the not too distant ocean. It didn't matter that everyone was pleasantly polite and compatible. It didn't matter because it was still a funeral and Polly hated funerals. She either didn't observe or she ignored most societal rituals and funerals fell into both groups. She found that most traditionally accepted behavior at times like this was part of built-in obligatory reflexes that others responded to without asking themselves why they did or even if they believed in the ritual that started the behavior. She was here unwillingly to participate in a behavior she had denounced long ago as being inhumane to the survivors.

Mrs. Goldman didn't drive and neither did the Gotjciks so Polly had agreed to drive them to the funeral in Sara's sedan. She hadn't intended to stay, but once there it seemed impossible for her to find a tactful way to leave. The service was to be short and at the grave site per the simple handwritten will that had been found in the Jacobsons' safe deposit box. The Jacobsons had attended a local church every Sunday and the minister, Reverend Haley, had agreed to say a few words at the cemetery. He was eighty-two and had lapses in concentration which sometimes happened in mid-sentence. When introduced to Polly it had been necessary for her to repeat her name three times in five minutes and he still walked away from her asking Frieda "Who was that nice young woman we were just talking with?"

The cemetery was small and isolated from the city's activities. The grounds were cluttered with large odd-sized concrete headstones that stood one after another and appeared to weigh heavily on the uncaring dead beneath. In between the stones were patches of crabgrass interspersed with a clover-type weed which grew untrimmed between the randomly spaced concrete markers that prevented any kind of large-scale maintenance. The Jacobsons had purchased their plots when they had first come to Florida and rented an apartment from Frieda. Stephen had been paying for the plots with monthly payments all those years and ironically had made the final payment the week before they were murdered.

There was an unusual gathering at the cemetery. The two open graves were on a small patch of high ground under one of the few trees that did not grow in a line at the ground's periphery. Since most of the mourners were elderly, Frieda had seen to the rental of fifty folding chairs which formed a wide semicircle behind the graves. A few of the chairs were occupied now by people Polly had never seen before. Polly guessed these other guests must have known the Jacobsons from church or from the seniors club they attended. Small groups formed near the chairs, each one a faction of some part of the murdered couple's private or social life. At the center linking them all together was Frieda moving freely from group to group uniting the grievers with stories they all had in common about her deceased tenants.

In spite of the intermingling of friends on the grass Polly felt a chill jolt her body as she viewed the scene. Funerals meant inevitable depression, meant bringing death into her mind and with it the pull of nothingness she was to become. There was the chrysanthemum so significant in every arrangement. She couldn't see them or smell them anywhere else and not think of them as death flowers. These had given up their lives to rest here alongside the dead people they honored. Polly felt instinctively that she had been staring too long at the graves, been standing apart from the others too long, been pretending to engage in silent meditation about her own mortality too long. She pushed back her dark memories of other funerals she had not wanted to attend and the foreboding feeling she felt at this one and walked over to stand with Frieda as the landlady removed each card from a flower arrangement and wrote on the back what had been sent and by whom.

"Isn't this arrangement of red carnations and stocks beautiful, dear?" Mrs. Goldman commented as she wrote the description of the flowers on the back of a small blue card that had been enclosed by the florist.

"They're all quite lovely." Polly replied automatically while physically gagging over the asphyxiating smell of so many heavy-scented bouquets. Flowers were one of the scents of death. There were too many gladioluses and lilies fighting each other to spew their individual scent until it became a battle of each flower racing to devour the oxygen quicker than the next. And behind her was the dank smell of the overturned earth as an even more insistent reminder of death.

"What did you say Frieda I'm afraid my mind was wandering again?"

"I said the Jacobsons got flowers from everyone at *the Oaks* even the ones who weren't up to coming today. Then there's one from the lady who did Harriet's hair; one from her doctor's office; and even a large colorful one from Mr. Henry."

Of the mourners from *the Oaks* only five besides herself and Frieda had made it to the funeral. The others had begged off for one reason or another. Most appeared fearful of acquiescing to a fate that would come to each of them in turn all too soon. Herbert Norwich and the Stangely sisters had arrived together in his old red Ford and Polly wondered again how he managed to hold each of them at bay while blatantly wooing them both along with every other woman at the ceremony.

Reverend Haley was slowly negotiating the small hill to stand at the head of the graves. He used two canes to walk and positioned himself firmly in place by digging them into the grass with his skillfully deft fingers on the brass handles. Once in place he spoke haltingly of Mr. and Mrs. Jacobson's devotion to God and of their generous donations to the church. It was a clerical eulogy that could have sufficed nicely for any of his loyal parishioners. There was nothing personal about the couple as individuals, no anecdotes or remembrances of special moments in their lives. He was appearing as requested to deliver a benign message of good will that he had tendered hundreds of times before. The small audience may have noticed the impersonal nature of the message as some seemed to be silently imagining whether such a generic message was all they would receive in departing this world. More than a few may have made a mental note to amend their wills in favor of eulogies to be delivered by family or friends or perhaps the preparation of a final text specified in writing prior to their demise which would truly allow them to *rest in peace.*

There was a pause and all eyes looked at the Reverend unsure whether the ceremony was over or whether he had merely stopped speaking again to regain some new thought that had eluded him. Reverend Haley nodded twice in finality and began to turn to walk away from the grave site. A universal rise to leave began and Polly looked through the departing faces for Sgt. Savitch. Earlier he and his two detectives had been standing near the parked cars on the road just off the funeral site. As the three had approached for the message from Reverend Haley the sergeant had moved to stand behind the rows of chairs near the

Once Upon a Murder

graves. He had stationed his detectives further away so that their view encompassed the whole scene and could take in those coming and going anywhere in the vicinity.

Savitch was once again engaged in conversation with the unpleasant looking man in the oversized jacket. The man had been standing off to the side during the ceremony and Polly was certain he had no way of hearing the Reverend's words. He had since put on the baseball cap that had been hanging at his side and continued his animated discussion with the officer. Polly saw Savitch start to physically restrain the man then think better of it and eventually let the angry man move away from the scene after the sergeant had gestured an O.K. to the watching detectives.

Polly looked around for Frieda and the Gotjciks. Sonia and Flo had descended on the Reverend after the service, each taking one of his hands in theirs thereby seriously endangering his equilibrium. Even though their actions caused his canes to fall to the ground he appeared to be enjoying the astrological future that was no doubt being imparted to him.

A short distance away Frieda was continuing to act as hostess to the mourners as they left, giving each a hug and thanking them for attending.

Polly turned around to go speak to the sergeant only to find him approaching her with the same intention. She spoke first hoping to end her curiosity about the man who had angrily severed his conversation with the officer.

"Is the man I just saw you talking with another detective assigned to this case?"

"No. If he was I would have been able to detain him with a look or a few well chosen words. Neither seemed to work on Phil Jacobson."

"Related to the deceased?"

"Yeah, Stephen's non-grieving younger brother."

"He didn't seem to care for you or the services for his brother. Why did he bother showing up at all?"

"I brought him. I was interrogating him at the station this morning before the funeral and I wanted to continue after it was over. He told me he was finished answering my stupid questions a few minutes ago and took off. He's evidently not a man to stay in one place long and he made it no secret that he and Stephen were not close. Judging from the way he talked about his brother's wife I gathered that he was quite fond of her. Not to completely change the subject, but since you're obviously the youngest and the most attractive resident at *the Oaks* I was hoping you were also the most observant and the cleverest of the group and had discovered some incriminating evidence for me on one of your temporary fellow tenants."

Once Upon a Murder

"As a matter of fact I do have something to contribute and I'll gladly tell all for even a small part of Phil Jacobson's story and anything else you may want to confide about your investigation. After all, those of us under fifty have to stick together. Sergeant Savitch?....I'm sorry....I didn't mean to presume....Sargeant?"

Polly thought he was fixing her with a stony stare because of what she was suggesting as his eyes moved away from her face to look behind her and back to the open graves. She turned to follow his gaze and to watch what had caught his attention and had made him focus so intently away from her. In her line of vision she saw two figures: one a sobbing woman who held a few red roses tied with a black ribbon as she stood looking at the caskets; the other was Mrs. Goldman rushing excitedly toward Polly arriving too breathless to speak.

"Goodness me I can't seem to catch my breath. Did you see her? How could she have known? She must know everything. But how? The poor dear. To find out like this. Poor Marilyn!"

"Marilyn?" Polly and Savitch parroted the name together--he questioningly unaware of the relationship between Marilyn and the deceased; she in astounded disbelief at Marilyn turning up at the funeral.

"Marilyn, Harriet's daughter. I'm afraid our little secret is out now. I just had to let you know about Marilyn being here after our little chat yesterday, but now I must go back to be with her. You understand don't you, dear? She has lost two mothers now and she'll need me."

Frieda turned and rushed back to take Marilyn in her arms, turning her slowly and leading her to the chairs that had recently held the mourners during the service at the grave site.

Sgt. Savitch started to approach them but Polly took his arm and begged for a moment to talk to him and a moment for the two women to talk to each other before he interrupted their emotional reunion.

NINE

"She should have told me about Marilyn the other night when she was questioned about the Jacobsons' personal life. She could at least have mentioned that there was an estranged child, a daughter that had been adopted. Chances are, under the circumstances, I would never have had to go to the Henry's house and question them. Now that Marilyn knows about her real mother, now that she's here, I'm afraid she's in it whether she's up to it or not. Don't worry I'll go slow with her, but you can see that her being here opens up a whole new angle on the murders. She could have been in an angry rage and killed Mrs. Jacobson for never keeping her natural child and him for not being able to accept the way she was conceived. Her adopted father too could have been involved because he was afraid to lose his place in Marilyn's life. He had already lost his wife and now he

Once Upon a Murder

would hold onto his adopted daughter at any price. You see the possibilities? Motive for these murders has seemed to materialize out of nowhere today. I had lots of suspects before but very few genuine motives there. Now I have a story just begging for investigation. It could turn out to be another red herring or a dead end, but it's the best lead with the exception of Phil Jacobson that we've been given since the murders were committed. He's such an obvious candidate that I almost hope he's innocent. He's ornery enough to be guilty, but I'm just tired of talking to him and getting nowhere!"

"You said he had a motive and you implied it might have been over his interest in Harriet. Don't you think that two murders are a pretty radical way to solve the problem of infatuation over his sister-in-law?"

"You'd be surprised what some people will do if they're just a little ticked off, not to mention what they're capable of when someone else has what they want."

Sgt. Savitch wasn't really paying complete attention to Polly. While he and Polly stood a little removed from the two women sitting near the graves the sergeant had not let his eyes leave that scene. He had been given an unexpected bonus at the funeral and he didn't intend to lose sight of it. He had earlier sent one of the detectives after Phil

Once Upon a Murder

Jacobson and he motioned now to Burch to come closer on the other side of where the two ladies were sitting. He was getting impatient and wasn't going to wait much longer. Amenities be damned. Polite distance from emotional outbursts was not what he had in mind. He had used those outbursts against the people having them time after time. He was a cop, not a handholding counselor.

He put his left forefinger inside the front of his collar and ran it around to the back of his neck as if to give the sweat that had gotten trapped there free rein to run down and puddle in the hollow of his collarbone. He could sense the humidity building up again promising to be one hellova hot one by tomorrow. He wasn't listening to Polly and yet he was interestingly aware of her presence as he corrected his lazy slouch and pulled in his recalcitrant pot belly to feel his pants readjust lower on his hips.

He disliked these formal occasions outside the office that required him to wear a suit or a sport coat and slacks. There was only one season in this city and he had bought two summer suits for days like this when he knew in advance he would need to be dressed like this all day. For the office he had a sport jacket conveniently draped over the back of his chair for when he needed a temporary dress up to his wardrobe or when the brass occasionally popped in to check things out. It didn't matter that what he was wearing was a lightweight suit. He was stifling in it and knew he looked like an overheated civil servant. The confinement of his clothing only made him edgier.

He'd waited long enough. He stretched himself out to his approximately six feet and approached Marilyn and Frieda using his most confident cop swagger. He was determined not to end this day as defeated by the case as he had felt when the day had begun. He noticed Burch relax against the tree as he saw his superior move to confront the newest suspect. Sgt. Savitch felt rather than saw Polly follow him to the folding chairs and take a seat next to Frieda as he pulled one of the uncomfortable chairs away from the row and banged it down in front of the three women, an action that commanded their attention and set himself up as the controlling influence of the group at the same time.

"I'm Sergeant Savitch. I understand Harriet Jacobson was your mother. I'm very sorry about her death and sorry too that I have to use this indelicate opportunity to ask you some questions. You were a complete surprise to me," he said while giving Mrs. Goldman a glance that made her stiffen, "and if I had known about your existence before I would have had you in my office for questioning days ago. So you see I'm already behind in finding out what you have to say. Shall we begin?"

"I-I-I don't know what I can tell you. I never knew her and she didn't know I knew about her so I really have nothing to say."

"Let me be the judge of that. Let's start with what you know that I don't about you and Mrs. Jacobson. When did you find out that she was your mother?"

Marilyn looked down into her lap. Her hands toyed with the black ribbon on the flowers she had brought to the funeral as she hesitated to speak while she considered whether to create a lie or to reveal the truth.

Savitch took it all in and didn't miss the delay or the contrived answer that followed.

"My father told....I mean my adopted father told me after she died. He thought I should say good-bye even though I had never known her."

Savitch couldn't help but pounce. It was second nature to him and somehow he knew she could take it.

"He encouraged you to come to the funeral? He had kept her existence secret from you for what, over twenty years, and all of a sudden he tells you when she dies, when he has every reason to believe that with her dead you would probably never find out who she was?"

Once Upon a Murder

"I don't know why he told me. Maybe it was because I saw the letter that Mrs. Goldman wrote him about her death."

"But I didn't...." Mrs. Goldman put her hand over her mouth as if to stop the officer from hearing what she had let escape unintentionally in her excitement.

"Mrs. Goldman," the sergeant spoke barely able to control the aggravation he was feeling toward Marilyn for lying, "did you write Mr. Henry a letter telling him about the Jacobsons' deaths?"

"I, well, I don't really remember. Harriet and I wrote to him every month before she died. I could have told him in my last letter. Since the murders I'm afraid I have been retelling the horrible story to most of my friends and I do remember writing about it to a few who live out of the city. I honestly can't remember if I wrote him before or after the deaths. Maybe I just thought I would have written him. I just can't remember."

"Frieda," Polly interjected, "when you told me about Marilyn yesterday you mentioned that you had phoned Mr. Henry with the news of Harriet's death. Did you feel you needed to write something more to him after the phone call you made? Did you send a letter that could have been received this soon after the deaths?"

Once Upon a Murder

"No, that's right! I was muddled up in my head. Sometimes days and happenings get changed around in my head and sometimes I don't know if I did some things at all. But I have my good days. Thank you Polly for jogging this old memory. I can tell you now sergeant right out and for certain that I did call Mr. Henry to tell him Mrs. Jacobson had died and I know I haven't written to him since. I know that because my letter writing pen needs a new cartridge. It's right here in my purse. I dropped it in here so I would have it with me when I went to the store."

She had been fumbling in the bottom of her bag and now held up the pen triumphantly as proof of her credibility. A look of pride came to her face as if her producing the pen was a symbol of her competence. The look of pride was replaced by a look of relief, the relief of knowing her moment of lucidity was validated. The second look and its accompanying feeling might not automatically follow so easily for her the next time she questioned her memory.

The sergeant lingered in his looks at Frieda and Polly as Marilyn regrouped. He wondered what she was planning to tell him now. It was cool under the tree where they sat and he suddenly felt more charitable toward the child who had come to pay her last respects to a mother who had said good-bye to her as a baby and had virtually denied her the right to be here. He recovered from his reverie in a moment as he picked up a dry leaf that had fallen on his pants and crushed it. The effect was immediate. Marilyn came out of her thoughts with a start and met his stare.

"So I knew about her. Does it really matter how I found out? I'll tell you how it happened. I found the letters. He'd been keeping them in one of my other mother's trunks. He never could give away her things after she died. Anything that had been hers is still in the house. When she died he never offered them to me, he just packed them away in two trunks and put them in the spare room closet. I guess he thought there would be a time when he'd be able to give them to me or a time when I would ask about them. But still, even now, we both avoid the subject as if the trunks don't exist. That doesn't mean I haven't wanted to go through her things and remember the way my mother, Mrs. Henry, looked in the familiar clothes and jewelry and the way she always smelled of a kind of creamy soap. It wasn't the smell of perfume or cologne or makeup or any number of smells you get from other women. Just the smell of sweetness, a pink smell I used to call it. That's what I thought from the time I was a little girl. I'd tell my friends, 'My mother smells like the color pink.'"

Once Upon a Murder

Frieda had her arm around Marilyn, but Marilyn didn't notice that she was being comforted, that she could be comforted. Her gray-green eyes looked fathoms deep, as if she had fallen into them and was fighting her way slowly out of their depths with each fresh memory. She finally reached the surface hard and gasping.

"All that's over now. What good does it do to remember things that weren't mine? She was never my mother just an available substitute. My memories of her should be dead like she is. She was my caretaker. I'll remember her that way from now on. And Mr. Henry. I never felt close to him and now I know why. He was never as good as she was at pretending to be a real parent and I sensed it. When I go back to the house it will be to pack and leave. I only stayed to keep what I thought was left of my family together. Now I don't feel like part of his family or any family. There's just me. I told him I was coming to the funeral. I told him I was leaving him, his house, and the two trunks behind. Leaving everything behind."

Savitch could see that Frieda wanted to immerse Marilyn in stories about the love her real mother always had for her and tell her what a lucky girl she was to have had two loving mothers not just one, but he couldn't let her do that now. This was an interview with a murder suspect and he was pushing patience to allow her companion to remain. The two women could patch up Marilyn's way of thinking later. He needed facts and she was in a perfect state of mind to give him those.

"When was it you discovered the letter. How long ago?"

Marilyn held herself stiff and unyielding as if she would not allow the questions to penetrate her protective exterior.

"It was several months ago. Mr. Henry had to go out of town for a few days and a strange letter came to the house. The return address label showed it came from Mrs. Goldman. She and I had become friends after my mo-- after Sharon Henry died so I didn't think there was any harm in opening the letter. After the first few lines I realized the letter wasn't from Frieda at all but from another lady, and there was a check in the letter--money to buy me a gift from her--from this other lady. I didn't understand why this lady who I had never met before would be buying me a present. I read that part again thinking I must have misunderstood and that the money was from Frieda, but no it was a check from the account of Mr. and Mrs. Jacobson. She asked in the letter for my stepfather to send another picture of me and I felt funny and scared all together, like I was unknowingly being used for some secret purpose.

Once Upon a Murder

I didn't like the way the letter made me feel. I went to the desk and looked through the address book. I found her name and address. She lived at the same place as Mrs. Goldman only in another apartment number. Who was she and why didn't she use her own name label as the return address? I started going through the things on the desk. There was a large daily calendar Mr. Henry left at the house so I would always know where he was. He writes everything down; he has a terrible memory. I flipped the pages and each month was the same. He had written at the end of each month *write letter*. I sat there imagining all kinds of things but none of them seemed to be the possible truth. I finally settled on the idea that she must have been his mistress."

Marilyn looked around at the faces sitting with her to see if that conclusion seemed logical on her part, trying to force her mind back to the time when a mistress for her father would have been so easy to contend with compared to the reality she discovered later that day. The faces offered no break in her story only a stoic acknowledgment of her attempt to find out the truth and an unspoken encouragement for her to continue.

"I opened the desk drawers one by one but everything was as I remembered it, familiar and expected, until I shut the center drawer hard and heard the tinkle of something in the drawer. I opened it again and couldn't find the cause for the noise. I took out the drawer and looked underneath the desk. Hanging on a nail at the back of the drawer were two keys on a chain. They were small and similar in shape and I didn't recall having seen them before. I took them and stood there wondering what they opened. As I held them I went frantically through the house looking for something the keys would fit. Something was being kept from me. What was it and why? The keys had to be for something of his in the garage. I looked through everything, all of his tools, things in the drawers of his workshop. There was nothing to use the keys on. I tried to calm myself. I looked at the keys again. They were not safety deposit keys or any regular house or car keys. They looked more like keys to a suitcase and then I remembered the trunks. I relaxed a little knowing now that the reason he had hidden the keys was to keep the trunks and what they represented out of his mind.

    I almost put the keys back. I had the drawer out. I had almost forgotten about the mysterious Mrs. Jacobson but now I remembered and got the idea that maybe this would be a good time to go through the trunks. It wouldn't upset my father and I would be free to cry if I wanted to. I went to the spare room and dragged the first trunk out. There was no dust on the top like there was on the

Once Upon a Murder

other one. It had been opened, cleaned off, used recently. My heart was racing again. When I finally made my shaking hands open the trunk I cried out when I saw bunches of letters on top of the clothes, letters just like the one I had opened earlier. I sat down and gathered the letters in my lap. The postmarks went back years and years. I found the very first one addressed to Mrs. Henry and began to read words about me as a baby and as a little girl, words written by this Jacobson woman to my mother.

I read three letters before it hit me. The *our girl* Mrs. Jacobson kept referring to was me--I was the shared child--the child given up by my real mother for adoption. I put the rest of the letters in order and began to read them. I sat there for hours remembering my life as the letters went back over the years. Every few letters Mrs. Jacobson would beg to see me. She wanted to come to the house as a stranger or a friend, anything to meet me, and I guessed from what she wrote that Sharon Henry threatened to move, to take me away and break the contact she had made with my real mother. And so the letters went on. When I was through I didn't cry or feel sorry for myself. I was angry. Damn them all for keeping this from me! All the closeness and trust I had felt all those years with my mother and father fell away at that moment since its foundation was gone. I was more alone then I had ever been. I had no one to talk to. I had lost a real mother and an unimagined one and had an adopted father I didn't want to confide in. There was nowhere to go where I couldn't expect more lies. I went to sleep that night with the light on, something I hadn't done since I was five." Marilyn let her head and shoulders sag as if the burden of her memories was too much to fight against.

"Are you still that angry, Marilyn? Did that anger make you confront the Jacobsons last Friday night in their apartment? Maybe you confronted them with more than the truth. Maybe threats got in the way of the reason you had gone there to use against them. Did actually seeing them, seeing her, drive you to violence? And then when the violence had spent itself did you realize too late that you hadn't gotten the answers about your adoption that you had come for? Weren't you too upset to try and understand the reasons she might have given you anyway? Didn't you just want to hurt her for giving you away, to strike out and hurt them both when you found them together."

Savitch pushed for a quick confession out of instinct and under an adrenaline high he always had at the build up of his own questioning techniques. When he took a breath after this last push at Marilyn he wondered why he had even bothered when he already knew that if she was the

Once Upon a Murder

killer a jury would probably let her off quickly and lightly for a crime committed under emotional duress.

"I was mad as hell at them, at my real parents, but I didn't kill them."

The sergeant looked at Polly and then at Frieda. Marilyn didn't know all of it yet. The three of them realized she would be in for another shock. Mr. Henry hadn't told her about her real father. She still thought it was Mr. Jacobson. Even Savitch had no heart or adrenaline left for the telling of the rest of Marilyn's nightmare. Phil Jacobson and Marilyn, both were promising suspects, yet both were trying prospects to question in their own way. He turned to Marilyn with his eyes finally softened in expectation of another blow she would have to take today.

"I want to talk to you again tomorrow. Call me and let me know when you can come in." He placed one of his cards gently next to the flowers in her lap and got up to leave. "Mrs. Goldman needs to tell you something else you should know, something that wasn't in the letters."

He didn't have to tell Polly to follow him. She got up automatically to join Savitch, unwilling to be part of the young woman's new pain, as they walked away and then stopped a short distance from Marilyn and Frieda.

Once Upon a Murder

"This is going to be even harder for her to hear than everything she already knows. I can't imagine what this last confession is going to do to her. Now she'll want to get to know about her real father and the build up of pain will start all over again."

Polly knew as she said the words what an endless and dark life that would be for her under the circumstances. Marilyn would possibly want to dedicate her life to digging in the past instead of creating a new life by using the discoveries she had made to strengthen herself in the future.

Polly and Savitch watched as Frieda took the younger woman's hands in hers in the hope of containing the emotion that was to come within her own clenched fingers. But nothing could contain the wounded cry from Marilyn as Frieda told her she was the child of a rapist who had died in prison ten years ago.

TEN

In Polly's opinion everything she had seen and heard since she walked in the building was classic cop. All the images, the chaos, the stereotypes fit from old TV shows, old paperbacks and old movie renderings. There were attempts to tone down language and spruce up clothing and posture as she passed but they were haphazard and lackadaisical. The detectives were the fixtures; she was just passing through. Perhaps they gawked because she was comparatively overdressed in her pastel silk suit, but what did one wear to a police station? What was proper attire if you hadn't been summoned or you weren't escorted here in handcuffs? She'd thought enough not to wear any *hot colors*, nothing that would cling to her body, and definitely nothing revealing. As she walked toward the office she had been directed to she thought to herself that this is what catcalling

Once Upon a Murder

construction workers must be like when you get them down from their high-rise buildings and put them on the ground.

As she maneuvered between the green metal desks and the odd assortment of victims, suspects, and investigators, she noticed Burch waving to her from his niche off to the right. She returned his wave and kept going in the direction he was indicating, hesitating briefly before entering the empty office that belonged to Sergeant Savitch. According to the lettering on the door it was H. E. Savitch. Not much of an office, technically only a glassed-in green metal desk like the others. In addition to the desk he had two metal chairs, a file cabinet, and venetian blinds to accessorize the room; but it was an office nevertheless and she was sure that it was significant in the pecking order of police hierarchy.

She was a little late and wondered why he wasn't sitting in his chair waiting to chastise her for it and give her a short monologue on the value of a sergeant's time. It was noisy as she waited inside the uncarpeted office. Everything and everybody made sounds and those sounds were amplified as they scrambled off the walls and the ceiling and the floor looking for and not finding something soft to absorb them.

She sat there nervously questioning herself for staying. After all, what information did she really

Once Upon a Murder

have to give him? He was busy with a criminal investigation and the Jacobson murders must have been only one of the cases he was working on. He had plenty of witnesses and suspects and now he had Marilyn and her unexpected involvement. How could Polly think of presenting him with yet another aspect of life at *the Oaks*, of opening yet another direction in his investigation and one that might be completely unrelated? She was just about to swivel around in her chair to leave when he stepped through the door and audibly sighed as he mentally logged another interview into his already full schedule.

"Good morning, Mrs. Sloan. I thought you might not show up just like my new acquaintances Phil Jacobson and Marilyn Henry. I thought you might have had enough police contact yesterday at the funeral." He lit a cigarette from one of the two opened packs on his desk with a silver flip-topped lighter without asking if she minded him smoking.

She didn't care that he hadn't asked before lighting up. It was his office. He inhaled long and hard several times as he relaxed in his chair, smoking as if he were trying to catch up from having been deprived earlier. Suddenly she didn't know how to approach the subject of the letters. Every way that she had reasoned they might be important in the case seemed unimportant and frivolous to her now that she was in his office. As if she would know something no one else knew. As if the letters had some legitimate place in the thick file on Savitch's desk, the one with its tab jutting out and the heavy black ink that spelled out the murdered victims' names. She decided quickly just to let his behavior and interest guide her to reveal or not what was in her handbag.

"I'm much too curious. It's more police contact not less that will answer my questions. And since I've been thrown into this case along with the others at *the Oaks* I can't avoid what's happening just because I'd rather not face the unpleasantness. Not only that, but my closest friend may have ended up in the same way had it not been providence, luck, or the mere randomness of the murderer's choosing."

Polly had blurted this last part out not because she wanted to make Sara a possible murder victim, but to force her way further into the case with her anger about Sara's accident, an anger she knew would put Savitch on the defensive and cause him to relax his protective guard with what little sympathy she thought he could display.

"What about Sara, Mrs. Sloan? Just because she lives in the same building are you implying....? No. There's nothing to indicate so far that these murders were specific to the tenants at *the Oaks*. Everything we've found out so far indicates that the murders were because of something in the

Once Upon a Murder

Jacobsons' past and I certainly have plenty to go on there after yesterday."

"Sergeant, please call me Polly. I'm not a Mrs. and Mrs. Sloan is my ex-mother-in-law so please don't take me down memory lane by giving me a title I left behind a long time ago and have no desire to reattach."

"Okay, Polly then. I might as well be on a first name basis with you as well since for some reason or other I seem determined to talk to you about the funeral and the case in general without of course giving you any restricted information which I can't divulge."

Polly felt her body shift to relax and tense with excitement at the same time. Before she could hear anything further the sergeant had to say, she heard someone calling from just outside the office and saw Savitch's features grimace at the words. Koslovsky stuck his head in and politely greeted her and then signaled for Savitch to come out of his office for a minute. He walked back to his chair after a few minutes holding a printed copy of data from the police computer. He appeared lost in thought about this new information and Polly wanted to get back to the ease that had begun to settle between them before the detective's entrance.

"What was it the detective called you before?"

Once Upon a Murder

"It's a nickname. No one is immune to tags here. They gave it to me after I got this office. On the door H. E. Savitch. What he called me was *he-man*. It's a stretch I know but it stuck. These guys don't know from perfect; if they think it bugs you they keep it up. I never encouraged it but I can't stop it either."

"What do the initials stand for?"

"Hartley Edward. My mother wanted me to be a lawyer so she gave me a lawyer's name. The Captain calls me Hart when he's not using my nickname and to every one out there I'm just Sarge or he-man. Believe it or not most of the time it's said with respect."

Polly could tell that was true just from the interplay between him and the two detectives she had met at the crime scene. Looking across at him now she suspected he was an uneasy combination of the lingering hard-hitting investigator type that was becoming passé in modern police work and the sensitive psychological investigator his Criminal Science Degree dictated he should be.

He lit another cigarette and started talking about the case. The interviews in general that he had been through with the Jacobsons' seniors group turned out to be routine with no concrete new leads. They had been well liked as a couple. Interviews with their church group same thing. A few people had mentioned Mr. Jacobson's link to a farm run by his brother in Kansas, and the women repeatedly said that Harriet was uncomfortable when asked about her family. As he ran down individual names, occupations, and comments from several pages of condensed notes he had pulled from the file she realized he was only summarizing his thoughts aloud for himself and not really confiding or explaining the nuances of the case to her. She was content to listen and be a silent sounding board for his dialogue.

If the opening never came for her to offer what she viewed as possible evidence in the crime maybe she'd present a hypothetical situation of supposed evidence and see if he was interested enough to draw her out. Then she could present the chain letters as a less than foolish bid to be helpful and cooperative.

The monologue got interesting when he delved into the bio on Phil Jacobson. Evidently the feeling of dislike Savitch had felt toward the suspect at the funeral continued in his assessment of the man's habits and life on the farm in Kansas. Besides the attachment Phil had shown toward his dead sister-in-law there was also an undercurrent of hate toward his dead brother based, Savitch believed, on that jealousy and simple monetary greed.

"....Phil has a great setup in Kansas but the big time farm owner in Kansas was just a hick to his brother Stephen. They didn't get along because of the tension between the two brothers over Mrs. Jacobson and because Stephen actually owned the farm. It was in the father's will. Stephen as the oldest son held the title as was family tradition. Property's been in the family for four generations. Always done that way back there. Property's passed from eldest son down to his eldest son and so on. Evidently they weren't a family big on having girls. Oh there are a couple in there all right, but the boys always outnumbered them. Phil ran the farm just as if he owned it. He didn't have to pay Stephen what the farm made; the profits were automatically reinvested in the farm. The Jacobsons had plenty of money coming in every month from pension and social security. But there was always this lever, this control Stephen had over Phil, to exercise at will if Stephen felt his brother was handling things wrong. Jacobson here had final approval over the way Phil spent the money and that along with the brother's feelings for Mrs. Jacobson could have pushed him to do something completely on his own with no final approval from brother, something like kill the goose that had the golden egg in his name. I know. What about Harriet Jacobson? If he loved her why kill her? Suppose she spurned him in front of Stephen, major confrontation, all the ugliness and the way things really were spelled out

Once Upon a Murder

for Phil in the presence of his long time lady love. Phil kills Stephen to get the farm and kills her as an afterthought when she wasn't supportive. It's weak at this point, still an unproven theory."

The way he analyzed the motivations and simplified death away made Polly wonder whether the evidence led to the theories about the crime or if one or two main theories grew and branched out to encompass the criminal evidence. And once again she found the objectivity incredible. It wasn't exactly cold and detached but the bodies had somehow slipped from having once been people to now being building blocks in a larger picture. Murder was the most important crime, the most heinous, and at the same time the most exciting to investigate. At least that was the way it appeared to her, that's what she got from his voice and his enthusiasm. She could see what he felt about it in his eyes. Savitch was in a struggle, a challenge match against a killer, and despite what he had just said about Phil Jacobson she felt that this was not the theory he firmly believed in.

"You believe it's as pat as that? Younger brother kills older brother for clear title to a farm?" Polly ventured to ask as Savitch seemed to be letting his own explanation of the crimes sink in and consume his doubts. "Was Phil in town the night of the murders?"

Once Upon a Murder

"He was here all right. He left his farm two days before the murders and apparently heard about them the morning after over his motel radio. He called in to us and I sent a car to bring him to the station. That was my first meeting with him; yesterday at the funeral was the second."

"His appearance at the funeral was less than remorseful or respectful toward his dead brother and sister-in-law. He was obviously agitated about something. What's he like?"

"He's sporadically noncommunicative. He's moody and broods about something inside all the time. Never smiles. Introverted and underdeveloped in the social graces. Somewhat of a recluse. Just works the farm. Has his small town prejudices about the outside world. Very superstitious. Believes in the weather as a force, a power that he talks to and guards against. I guess that's the farmers' lot, worrying all the time about nature dumping on you more than people do. The day after he came in we heard from the Farmers Franchise Bank in the small town closest to his farm. He'd been in to apply for a loan to help pay for two new pieces of heavy equipment. Manager told him he had exceeded his authority for purchases for the year, the contract with Stephen again, and that he'd have to have a notarized letter from his brother to make the purchases. According to the bank manager Phil was *very hot*

Once Upon a Murder

under the collar and saying things like 'I'm tired of begging from him; he doesn't run the farm I do.' And get this, the manager distinctly remembers Jacobson saying 'When will he die and quit messing with my life?' Good witness if we need him.

Evidently Phil hitched his way here, claims he arrived the afternoon of the murders. The trucker team who gave him his ride into town insisted he have dinner with them and see a show at a club out on the highway. He conveniently doesn't remember the trucking company name. The two good ol' boys only gave him nicknames so we're having trouble running them down. Have to check trucking companies based on the color of the truck through unions and other truckers to see if we can locate these two and substantiate his alibi. He says he didn't see his brother and sister-in-law but he did call. Stephen knew he was in town and that he was angry and demanding."

"Why now? The farm's been in Stephen's name all along and the physical distance between the two brothers paralleled their personal distance from probably the time of Stephen's marriage or even before. Phil must have had to come to his brother other times over the years even if he didn't like it or accept it. Why now? Do you think he's capable of murder or is he just irrational and easily riled? He sounds to me like a man who reacts on a very basic level guided by beliefs and habits deeply embedded in his personality. If he'd done it wouldn't he have trouble with his conscience if he returned to his farm as if nothing happened? I don't think a man who acts more from instinct than motive or violence could go against nature like that. It's too much a factor in his life. He respects nature and acknowledges its power. He could kill to eat, to survive; but not to gain financially. I've known some farm families. They wouldn't kill to gain something material and I don't think from what you've told me Phil Jacobson would either."

"I feel the same way you do about his chances of being the murderer, but until his alibi is verified I'm leaning toward the possibility that he's a psychopathic farmer acting in character."

"The man did seem unpleasant to me from a distance and I haven't even met him yet. His actions at the funeral may just have been those of an uncomfortable country man reacting to the rituals and laws of the big city which make little sense to him and which he feels have no right to dictate his actions and certainly no hold on him here longer than necessary. Now that Stephen is dead will the farm revert to Phil as the eldest living son?"

"We're looking into that. Neither Stephen or Phil has any children so it won't be passed down another generation unless Marilyn wants to file a claim for it. I'm sure there must be a provision covering the eventuality of no natural children, but the lawyer who drew up the will is on vacation. His law office is closed. The County Recorder's Office up there doesn't have a copy of any new will for the older brother. We were able to contact the secretary and expect a fax of the codicil to the will we found in the apartment. All we know is what Phil told us, or what he wants us to know, and Stephen's handwritten will refers to this Will of Property that was kept at the lawyer's office. We'll have to wait until tomorrow to find out the status of the farm as it stands now. Meanwhile I have had my men concentrating on alibis for the people from the seniors group, the Jacobsons' church, and *the Oaks*. There are a lot of calls to make. The tenants that you haven't met yet have to be alibied along with all the ones who are still in town. We do have a good start on the three missing apartment dwellers though.

"Apartment two resident, one Larry Stone, a retired metal worker and ex-bodybuilder. Pretty much a loner. Stays in his apartment. Watches wrestling or boxing or other sporting events and drinks beer and smokes cigars. He went to Hawaii for ten days on a tour package. Likes to swim. Used to be a competitive swimmer in high school. Goes to the Islands to snorkel and scuba dive every year. He's still partners in a health club with

Once Upon a Murder

one of his cronies, a guy named 'Flasher' Hiltz. No, I don't know how he got the name. The tour is loosely controlled time-wise, a few group dinners and tours and a lot of time for individual recreation. Nothing planned for the day or evening of the murders. We're checking airlines and time frames to see if it's possible for him to be involved. He left the hotel the day before the murders to visit one of the other Islands and hasn't shown up back at the base hotel yet. No conceivable motive for him to have done it according to residents at *the Oaks*.

Apartment 10A, Chrystal Langford, went to a reunion of old hoofers in New York. A vaudeville routine get together. We tracked her down at an evening performance for charity at the Courtland Convalescent Hospital. She was doing another benefit for servicemen when the murders were committed. Scratch her.

Apartment 10B, Mr. and Mrs. Kearney, Tom and Ruth. The couple took their R.V. out of storage and went to visit grandchildren, two in Indiana and three in Illinois. Going to be gone about one month. They're traveling between grandchildren now but the oldest daughter has been contacted and will have them call us when they arrive. Again no possible known motive. The Kearneys are well liked and they're the organizers for activities at the apartment house.

Once Upon a Murder

They plan get-togethers and short trips with the other tenants and Ruth regularly visits with them all at *the Oaks*. She could have known more about the Jacobsons than anyone else, but we won't know until they call in. I don't expect them to be guilty but maybe they'll be able to add something to what we already know about the Jacobsons, maybe another motive we haven't thought of yet. And then there's this." Savitch finished while waving the computer sheet enticingly at Polly.

"I've been wondering about that ever since the detective gave it to you. New evidence about Phil or Marilyn?"

"No, but I think I'll keep you in suspense for a while. It's your turn. You're not here to observe police methods and you haven't been summoned as a suspect since you arrived in town after the murders were committed. So you think you know something, don't you? Something I've missed?"

"It doesn't sound to me that you could have missed much, a.a.a.nd you might find out anyway if there are others or if any of the other tenants volunteers a letter...that is, if they got one..."

"Whoa! What letter? If you've got pertinent physical evidence from this crime give it up. I'll try to forget how you got it and that you're offering it a little late in the game."

"It's nothing I'm not entitled to have, nothing I came by deviously or illegally. Actually I would

Once Upon a Murder

have given it to you at the funeral but you seemed to have your hands full with other new information then."

"You've got my full attention now. Give."

"Just a few words of explanation and then you'll know and see what I found out and what I suspect. Maybe it's irrelevant, coincidental, and of no value, but at least that will be for you to decide now--I simply can't stand speculating about it any more. Before I made this trip Sara sent me a note and included with it a letter she had received. She sent the note because she had fallen down the second story stairs at *the Oaks* under suspicious circumstances. The letter she included was mildly threatening and she feared some connection."

Polly pulled the first letter out of her purse and offered it to Savitch.

"It's a chain letter. O.K., I can see the skepticism in your face and feel you're ready to laugh this off. Read it. It's sort of standard format. Notice the four names and addresses on the list. All local. Unusual for a legitimate chain letter. After the funeral I drove around town before it got dark. I was only able to go to two of the addresses, the last two. They don't exist. Why? Why send a letter with non-existent names and addresses? The second name and address isn't listed in the city street directory. I was going to

Once Upon a Murder

go to the library and try to investigate the street name today."

Savitch shook his head.

"Maybe not then. The first name, the one Sara would have mailed her letter to, is a P.O.Box under the name R. Rodriguez. There are eleven R. Rodriguezes in the directory. That's where you and your detectives come in....."

"Very thoughtful of you to need us. Chain letters usually originate and continue for personal gain, anything from getting recipes from a hundred housewives to pyramid schemes worth thousands to the participants. This one does sound a little different. No chance of fingerprints now. Where's the envelope?"

"Sorry, I don't have it. I asked Sara about it after I arrived. She thinks she used it as a coaster for a drink and threw it away. But of course that was before she fell and reconsidered the importance of the letter as a serious threat to her health."

"Tell me about the fall. I'll also call her and get it firsthand, but go ahead and tell me what she told you as completely as you remember it."

"Remember Mrs. Sotheby, apartment #7 upstairs? She can create a guilt complex in anyone and has a tendency to whine appealingly to get a regular flow of visitors through her apartment. Sara went upstairs to visit one evening. It was

Once Upon a Murder

dark outside but she swears the overhead light at the top of the stairs was on when she went up. When she left it was out but she didn't think anything of it at the time--just a burnt out bulb that needed to be replaced. There was something on the stairs that hadn't been there on the way up. She turned her ankle and fell to the bottom landing hard against that terra cotta potted palm in the corner of the courtyard. Just an accident? Maybe. And afterwards she only felt like anyone would, foolish at having fallen. Thought she hadn't been paying attention and just tripped on her own feet even though she had made the trip upstairs to that apartment dozens of times. The more she thought about it the more she was sure the stairway had been intentionally dangerous. She went back hours after the fall, after she had soaked and bandaged her foot. The light was on and the stairs were clear. That sounds contrived on someone's part to me and I more or less convinced her of the same thing."

"It could have been perfectly innocent. The light bulb could have been loose and someone came by and tightened it. The stairs could have been clear all the time. Sara just thought, like you said, that she tripped or slipped without anything having been there."

"Okay if you want to excuse it as an accident go ahead, but nevertheless two people were

Once Upon a Murder

murdered a few days later and I don't think they were killed by a discontent and greedy brother or a resentful adopted daughter. I was there after the murders in case you forgot. What was done to their faces had a purpose for the killer and I can't see either Marilyn or Phil staying around with the bodies long enough to practice that kind of artwork."

"That bothers me too. But murder is very seldom logical or reasoned except to the murderer and until I can find out what he or she meant by the face drawings I'm inclined to believe it was an afterthought, just something the murderer did to throw us a curve and make us suspect it was a psycho."

"When I saw their faces I subconsciously flashed back to when my daughter was a little girl. The exaggerated features drawn and the way they simplified the complex shapes and angles of the features made me think about my daughter's drawings of people at that age. The faces were colored like a child would make a drawing of people for school, exaggerated facial features at that age is what kids concentrate on because most of them don't have the sense of proportion yet to do a complete body picture . I'm sure you know by now what made the lines. It wasn't crayon by any chance?"

Once Upon a Murder

"It was crayon. Playhouse Brand Crayons red number two to be exact. Anyone can pick up a box of them at any drugstore or toy store in the city. It was crayon though and I have to lean toward Marilyn trying to relive something from her childhood with her dead parents, something another set of parents had witnessed with her as she was growing up. She didn't know until yesterday that Jacobson wasn't her real father. She killed them both as being equally guilty of giving her up for adoption, froze them immortal in time for her purposes, and then spent private time with them which had never been an option for her before. Strictly amateur psychology granted but I'll throw it out for the shrink this afternoon and see what he has to say.

"And about the chain letter....the vague threat about guilt....that is unusual. What did the writer hope to achieve? Was he going to go around punishing anyone who didn't return the letter by making them fall down a flight of stairs or with some other mischievous accident? Chain letters involve other people. According to my recollection of them doesn't the last name on the list have to be the person who sent the letter to her? You say the address is a phony? I'll check out the names and addresses. It won't take long, but really the letter could have been perfectly

Once Upon a Murder

harmless and there's nothing to make me think there's a connection with the murders."

"Then maybe this will change your mind." Polly opened her purse again and withdrew the second letter and envelope encased in plastic and handed it across the desk to the sergeant.

"After Mrs. Goldman told me about Marilyn she showed me the box of letters she kept for Mrs. J., letters from the Henrys about Marilyn. Frieda Goldman also kept anything else that Mrs. J. wanted to keep from her husband. This letter was the last thing she gave Mrs. Goldman before the murders. Frieda told me Harriet Jacobson thought it could have been about her particular guilt at giving away her child. She was terrified that someone else had found out. She couldn't confide in Stephen so she went to Frieda. Frieda told her it was probably sent to her because her name was on a list from a company she had patronized or that her name had been taken out of the telephone directory. Mrs. Goldman advised her tenant not to send it back and assured her she had nothing to feel guilty about. Mrs. J. insisted Frieda keep the letter anyway. And to anticipate your next question, no, Frieda didn't get a letter herself."

Now the sergeant's face formed a deeper frown as he carefully removed the second letter from its envelope. He laid the two side by side and compared them.

Once Upon a Murder

"The letters are identical. That means both came from the same name on the list, presumably the last one. Detective Koslovsky is going to love following up on this clue. One letter sent to a teacher whose name is on dozens of lists isn't anything unusual and deserves no special consideration. A second identical letter received by a tenant at the same apartment building as the teacher, a tenant who is shortly thereafter murdered, is possibly significant. Even so, if all the names on the list are bogus I'm afraid we're stuck with a dead end. It's conceivable that the sender didn't expect the letters to be returned. He could have sent them strictly for their nuisance value, and yet, if we get any validation from the names and addresses on the list to the effect that they were randomly sent, maybe we can at least get the post office to lean on this person and threaten him with some mail fraud statute to get him to stop. I'll have to check all the remaining tenants to see if they got letters too. Thanks to you, now I have even more loose ends to tie up than I did before you came in."

"I'm sorry if the letters mean more work but I thought you should know about them. How far you take it from here I guess will depend on what you find out about the names on the list. I hope it turns out to be a dead end because at this point I don't think there are just two letters and if any

Once Upon a Murder

others were sent to *the Oaks* I don't like to think what that could mean. I'll confess to you that I have been very careful since I've been there. I'm always expecting something else to happen and I carry a flashlight when I walk around at night in case I find any loose light bulbs. Well, I've delivered my evidence so I'll leave now so you can get Detective Koslovsky going to check the addresses. Will you let me know what happens?"

"As a matter of fact I have to go see one of the other tenants later today." He picked up the previously ignored computer sheet again. "Two of my favorite people from *the Oaks*, Flo and Sonia, have been less than candid about their past. Mrs. Gotjcik had a previous brush with crime. She went all the way to involvement in hit and run to make one of her predictions come true. It just came over from the Georgia Police. She spent only six months in jail thanks to the support of another influential client who had connections. I think it's time to see how far she would go to change other predictions to reality. If I know anything about the letters by the time I drive over to the apartment building I'll stop by."

"I hope you do and thank you."

"For what?"

"For not coming right out and saying that the chain letters have no possible connection to the murders and for not dismissing me as a

151

Once Upon a Murder

meddlesome pest in your case. And while I'm at it I would also like to thank you for letting Sara go to New Orleans. You could have been unreasonable and demanded she stay here during the investigation."

"I don't think she had anything to do with the murders and I honestly felt no compelling reason to force her to stay in town and risk the anger of the whole University being turned against me. I feel bad enough knowing that I spoiled the vacation the two of you had planned. I really ought to be thanking you for being so cooperative in spite of the fact that I've ruined your long awaited and deserved vacation cruise. Our city locales can hardly compete with the sites you would have seen on your vacation, but I hope you will find something pleasant in our city to make your stay more enjoyable."

As they both got up to leave the office Polly noticed Savitch extend his torso with an intake of air to stretch his true height. He was only pushing six feet but she was sure that he claimed every inch of it and his thick, wavy, brown-gray hair made believers out of any skeptical audience including herself.

ELEVEN

On the drive back to *the Oaks* Polly's head was filled with the information the sergeant had given her and the numerous possibilities the information generated. Had Phil killed his brother and his sister-in-law to rid himself of their involvement in his life? Had Marilyn been so distraught over the discovery of her real parents that she had grotesquely eliminated them from her life? Did one of the missing tenants kill the J's and then go off merrily on vacation? Were the chain letters directly connected to the murders or did they pose a separate and unrelated threat? Or no threat at all? Would all the leads away from *the Oaks* fall through and prove that she must be spending her vacation in an apartment building with a murderer or maybe several murderers with a common purpose? She tried to put a halt to the swirling questions that each took their time coming to the forefront of her thoughts before receding into the background of her mind to make room for replacement theories.

No fingerprints found at the scene could be matched by the police to any known criminals and the fact that the tenants visited each other regularly and cross-contaminated each others apartments made it impossible to quickly sort out the prints that had been taken the night of the murders. She didn't envy anyone that job.

As she drove Sara's car into the spot marked apartment number five she contemplated how to spend the rest of her day. She had promised Sara that she would take care of several errands for her and then there was the growing mound of her own laundry that needed attention. She entered the apartment courtyard from the garage, walked through to the entry next to the manager's apartment and up to the numbered slots that held the tenants' mail. She opened number five with the key Sara had left her and took the handful of envelopes to Sara's apartment. As she walked along the stuccoed hall to the apartment she couldn't help but pause at the foot of the stairway right at the spot where Sara had landed after her fall. Even though it was the middle of the day, the light which had been off when Sara had fallen shone brightly down on the stairs eliminating any shadows or dark corners on the stairway. She continued to her door and entered the apartment. She dropped the mail along with her purse and keys on the couch and went to the kitchen for a glass of iced tea.

Returning to the couch, she kicked off her shoes, leaned back against the soft cushions, and closed her eyes. She felt like taking a nap. Usually she could get by on five hours or less sleep but since she had been in Florida she couldn't seem to get enough. It must be the climate. The weather was making her lethargic and causing her to tire easily. Before she found herself dozing off yet again she reached for the mail. One of the things she had agreed to do for Sara was to check her mail for anything important, anything that had to be answered immediately, and call Sara every day to let her know what needed to be handled from New Orleans. Sara corresponded regularly with teachers in her field whom she had met at seminars and not all of them had faxes or computer message capabilities. Some of the teachers were as far away as London and Frankfurt.

Sara's mother was a patient in a convalescent hospital in Virginia near where Sara's brother lived. Sara sent letters and cards but didn't visit frequently since her mother no longer recognized her. Her brother wrote her a letter after each one of his visits, letters filled with remembrances of their youth and of the times in past years when their mother had been well. He didn't like the telephone for the commercialized progress it represented and because it went against his monk-like antimaterialistic lifestyle. Polly and he didn't get along.

From the return addresses on several of the letters, letters she mentally categorized as occupant for teachers, she was temporarily relieved to agree with Savitch that Sara must be on numerous mailing lists because of her profession. Then she saw it. A white envelope with her name spelled in red letters. She unconsciously released her fingers letting the letters fall in her lap as if they had burned her hands. Shock and realization of what she was holding made her drop them. The letter hadn't been sent through the mail. Only her first name was on it. Someone had stood in front of the bank of mail boxes and personally inserted the letter in the slot. The mailman had a key. Whoever had slipped this letter into the box had no key. Her name in red ink glared up at her. It hypnotized her with its malevolent aura. She knew what it contained had something to do with the murders and at least this time she hadn't handled it except at one corner.

Savitch. Have to call and tell him now. He could get fingerprints. But if it was nothing she would feel so stupid getting him all the way over here. Even as she thought logically her mind raced ahead to rationalize a way to open it. She was overreacting. It was a note from Frieda or one of the other tenants just wanting to talk. Why then not just slip it under her door or better yet tack it to the outside screen for her?

She knew she had to open the letter, wanted to open it. Needing to protect the envelope from her fingerprints and to preserve any others that might be on it she went to the kitchen and sorted through a drawer of utensils looking for something to use. She returned to the couch with a pair of tongs and a thin filleting knife. She held one corner of the envelope with the tongs and inserted the blade tip of the knife into a hole at the opposite corner slowly cutting down the side opening of the envelope on one end. She shook out the single piece of paper and knew before she unfolded it that this letter was including her in whatever was happening at *the Oaks* . Using the tongs and the knife in place of her fingers she unfolded the paper and held it down as she read:

Two are gone now by a deed to
                    strengthen and embolden;
I can tell you now that only
                    a child's life is golden.

Once Upon a Murder

This was very specific. This was about murder. Murder here in this building. Knowing she and the murderer had touched this same piece of paper made her feel like she was being forced into the accomplice role by the sender. Savitch's words came back to her and made no impact on the tangible reality of her personalized chain letter, "There's nothing to indicate so far that these murders are specific to the tenants at *the Oaks.*" Bullshit! It was his words that were just so much nonspecific bullshit now.

What in the hell did it mean about a child's life? This second letter really seemed to point at Marilyn and now Marilyn or whoever had pointed a hateful finger at her. Why? She had a daughter but had never given her up for adoption. What in God's name was she guilty of? Guilty of knowing about Marilyn? Blamed by a latently deranged mind for being in on the deception? Surely Marilyn must know she had never met any of these people until a few days ago.

She looked at the letter again. Just the two lines printed as if copied by a child on a grade school tablet. Each letter absolutely perfect. Just like the letters on the chart above Mrs. Ferguson's blackboard in grammar school. And then the same four names. No, the last one was different. Oh my God.....Mr. and Mrs. S. Jacobson. Somebody wanted her to believe the letter came from them or wanted her to fear joining them or blamed this mess on them. Impossible. She was just being pulled into this puzzle deeper and deeper; being linked to them, being suspected like them.....but of what?

She got up and started to search the apartment in a panic. Still holding the filleting knife she ran through the rooms looking in closets, looking in the shower, checking to make sure she was alone. She wasn't going to be attacked by someone hiding in the apartment. If there was someone here she wanted a face to face confrontation. Him and his weapon against her and her knife. Unless his weapon was a gun. She hadn't thought about that until she had completed her search and made sure the door was double locked. The murderer hadn't killed the Jacobsons with a gun. That fact would have been of little consolation had she been shot while running around like a fanatic with only a piece of kitchen cutlery to protect her.

Why didn't Sara have a nice big dog to bark if anyone tried to get in and to sniff out anyone in hiding? Because Sara was not an animal person. Sara didn't want the responsibility of a pet when she traveled so much and had never seen one she couldn't live without. Polly shook her head and smiled, momentarily taking a break from her panic, wondering how she who loved animals and would

Once Upon a Murder

digress into baby talk at the sight of anything furry had been friends with Sara for so long.

Shifting mental gears again she went to the phone and noticed that, as she bent her head over it to dial, drops of perspiration from her recent activity fell on the black plastic case. It rang thirteen times before an unfamiliar voice, a female voice, answered the phone.

"Sergeant Hartley Savitch please."

"I'm sorry but he's out on investigation. What's your name? I'll tell him you called."

"Polly Sloan. It's quite urgent that I reach him. Can you call him in his car?"

"Lady, I'm just a clerk. Clerks don't have authority to do that. No one else is around. Gimmee your number and I'll see he gets the message."

"How about Detective Burch or Detective Koslovsky. Are either one of them in?

"They went with the sergeant."

Dammit. She would have to sit here and wait for him to call her. Sit here in Sara's searched and locked apartment waiting for him to call and hoping nothing more serious than the letter happened in the meantime.

"All right, you win. My name is Polly Sloan at Meadow Oaks Apartments. It's regarding the Jacobson murders. The number is 555-5881. It's urgent. Thank you."

Once Upon a Murder

Returning to the couch she avoided touching or reading again the letter or its envelope and focused only on the unopened mail to pass the time. Trying to get her mind on the lighter side she started by opening the junk mail: a mortgage company that understood the financial demands made on a teacher's salary by pitching in a buddy-letter format to try and get gullible teachers to borrow from their friends at McMahon Mortgage, Inc.; a discount computer company offering 25% off for full-time teachers; and a machine-printed envelope with a credit card offer that simply requested Sara's signature in return for the card. Next she opened an envelope with a see through window revealing a rectangle of orange which denoted the notice inside. Sara's utility bill was overdue. Polly would pay that for her later today if she got the chance. Two of the envelopes looked personal. The first was from a woman in New York, another professor, writing her to visit and be a guest at several lectures to be given at the museum. The other envelope contained a similar invitation from a Dr. Ernest Strong in Cleveland. This time she was asked to give a lecture. The rest of the mail was bills that could wait.

It had been twenty minutes since she'd called the precinct and no return call yet. Remembering the comforting adage *safety in numbers* she went to the phone and called Frieda.

Once Upon a Murder

"Frieda? It's Polly"

"Hello, dear. Are you back from the police station so soon?"

"Yes. How's Marilyn doing?" Polly knew Frieda had insisted on having Marilyn with her while she was in town. Polly was definitely not in the mood for any company that required gentle coddling. She wanted to talk to Frieda alone and needed to stay by the phone in case she got a call.

"She's pretty shaken up by everything I told her. We were up all night talking about her mother and I tried to answer all the questions she had. I'm afraid she will never believe that her real mother had a good enough reason for giving her up for adoption, but she is trying to understand. It's just that she never got to talk to her mother directly, to confront her and hear the answers from Harriet herself. I think it would have been so much easier on her if she could have spoken with her mother before Harriet died."

"Are you all talked out and too tired to come over and talk to me?"

"Well, I don't know if I should leave her. She doesn't manage to keep herself together long all alone. Why don't you come here? She's asleep. We can have privacy here just as if we were alone."

"I'm waiting for a call from the sergeant. I shouldn't leave."

Once Upon a Murder

"Can't he call you here?"

Polly couldn't just sit and wait for a call. She had to tell someone she could trust about the letter. She'd call and give the police department one more chance to get the information first, then she was off to Friedas.

"If I don't call you right back expect me in ten minutes."

"I'll put some tea on for us and I have a freshly baked cake. Marilyn bought it for me. She knows me already. Me and my sweet tooth."

Polly made her call to the station and had to settle for exchanging Frieda's callback number for Saras. She went to the couch to get her purse and keys and glanced at the pile of mail. Beside the new chain letter the orange notice caught her eye. She picked it up and looked for a number to call. It was the 20th and the bill said to pay by the 18th. Wasn't it just like them to date the notice after the possible delivery date of the mail? She called the utility company and arranged for an extension to pay the bill in person the following day. She didn't want to leave the chain letter in the apartment. She got an empty gift box out of the hall closet and, using the tongs, dropped first the letter and then the envelope inside the box. Having reasonably protected the evidence she left the apartment and went to Friedas.

Once Upon a Murder

*　　*　　*　　*

Frieda was bustling around the kitchen in preparation for her guest. She was totally in her element as she cut the cake and then arranged it, the china teapot, and the matching cups on the tray as if nothing had touched the tranquility of her daily routine-- nothing like murder. Humming as she worked she finished the tray with two neatly folded cloth napkins in a gay blue and yellow plaid fabric. She picked up the tray and entered the living room and was surprised to see Marilyn exiting the room and continuing down the hall.

"Marilyn, Polly is coming over for tea would you like to join us?"

Marilyn didn't answer but continued to walk down the hall toward the room Frieda had given her to use during her stay. Frieda placed the tray on the table and followed Marilyn to the back of the apartment. Before Marilyn could close her door Frieda caught up with her.

"I thought you were sleeping, dear. Why didn't you come into the kitchen and talk to me when you woke up? You've changed your clothes. Are you planning to go out?"

Marilyn stood there not registering anything Frieda was saying. She turned and went to the bed, sat down, and took off her shoes.

Once Upon a Murder

"I'm tired. I think I'll take a nap. Would you close the door when you leave please?"

"But I thought you....." Frieda had started but Marilyn had laid back on the quilt and closed her eyes as if to close the conversation as well. Frieda retraced her steps into the hall and closed the door. Confused by Marilyn's behavior she returned to the living room and heard a quiet knocking at the front door. Still puzzled, she went to let Polly in and discovered the front door was unlocked, something she never would allow when she was alone in the apartment. The door was opened to Polly by a perplexed looking Frieda and it was several greetings to the woman by the guest before Frieda acknowledged Polly's presence and let her in.

"Is anything wrong, Mrs. Goldman?"

"No, nothing except you not calling me Frieda. Come over to the table, dear. I made some tea. And these days I need my tea to calm me down. I don't think I'll ever be the same again. The murders have disrupted my life and I can't help but admit that I find it hard to trust my tenants any more like I used to. And just now I became very suspicious of that poor child Marilyn who lies asleep in the back bedroom."

"Suspicious? Why? What happened?"

"After you called I went to the kitchen to fix this tray and when I came out I saw Marilyn

Once Upon a Murder

heading down the hall toward her bedroom. I followed her to ask her to join us for tea. She said she was tired and wanted a nap. Funny thing is I thought she had been in there all along sleeping since before you called. She had changed her clothes and when I went to the front door just now to let you in it was unlocked. I locked it when we came home from the store earlier today. It should still have been locked since I didn't go out and I didn't see Marilyn go out but....I doze....you know, in my chair from time to time. It's possible that she unlocked the door while I was dozing and went out then. After all she isn't a prisoner here."

"Of course not. She might have just gone out for a walk to think over the things you told her."

"Let's not imagine trouble or suspect our friends without cause. Tell me what made you call. What was so important you couldn't wait to share it with me? This time I'll be the secret keeper."

Now that Polly was in Frieda's apartment she was uncertain how much to tell her. True, Frieda was a great confidante and appeared to be a strong supporter to her friends in time of need, but this new letter would make it impossible for Frieda to believe that the murders were just bad luck or coincidental happenings in her building. Polly didn't want to alarm Frieda with a new threat to add to the manager's burden, but she needed to

Once Upon a Murder

find out if there were other letters. Frieda hadn't received the first one and Polly was doubtful that she had received a second, but could the same be said about the other tenants? Polly felt she needed Frieda's help and approval to ask the others about the chain letters.

"Have you picked up your mail yet, Frieda?"

"Why no. He hadn't delivered yet when we returned from the store and, as I said before, I haven't been out of the apartment since then. Why do you ask, dear?"

"When I got back from the police station I went to Sara's mail slot to collect todays mail. One of the envelopes had been hand delivered to the box by someone other than the mailman, and it was addressed to me not to Sara. No one but the tenants here and a few police officers know that I'm staying at Sara's place. Remember the chain letter that was in Mrs. Jacobson's things--the duplicate to the one Sara received?"

"Yes. I remember."

"The letter with my name on it was another chain letter. I have it with me. Let me show you. But first, and I know the police have already asked you this before, have you received any strange or unexplained letters within the last few months?"

"No. As I told you the other day, Harriets was the only one I knew about besides the one you told me that Sara had received."

"Have any of the other tenants complained to you about unusual mail or anything being slipped through their mail slots?"

"No. I haven't had any complaints about my tenants getting odd sorts of mail and definitely no chain letters."

Polly hesitated to take the second letter out of the box. After giving Frieda a calming verbal disclaimer about its contents which she hoped would tone down the effect of the letter on the landlady, she carefully opened the box. Polly spread the letter open inside the box for Frieda to see and gave her a gentle reminder not to touch either the envelope or the letter.

"Oh my, it looks like this nasty business at my apartments is going to continue. I'll tell you, Polly, this makes me furious. How dare anyone-- especially someone I have let live under my roof-- be involved in murder and threats of murder against innocent people! I know you probably thought this letter would scare me to death and send me packing to the nearest hotel, but it only makes me fighting mad! We have no time to waste now. This is a warning we can't ignore. We must call that nice sergeant and get him over here right away so he can get to the bottom of this nonsense. I'm going to demand an arrest this day or my name isn't Frieda Maybelle Goldman!"

Once Upon a Murder

She went to the telephone in a huff, but it rang before she could make her call.

"Well, I'll be.....what now? Hello, oh hello Delores...how nice of you to ask me...I haven't seen her today, but if she had an appointment with the doctor I'm sure she intended...of course, she could have forgotten. You called several times and she didn't answer?...well that's no problem at all...I'll just go upstairs and see if she forgot or maybe she fell asleep.... and give you a call...not at all Delores, dear. Good-bye."

"That's odd. Dr. Spellman's nurse says Helen Sotheby had an appointment half an hour ago and hasn't shown up and they can't reach her by telephone. I promised to go check on her and let the office know if she is planning to come see the doctor today. The doctor started her on a different heart medicine recently and he's concerned about the dosage he prescribed and needs to monitor her progress with it every week."

"I'll go with you to her apartment. And just to satisfy my curiosity about the chain letter can we go by the mail slots and see who has picked up their mail? If Mrs. Sothebys is still in the box we can take it to her and save her the trip. It will also give me the chance to look through her mail for any unwanted poison-pen letters."

"I hope you're wrong about anyone else getting a second letter, especially old Mrs.

Sotheby, I'm afraid just reading the letter might give her feeble heart a reason to stop and do that evil murderer's job for him."

TWELVE

Frieda saw her first, the little white dog preening herself on the low window sill of Mrs Sotheby's living room. Polly didn't notice the dog until it stood on its hind legs and scratched on the window with its front paws. Then she jumped involuntarily as the movement of the animal startled her. The curtains and the window sill were white and the dog was white. She just blended in. Frieda stepped close to the window and tapped on it to attract the dog's attention. It was when the dog turned her head toward Frieda that Polly noticed the patch of brownish matted fur at the back of her head.

"You little imp. Quit your barking and carrying on. Helen can't be home. She would never let Snowball carry on this way and disturb the tenants. And just look at her head. The little miss has gotten into something. If Helen was

Once Upon a Murder

home Snowball would just be asleep on the sill. Well, I guess she must have realized she was late for her doctor's appointment and rushed out leaving Snowball all alone in the apartment. Usually she brings the dog down to stay with me while she's gone. Let's go in and get the dog and I'll leave a note for Helen."

Polly stepped out of the way so that Frieda could unlock the door. As Frieda entered the room the little dog jumped off the window sill to greet her. The dog ran around Frieda wagging her tail, but as soon as she spied Polly the dog took an angry and protective stance and began to bark again. Polly spoke to the dog, trying to calm her while at the same time she bent down to get closer to the dog's level, to convince Snowball it was all right and that she could stop barking.

"Stop that now! She's a friend." And to Polly. "She insists on making a little fuss every time someone new comes to visit. After the first time she'll be friendly to you. It's just her way to make you pass muster you see. The next time she sees you it will be proud as you please around and about the room to show you that you're old hat and that she can live without you.

"If you don't mind, Polly, I'm afraid we'll have to take her out. She does seem to be in an excitable state. Okay Snowball, down girl. My but you've made a mess. Helen will have a word or two for you when she comes home. What on earth have you gotten into? Just look at that dirty fur and Helen so particular about your grooming. Her leash, Polly. It's in the kitchen hanging just inside the broom closet. Come here you little devil. Oh, so you want me to chase you. Is that it? You want to torment an old arthritic woman by playing games?"

"I've got the leash, Frieda, don't bother with her. I'll catch her for you. Mrs. Gold....Frieda? Come here Snowball. Frieda, I've caught the dog. You little rascal stop squirming. I've got you now so you can give up your efforts to get away."

Polly snapped the leash onto the dog's collar. Looking around for the landlady and not seeing her, Polly mumbled under her breath to the dog something to the effect that if there was another kind of leash for wayward landladies the three of them could get out of there.

"Mrs. Goldman do you want me to take Snowball outside? Mrs......what's wrong? Frieda, have you hurt yourself? Oh Lord...Mrs. Goldman...Frieda, stop that, please stop beating your chest like that and tell me what's wrong."

Polly firmly grabbed Frieda's hands in her own and pulled them down and held them next to her body. Frieda responded by exerting an unbelievable strength against Polly's action and broke free to go over and collapse on the couch in a daze.

"You're scaring me. Are you in pain? Don't move. I'll get a cold cloth from the bathroom. You look so pale."

"NO. Don't go. I need a minute. Please?"

"Let me help you. Just tell me what you need. Do you want me to call your doctor? It's going to be all right. Stop that! It can't be good for you to continually pound your chest like that. Are you in some kind of pain? I want you to lie down. Now."

"....oh no."

"Frieda....please....tell me how to help you?"

"Helen, oh poor Helen." The closed hands finally slowed to a stop the self-flagellation she had started and stopped several times since she had returned to the living room.

"What is it? What about Helen? Please tell me what's wrong!"

"Go, go only and see what I saw. I want you to look again for me. Praise God it isn't so. Why did you do this thing? You are a cruel, cruel unfeeling face to us old women."

Frieda seemed to drift into some kind of silent reverie and promised no more prophetic or enlightened clues for Polly to grasp the sense of what had happened to the landlady. Convinced that she could do nothing further to comfort the woman, Polly left Frieda mumbling nonsense and gibberish to the dog at her feet. Pollys only chance for understanding was to follow Frieda's outstretched pointing hand entreating her to go into the other room where Frieda had previously chased the little white dog.

At first she saw nothing. Going from the brightly sunlit living room into the darkened bedroom she couldn't immediately focus from where she was standing at the room's threshold. Thick, heavy drapes covered the two windows on the far wall leaving only a slice of light seeping out on either side of the two fabrics. The four-poster bed dwarfed the room leaving barely enough space for an ornate dresser to be tucked into the few feet of wall space just inside the door. Her eyes were adjusting to the reduced light rapidly now as an open window under one of the drapes billowed the material enough to allow a longer slice of light to illuminate the room.

She felt for the light switch on the wall. No light came on. Polly stepped into the room intending to go across to the windows and open the drapes for more light. Only two steps had been taken when her feet were stopped hard by an unmovable obstacle and, realizing she was going to fall, she reached out to grab for anything that might help her maintain her balance. Her fingers could only grasp the flowing dresser scarf and her

Once Upon a Murder

fall was accompanied by the crashing and breaking of the bottles and jars that were yanked off the dresser along with the scarf in Polly's hand. Perfumed lilacs, lavender and honeysuckle-muted roses assaulted her nose as the fragrances ran together on the hardwood floor.

She tried to get up before the liquid reached and saturated her clothes and jammed a piece of glass into her hand. She sat on the floor trying to remove it as she felt the running liquid seep through her tangerine silk slacks. She had fallen where the light was best and, as she focused on the shard of glass in her palm, an image on the floor in the background demanded that her eyes refocus and make it the object of their scrutiny. The curtain was billowing more light less light more light less light like a neon marquee bright and then dull on the dead body of Helen Sotheby. Her eyes were open and staring as if to accuse Polly of the breakage all around them on the floor, but Polly knew that the woman would never say anything harsh or otherwise to anyone again.

Polly was still for a few minutes as each new expanse of light revealed another sight of the body. There was blood caked on her neck and her hands and her head was in the center of a halo of blood that had dried like paste. Helen Sotheby's face showed the horror of her fear and her last thoughts and the crayoned features superimposed

Once Upon a Murder

on her own only made those last thoughts and fears more garish.

Polly suddenly registered panic and had to get up and out of the room. The sickly-sweet smell of the blood from the dead body, the apartment's stagnant and oppressive heat, and the odor of so many rancid flowers from the perfumes made her move quicker than she thought possible. She ran to the kitchen and threw up the rich cake she had eaten at Friedas. When her body was under control again she stood with her back against the sink and tore a few paper towels off a roll on the wall to wipe her face.

Trying to steady her mind and her stomach she concentrated her attention on the side of the refrigerator where dozens of magnetized clips held recipes, coupons, and paper notes. The red lettering on a piece of paper being held by a magnetic poodle urged her to stare more closely. She didn't need to read the words again to know it was the first unreturned chain letter that both Harriet Jacobson and Sara Cornwall had received. She fingered through the rest of the letter-sized papers on the appliance's surface. No second letter. What difference did it make now? There was no need any more to threaten or try to scare a dead woman.

Frieda walked into the kitchen holding the white dog in a death grip. Snowball was content.

Apparently the dog didn't think the clutching gesture was unpleasant at all. Frieda was Helen's replacement to the dog and the animal didn't seem to be experiencing any grief at the change in her situation.

Snowball had been alone with the body how long? She had walked in the blood and gone to her mistress many times to try and revive her, to get her to play any special game that would interest them both. Now Snowball was just happy to have the attention she had been unable to enliven in her owner. Polly looked at the dog with her matted brownish topknot and self-consciously wiped her hands again on the towels to remove any traces of blood she had picked up from petting the dog and from being on the floor next to the woman's body.

Polly pulled out a kitchen chair for Frieda and pushed the woman down into it gently but firmly to make her sit without an argument. After bringing the phone over to the table Polly sat down and made the inevitable call to the police. If Savitch wasn't there then she would speak to someone else, anyone else, until someone with authority got the message. This time she was sure that whoever was on the other end of the police line would be fascinated by her report of another murder at Meadow Oaks.

Once Upon a Murder

"I'm not lying to you, lady....he called you....I gave him the message myself. I heard him talking to some Marilyn person and she told him she didn't know where you were....hold on a second and quit talking and I'll tell you where he is. He's on his way over there....said to tell you to meet him at the landlady's apartment."

"I can't do that, officer. You still don't understand. I'm guarding a murder scene! Send the coroner and whoever else you send when a dead body is reported....I told you before only you weren't listening....apartment number seven, Meadow Oaks, the corner of Jasmine and Woodley. And hurry!"

With that accomplished Polly experienced another shot of adrenaline and got up and walked around to take the action her body demanded. She paced between the kitchen table where her two live charges were and the living room window with its view of the courtyard and the entrance of someone who would relieve her of her dead charge. If Savitch entered the courtyard to go to Frieda's apartment she could see him and direct him upstairs where she would gladly relinquish to him her place at the death vigil in apartment seven.

In the corner of the wall next to the window was a triangular desk which displayed several photographs which appeared to be of the same woman over time. One of the photos was the

Once Upon a Murder

woman with two small children. Helen's daughter and her grandchildren. She had been so proud of them. Polly remembered her mentioning them the night the tenants had been questioned about the murders. The chair to the desk was pulled out and a few magazines and some unopened mail rested on the seat. When Polly and Frieda had checked Helen's mailbox earlier it had been empty. Helen had picked up her mail but had never had the chance to open it. Polly leaned over and fanned out the envelopes with the side of her index finger until she saw the one she had been searching for-- the one with the red lettering. The second letter.

She felt hot and sick and dizzy and oh so tired of being right. Here she was in a strange city thousands of miles from home, staying in someone else's apartment, and the most familiar thing she could associate with and depend upon was the appearance, on cue, of the chain letters and their subsequent promise of murder. A promise she wouldn't have been entitled to if she hadn't shown up here coincidentally and attracted the attention of the killer. Well, timing was everything, and hers had always been shitty!

The sirens outside interrupted her self-indulgent daydream and she reluctantly forced her mind back to reality and her body in line with the window again to see Savitch and one of the detectives standing at Frieda's door. She burst out

Once Upon a Murder

of the apartment anxious to be released from her unwanted responsibility in the upstairs apartment. Yelling from the railing down to the officers Polly gave no thought to who else might hear her and come running out of curiosity.

"Up here! Come up here! Hurry. Please hurry!"

Hart Savitch and Det. Burch turned toward Polly's voice and began to cross the courtyard at a run. Polly met them at the top of the stairs with a fresh fear on her face, a fear that they could just as easily be going to discover her body rather than Helen Sothebys.

"I've been trying to reach you for hours about the second letter. It wasn't mailed. It was from the Jacobsons. And then we found Helen. She didn't go to the doctors. The murderer is here; he has to be. How can he put letters in the mailboxes and have people let him in to murder them? He's here I know it!"

"Calm down, Polly, it'll be all right. I promise. I've got to go inside. We'll talk. Tell me everything later. Burch, I want you to call it in and get the team here, the same guys as before if they're available."

"I did that. I called and spoke to a man named Timmons and told him to call the coroner."

"Good. Timmons will send a couple of cars. We'll need them to handle the tenants." Savitch

Once Upon a Murder

nodded toward several of the upstairs tenants as they started to approach the Sotheby apartment, while downstairs in the courtyard others were staring up from the ground level to see what had happened.

As two officers appeared in the courtyard Burch leaned over the railing and yelled down to them, copying Polly's actions earlier. When the officers came upstairs Burch told them to stand guard in the hall until they were relieved or reassigned by himself or Sgt. Savitch. The tenants were starting to ask questions now and making a lot of noise as Polly and the two policemen sought unwelcome refuge in the dead woman's apartment.

Burch closed both the screen and the door with his handkerchief to keep the crime scene shielded from prying eyes and to protect it from entry by unauthorized persons. When he entered the apartment he stepped over and closed the white curtain over the window where Snowball had first caught Frieda and Polly's attention. He was being so careful about prints that Polly felt guilty about the things she and Frieda had touched without thinking in the aftermath of their horror at detecting Helen's body.

"I'm afraid I touched quite a few things. Frieda too before we knew there was a reason not to. And there's something else I did in the bedroom that you're not going to like." Frieda

Once Upon a Murder

started to get up from her kitchen chair to add to Polly's story but the sergeant gestured her to stay put. She sat again and continued to stroke the dog slowly and deliberately as if mechanically motivated.

The sergeant turned to Burch, "Let's go in." Savitch took out his handkerchief and covered his nose just in time to catch a sneeze. He sneezed two more times before explaining that he must be allergic to something in the apartment.

Polly asked him if by chance he was allergic to floral perfume and then went on to apologize for the broken bottles on the floor in the bedroom. Savitch couldn't hide the irritating look he gave her as the two officers went ahead into the bedroom to view the body, leaving her standing in the middle of the living room to guess at what he was thinking. Whatever it was she didn't need to add it to her own thoughts . She had been in Florida only four days and she had already seen three dead bodies. Not a good average she thought to herself but cold practicality had her admitting that being able to count the bodies was, however, a giant step above being one of them. With that consoling idea in mind she strained to hear parts of the conversation between the two men in the bedroom as it filtered out to where she stood.

"Who did what?....what part of this mess is a struggle? The damned perfume has run over onto the blood around her face. We better get our people in here fast before it gets worse if that's possible."

"A lot of blood. A stab wound?"

"No. I don't think so. The opening even from this distance looks too long and curved. Look at her hands. She put her hands up to the wound on her neck, maybe as a reflex when it first happened, and when they came away covered with her own blood...."

"....yeah, it could've been like that or maybe to prevent the assailant from attacking her again with whatever he used....or to close the wound if she could....or even as a futile attempt to stop the pain she must have been feeling."

"He did her face. Like the other two. Fuck this job." Savitch knew it was a momentary lapse of personal feeling that he couldn't afford, but he said it anyway. "Did he take her in here or follow her in? And those tracks. The dog has tracked blood all over the apartment. This place is an investigator's nightmare. I don't envy the tech team. They're the ones who'll say 'fuck this job' when they see this place. Let's leave the questions until we have some definite answers to go with them. There's no fresh air in here and my sneezing all over the room won't help matters."

The sergeant and Burch came into the living room just as a loud knock sounded at the front

Once Upon a Murder

door. Burch responded to the noise while Savitch finished up a series of sneezes caused by the concentrated perfume odor in the bedroom. Burch opened the front door to the apartment to admit a troop of professionals: a scowling man with a medical bag, another man and woman with a body bag and a stretcher, a police photographer, two men whose gloved hands held attache cases, and another detective and his partner who were immediately dispatched by Savitch to interview the building tenants.

Just then Snowball jumped from Frieda's lap and started to run around and bark angrily at all the strangers in her apartment. Despite many attempts to catch her she succeeded in eluding the outstretched hands until Burch grabbed her by the scruff of the neck which made her yelp in indignation. He deposited her once again in the landlady's lap with a patient admonition to hold the dog securely this time.

The small apartment was filled with people trying to do their job and Polly felt as if she were in their way so she went into the kitchen and sat with Frieda. Savitch stopped at the table briefly to clarify with her exactly what the sequence of discovery had been inside the murdered woman's apartment. He was specifically interested in the route each of the women had taken once inside and what they had touched. Polly retold the

Once Upon a Murder

events leading up to the discovery of Helen's body and then started to tell him about earlier when she had received the second letter and had called him at the station, but he wouldn't listen to anything except the details of the entrance into apartment number seven.

She told him about seeing the dog through the window before entering the apartment, about Mrs. Goldman's hysteria, about falling over Helen Sotheby's body in the bedroom and breaking the perfume bottles, about throwing up in the sink, and finally about calling his office to report the murder. She intentionally left out all the references to the chain letters in the woman's apartment since Savitch didn't want to discuss that issue with her now.

Savitch called over a man named Ralph who appeared to be in charge of the tech team. When Savitch relayed the information to him about Polly and Frieda's movements within the apartment Ralph started to swear. After a look from the sergeant the technician's dialogue toned down to a rhetorical mumbling about having to contend with a contaminated field of evidence caused by two inconsiderate females and one useless animal.

"Just be thorough and do the best you can with the perfumed areas, but I want to know where every print appears in that room whether it

Once Upon a Murder

belongs to the discovery persons, the dog, or anyone else. Understand?"

"I understand. I been doin' this job more than twenty you know. I understand. And that bit about being thorough. I'm always...."

"I didn't mean to imply that you weren't. Now go back and get to work. And let me know as soon as you're done in the bedroom. I want another look around in there before they take the body away. And can you do anything to cover that smell?"

"I have some special candles with me that'll help. I'll burn a couple in there when I'm done."

"Thanks, Ralph."

Polly was grazed again by a touch of guilt over the perfume she had inadvertently knocked from the dresser. She was getting that depression about self that wouldn't go away unless it was buried temporarily by positive factors, so she tried to conjure up a few. The perfume was an unfortunate accident that occurred as she discovered the murder victim, who might have remained undetected for hours or even days longer had she and Frieda not investigated the woman's whereabouts. She had been right about the importance of the letters. They were connected to the crimes and hopefully Savitch was well on his way by now to uncovering who sent them and ultimately the identity of the murderer.

Once Upon a Murder

"Sergeant, I am sorry for the perfume interfering with the evidence near the body. How much will it hinder the investigation? Will you be able to work as well as if the bottles hadn't spilled on the floor?"

"Being honest? It's a total mess in there. It could have been worse but right now don't ask me how. It's highly unlikely we would have found prints anyway one way or the other, but the dust or shoe sole particles that have been obliterated might have provided some kind of specific identification about the footwear or the footprints. Those we will miss. In order to do the work on her face the killer would have had to kneel or sit on the floor and I'm afraid any particles from his clothing or imprints of dirt from his feet have been wiped out or transferred to something else, maybe even your own clothes. I realize it was an unavoidable accident so you can rest assured that I won't be arresting you for destroying valuable evidence in a murder case."

"Thanks ever so much, Sergeant, for being so damned understanding!"

"Excuse me now but I want another look at the body in the bedroom before they take it away. It helps throughout the case if I memorize the room for myself in addition to looking at photographs I'll be seeing later. If one of the officers wants to take samples from your clothes or asks you to tell him the likely points of contact when you fell, please cooperate. Otherwise I want you and Mrs. Goldman to stay here in the kitchen and wait for me to release you to leave. Don't touch anything else away from the table."

Sgt. Savitch left the kitchen and met a haggard looking man emerging from the bedroom. They spoke for a few minutes and then Savitch entered Helen Sotheby's bedroom again and the other man left the apartment. He looked familiar to Polly and she remembered seeing him before at the Jacobsons' apartment the night she arrived. She had been pretending to be a journalist and he was there as the County Coroner who had spoken to her and the other news media at the first murder scene. That night seemed like weeks ago rather than just a few days.

Looking through to the living room she saw the two men with gloves work their way around the doorway of the bedroom and begin working the living room with their chemical mystique. As she watched their progression around the room they moved quickly and carefully--dusting, lifting, and labeling some of the prints and leaving others for the detectives to view before those too were removed to the lab. Polly saw a third man photographing the room, noting where everything was in all the rooms of the apartment with his camera. So many workers in so little space and yet it appeared to be a well-choreographed dance troop; each person knowing and keeping within his performance space and not interfering with all the other movement around him.

The few remaining detectives, along with Savitch, spilled out of the bedroom in a huddle sharing their theories and speculations. Just then a commotion could be heard outside the front door. Burch broke from the huddle and headed for the door to see what was causing it.

"Pardon me, officer, is this the Sotheby apartment? I have been getting nowhere asking my questions of these other gentlemen. Perhaps you can tell me what is going on here? I'm Dr. Arthur Spellman, Helen Sotheby's doctor, and I demand to know where she is!"

"Doctor, please step inside with me."

Burch was on the verge of telling the newcomer what had happened and introducing him to Savitch when Frieda, at hearing the doctor's familiar voice, jumped up from the table to greet him. Snowball had once again escaped from her untenable captivity and ran around the apartment freely disturbing the professionals trying to do their work. Polly tried to remain where she was in the kitchen as a *better late than never* gesture of compliance to the sergeant's request as everything in the living room seemed to be completely out of hand. The dog was playing havoc with the

Once Upon a Murder

fingerprint men and being a general nuisance until the doctor reached down and firmly picked her up in his arms and calmed her with his petting.

"Sergeant Savitch, doctor. I'm in charge of this investigation." He extended his hand to the bewildered physician who still had received no explanation for the official gathering in apartment number seven.

"What investigation? Please tell me what's going on. No one wants to answer that one simple question for me!"

"And I will have to delay the question's answer a little longer, I'm afraid, and ask that you answer one for me first. Why are you here?"

"Very well. I was expecting Mrs. Sotheby at my office at one o'clock. She never showed up for her appointment even after I had my nurse contact Frieda to find out if Helen would be late or couldn't make the appointment all together."

Mrs. Goldman moved next to the doctor and took the dog from him.

"That's right, Sergeant. It was after I got a call from Delores, his nurse, that Polly and I came up here and...."

"Thank you Mrs. Goldman. Go on doctor. You were saying?"

"Helen, Helen Sotheby, was my only afternoon patient today. I have been treating her for a heart condition and I recently changed her

Once Upon a Murder

medication. When I do that it's necessary for me to monitor the patient closely for side effects and to regulate the dosage. When she didn't show up as scheduled I went ahead and finished my work for the day and prepared to leave the office. As I was leaving I noticed that the pharmacy had bottled some pills for her and they were on the counter waiting to be picked up. It was important for her to have the prescription today so I decided to drop it off and give her a quick exam in her apartment if necessary. A kind of old-fashioned house call I make when necessary. Now Sergeant, I owe you no further explanation until you tell me this minute where my patient is."

"Helen Sotheby has been murdered." Savitch thought the doctor would want the direct approach after having waited so long.

"Impossible! Who on earth would murder a wonderful old lady like that? A burglar? Crime in this city is horrendous. I simply can't believe it. It must be some kind of a mistake. Surely she was mistaken for somebody else?"

"I'm afraid there's no mistake. Were you aware that there were two other murders in this building just a few days ago? You must have read about them in the paper or seen the story on the local news."

"I'm sorry, Sergeant, but I don't read the local papers and I only listen to cable news so you see I

Once Upon a Murder

haven't been aware of anything that might have happened here recently."

"Doctor, we're still examining the apartment for clues so, while I appreciate your late yet well-meaning concern for Mrs. Sotheby, I will have to ask you to leave at this time. If you wouldn't mind I'd like you to contact the coroner and give him her medical history including the latest medication you were prescribing for her heart. Det. Burch will give you the information and then see you out. Again, thank you doctor for coming by."

When the doctor left Savitch had another officer escort Mrs. Goldman and the dog back to the manager's apartment in order to prevent further disruptions. He had entirely too many uninterested parties at the scene. As Savitch looked toward the kitchen to see Polly sitting resignedly at the table, she signaled for him to come over to her. He stopped on his way to give additional instructions to the photographer and then went into the kitchen.

Polly couldn't refrain from disclosing her other discoveries any longer. She had already had one disciplinary lecture about evidence and she wasn't in the mood for another. She also wanted the technical people in the apartment to treat the letters with special care.

"Sergeant, on the side of the refrigerator is the first chain letter. On the chair by the desk is

Once Upon a Murder

Helen's unopened mail from today; one of those letters is the second chain letter. I'm convinced it's from the murderer even if you aren't. When you see it you'll notice that it only has her name on the outside. It was slipped into her mailbox by hand. I know because I got one myself in with Sara's mail today."

While Polly had been talking the Sergeant's face changed from barely maintained tolerance to frowning disbelief. He started to comment on her statements and thought better of it and turned instead to speak to the officers working toward the corner of the room where the desk was located.

"Don't touch anything on the desk yet. Martinez, stop what you're doing and go over to the desk. Polly would you mind showing the detective which letter you're referring to, being careful not to touch anything of course."

"Of course." Polly went over to the mail and indicated for the detective which letter was the important one.

The officer picked the envelope up with a pincer device and slipped it into a plastic evidence bag and sealed it. After securing the unopened letter the detective was likewise directed to the refrigerator to bag the single page of paper that represented the original chain letter three of the tenants had received.

Once Upon a Murder

The two officers Savitch had assigned to interview the tenants had returned to report to the sergeant on the whereabouts of the apartment residents during the day. They met Savitch over by the desk where the remaining police staff and Polly were in conversation. Detective Burch found it difficult to take his eyes off of the photos on the desk. He shook his head solemnly as he remembered Helen Sotheby's invitation to visit her apartment and see the pictures of her daughter and her grandchildren.

"I never thought I'd be seeing them like this, after her death, without being able to tell her how lucky she was to have them. I never would have guessed I'd be the detective who'd have to notify them of her death. And to have to find the dog she talked about as her closest companion a new home."

THIRTEEN

"Polly don't argue with me. Detective I want you to walk Ms. Sloan back to her apartment. I want you to check it out thoroughly before leaving and I want you to make sure she double locks her door. Is that understood? Polly? Detective?" The two affirmatives that followed and the departure of yet two more of the crowd that had gathered in Helen Sotheby's apartment left Savitch free to take the officers' reports with him and make his own rounds of the tenants.

According to what Polly had told him about the mail delivery, information that she had gotten from Frieda and that he himself had verified through police investigation, the mailman made Meadow Oaks one of his morning deliveries. The mail to the apartment building tenants was usually delivered around 10:30A.M.. Based on the coroner's preliminary assessment and the fact that

Once Upon a Murder

Helen Sotheby had already picked up her mail, the time of death was probably between 10:30 and the discovery of the body at around two o'clock. Mrs. Sotheby either got the mail, came back to her apartment and then had her murderous caller or; she went to get her mail, met one of the tenants, invited him her or them to her apartment, left the mail on the chair, excused herself to get something in the bedroom or to show the visitor something, and then was surprised from behind when some kind of wire or garroting device was slipped around her neck.

It was doubtful the killer lured the woman into the bedroom to murder her. It appeared to Savitch that the killer had used the first opportunity Helen Sotheby's back was turned to kill her. Did she even know why she was being murdered? The method used this time made it hard to believe the murderer had confronted his victim verbally first, unless she had been retreating to her bedroom for safety when she was attacked. More examination of the physical evidence, the coroner's report, and the photographs taken in the apartment might alleviate some of the guessing, but he doubted he would know for sure until the killer actually told him.

He scanned through the new witness notebooks the two officers had given him with the tenant interview information from earlier in the day. It wasn't the time for self-aggrandizement, nevertheless, he couldn't help but feel a sense of personal satisfaction when he looked through the sheets of neatly arranged data. The witness notebooks were his innovation. Each sheet had preprinted headings and subclassifications of facts that allowed the enforcement personnel to briefly fill in the necessary answers to standardly required questions. The sheets were carbonized and provided the correct number of copies for attachment to investigative reports thus doing away with the previous individualistic note taking habits of police officers who used various kinds of pocket pads to record information from witnesses in the field.

The notebooks, like the ticket books of the patrol officers, had a stiff back cover that turned into a divider to place between each group of sheets. His staff and the other detectives at the station had finally agreed that the witness statement information on these sheets tended to be more thorough, easier to read, and allowed anyone to pick up one of the forms and at a glance get the full picture of the interview without having been there. There was even space allotted for personal impressions and possible follow-up suggestions for each witness.

Savitch waited in the hall for Burch to join him before making the rounds of the building.

With Burch in tow Savitch wanted to start with the tenants upstairs closest to the crime. The Browns would be first.

* * * *

"First it was apartment nine now it's apartment seven. It's too close for me Miles, I want to move out of here or at least move downstairs. The climb up those stairs makes my heart palpitate anyway. It's not healthy!"

"I don't think there's any need for you to move, Mrs. Brown. I have every intention of leaving some of my men here at *the Oaks* when I go and I'm afraid I'll have to do my best to discourage you from leaving at this time. Your best protection is here and I will only have to detail an officer to watch both of you if you attempt to move. I assure you that you two are indispensable in this murder investigation and might even hold the clue we've been looking for and not even know it. I have to advise you also that you won't be allowed to go far until you and your husband can be cleared of suspicion in all three murders."

"Oh dear, you make it sound like we are criminals and like this apartment, our home, is a jail for us all. We have the right to try and get away from this dreadful killer, don't we?"

"Your actions will be restricted and your whereabouts will be monitored by the department as much for your safety as for our need to keep tabs on you. This doesn't have to be an ordeal for you at all. The answers to a few questions and I'll be able to let the two of you resume your normal activities. No thank you, Mrs. Brown. I don't care for any sandwiches, but you two go right ahead. They do look appetizing."

"Mr. Brown, you told Detective Burch after the Jacobsons' deaths that you're a retired naval officer?"

Miles Brown hurried to swallow the last of a sandwich half in order to answer the sergeant.

"Yes, that's true. I was on ship duty as a supply officer for most of my twenty-five years."

"Did Stephen Jacobson ever talk to you about your service time? Ever offer to you any information about his being in the armed services himself?"

"No he didn't. I might have talked to him about the Navy, but I really don't remember how he responded. Was he in the service?"

"No he wasn't. He had bad eyes. His vision couldn't be adequately corrected for enlistment or the draft. Did you ever have occasion to use any of your navy training in weapons or physical combat on anyone in civilian life?"

"Certainly not, Sergeant!" Olivia Brown answered indignantly. "Miles is a non-violent person. He couldn't harm anyone or I can tell you we wouldn't be married going on thirty-two years in October."

"Since you seem to be a good judge of character, Mrs. Brown, suppose you tell me who living in this building you consider capable of physical attack?"

"Well I...I really haven't thought about it. For the murders you mean? You think one of us did it, don't you?"

"I'm not saying that, but it would be a lot easier for someone here who knows everyone's routine to find an opportune time to catch any one of you alone."

"Oh my God! Do you hear what he's saying, dear?" Olivia tried to get her husband to respond as an outraged tenant, but almost immediately gave up the attempt to get him interested in anything but food.

"Mr. and Mrs. Brown, Mrs. Sotheby was murdered today in the apartment right next door. You could have seen or heard something that might have seemed to you completely ordinary and yet could be a valuable piece of information. Tell me what you did today up until the time you heard about Helen Sotheby's death."

Once Upon a Murder

They were eating in shifts now and this time Mr. Brown answered for them both.

"Livie, Mrs. Brown that is, and I got up about ten. We had a leisurely breakfast and read the paper."

"Is the paper delivered in the hall or downstairs?" Savitch interrupted.

"The boy has quite a few papers for this building and delivers them individually in front of each subscriber's door. He thinks he'll get a tip, I guess, or a couple of dollars at Christmas."

"What time, Mr. Brown?"

"Well, Livie was already pouring the coffee when I came in from outside. It takes about ten minutes for the coffee to go through the filter and she went to the kitchen as soon as we got up so about ten fifteen I would suppose."

Mrs. Brown nodded her assent.

"When you went outside did you glance either way down the hall or see anyone in the courtyard?"

"I looked up to see what kind of weather it would be today. I had to look out across the courtyard to do that. No. I don't remember seeing anyone. After I looked up I looked down at the paper. A headline caught my eye and I turned and came back inside the apartment while reading the story underneath the headline."

"Hear anything?"

Once Upon a Murder

"No. It's pretty quiet here. A lot of late sleepers and mostly folks mind their own business in their apartments at that time of the day."

"Did you pick up your mail?"

"Livie? You did didn't you?"

"Yes"

"What time?"

"Later. After we had breakfast and got dressed to go out. It was around noon. I told this to the officer already. Didn't he tell you?"

"Yes, Mrs. Brown, he told me. But I like to ask some old questions along with the new ones. That's okay isn't it?"

"Of course it is, Sergeant."

"In your mail today did you get any unusual letters, any non-addressed letters? Letters with just your name on the envelope?"

"Miles, you opened the mail. Where is it?"

"I threw it away except for this magazine."

The sergeant picked up the *National Geographic* and thumbed through it making sure no envelope was concealed inside and then he asked for the discarded mail.

Miles went to the wicker wastebasket across the room and before he could reach in for the mail Savitch told him not to touch it, just to bring the basket over to him. The basket was empty except for a few opened envelopes and their contents. Savitch moved them around with his pen after dumping the mail on the coffee table. He looked at the envelopes first.

"How many envelopes were there?"

"Three."

Savitch could see that all three were advertisements. Standard occupant name list stuff. A loan company. A solicitation for a local charity and one for a family dental clinic.

"This all?"

"Yes, that's it."

"I know this will be repeating myself, but have either one of you received any letters in the last four or five months that demanded an answer? Letters that asked you to return them to a name off of a list?"

"No. I really don't remember any. Olivia, what about you?"

"No, Miles. You know we don't get much mail. Just like these or our monthly checks and bills."

"Mrs. Brown, do you have any children?"

"No. Mr. Brown and I don't have any children. We never really thought about it until it was too late. We were well into our thirties when we married and we needed time for just the two of us alone together and that's all there's ever been, just Miles and me."

Once Upon a Murder

"According to this report from the officer that spoke to you earlier you left your apartment around noon and went shopping."

"That's right. I went downstairs to get the mail and brought it upstairs. Miles opened it, threw the letters in the trash, and then we went out. We drove to the Discount Fair Market on Selkirk Avenue. We were there about an hour or an hour and a half. We went to our regular checker, Barbara. Why here look," Mrs. Brown dug her checkbook out of her purse, "here's a duplicate of the check I wrote to her, I mean to the market."

"I believe you, Mrs. Brown. Then what did you do?"

"We came back here, put our car in the garage, and then came up here to our apartment. We put the groceries away. Miles and I take a nap in the afternoon so we can watch our television shows at night. He went into the bedroom and I sat here on the couch watching my favorite game show *Fortune Forever*. We both fell asleep and didn't wake up until I heard the commotion in the hall after poor Helen's body was discovered."

"Can you think of anything strange or out of the ordinary that has happened recently in the building or to any of the tenants? Any new solicitors or guests in the building? Anything you might have seen or heard that was not part of the daily routine here?"

Both Mr. and Mrs. Brown seemed to ponder the sergeant's questions for a minute or two, looked at each other, and then turned toward him and nodded negatively in unison.

Savitch and Burch thanked the couple and left their apartment.

* * * *

"On the Jacobson investigation who interviewed Mrs. Turnbull, you or Koslovsky?"

"Ed did. I haven't spoken to the woman before."

"Her apartment is right between the two murder scenes. I'm going to find it hard to believe that she doesn't know anything, didn't see or hear anything this time. Let's go."

Mrs. Turnbull greeted the detectives at her door wearing lavender and gray workout clothes. She was perspiring and out of breath when she let them in. She wiped her face and arms with the towel she had taken off a chair while explaining that she was too upset to sit still and had turned on her treadmill and been walking briskly to calm her nerves.

Savitch thought that a peculiar way to react in the aftermath of a murder but he withheld his

Once Upon a Murder

comments about her behavior and commented instead on her athletic demeanor and appearance.

"You are in amazing condition for a woman in her sixties."

"Sixty-seven last birthday, Sergeant, and I feel better now than I did at twenty-seven."

Mrs. Turnbull stood looking down at the two detectives where they had taken seats on her living room couch. Looking up at her imposing presence and her obviously healthy physique was unsettling for the two men. They were both thinking the same thing without having to acknowledge it to each other. This woman could easily have overpowered old Mrs. Sotheby and had the quickness and agility to have controlled and then murdered the Jacobsons.

"The officer who spoke to you a little while ago said that you have been home all day. Is that correct?"

"Yes, Sergeant. I was planning on going out this evening to a movie after my walk, but now I think I'd rather stay in and go out tomorrow during the day when it's light out. You can certainly understand my hesitation to put myself at risk in the dark, can't you?"

"Yes, but cover of night wasn't necessary for the murderer. He killed Mrs. Sotheby this morning after breakfast when you claimed to have been in this apartment. What exactly were you doing earlier today, say between ten o'clock and about two this afternoon?"

"Got up at seven as always and went outside to get the paper. I don't know why I bother to look for the paper that early; that odious paper boy never arrives until most of the morning is gone."

"See anyone in the hall when you went out?" Burch questioned.

"No one. I'm the only one around here up at that time except for Sara downstairs who I see sometimes trying to make the paper magically appear when she wants it like I do. But she's gone now. There was no one in the hall. I would have sensed it even if I didn't look."

"Go on with what you did after that."

"I had hot tea with honey, a bowl of bran, and two pieces of dry whole wheat toast. Doesn't everyone? I dressed and went downstairs to do a load of laundry before the laundry room is taken over by those sisters and all the ridiculous clothing they wash all the time. Sorry about that. I had forgotten that I did leave the apartment. Went down around 8:30, put a load in the machine, and then returned to the apartment. The machine takes about thirty-five minutes. I came up to watch a morning show on TV. The show was all about lifestyles of senior citizens who are still caring for themselves, like me; people not living in retirement homes or with their children. It started at nine and

Once Upon a Murder

I ran down to the laundry room at the first intermission to throw my wet clothes in the dryer. They must still be there because I watched the rest of the show and then picked up a book I had been reading the night before off the table by my chair and read until lunch. I might be in pretty good shape for my years, but exercise can't improve my memory. It gets worse every year. I'm sure someone probably took my things out of the dryer and left them on top for whenever I would return to claim them."

Burch asked first, "See anyone while you were out of your apartment?"

"Not the first time when I went to load the washing machine, but when I went down to put the items in the dryer I saw the woman who's staying with Frieda coming out of her apartment."

"Marilyn Henry, Mrs. Jacobson's daughter?"

"Yes, that's her name, Marilyn. I didn't see where she went and I don't think she saw me. I really just had a glimpse of her back. I ran to the laundry room and back because I wanted to see the rest of the program uninterrupted. I saw no one actually skulking around that wasn't supposed to be here."

"You were here then, sitting in that chair, watching TV or reading from nine until around noon, except for the two trips to the laundry room?"

"Yes, more or less, I got up a couple of times I'm sure, but yes."

"Mrs. Turnbull, in the next apartment, more than likely during the time that you were sitting in that chair, a murderer entered Helen Sotheby's apartment, put a wire around her neck, and sliced her throat open from ear to ear. Didn't you hear anything coming from her apartment, any sound at all?"

"Well, she uses, used a walker, you know. She wouldn't have needed it if she'd taken my advice and exercised those pathetic legs of hers, but never mind. She only used it when she was very tired or when she had to be on her feet for a long time. I can usually hear the rhythmic thump on the floor when she's using it. I didn't notice it today. And then there's that creature, that *Snowflake* or whatever it is she calls that pest, forever jumping off of things in her apartment. The sound does carry but I try to tolerate it. That must have been what I heard today. I was reading Sean McGowan's latest mystery, *A Phantom Dies Twice,* and the part that I was reading was quite frightening. All of a sudden I heard this thump. It scared me out of my wits because it came right at the moment when Harold accidentally knocks over the casket in the novel. When I recovered from my fright at the noise happening at that precise moment, I realized that I had foolishly overreacted and the thump must have come from the dog jumping off the bed. That's where the noise came from, the bedroom. I even wondered if Helen might have fallen, but that couldn't have been the case because I recovered from the scare about the book and all and, while I was seriously thinking of going over there to check on her, I heard movement in her apartment and knew she was all right. Shortly thereafter I heard the door open and close and assumed she had gone out."

"The time? Can you pinpoint the time for us when you heard that thump?"

"Well, looking back on it now I can make a guess at the time. I started reading after the TV show was over at ten o'clock." She picked up the mystery novel that had been lying on the table. "That part with Harold was in chapter fourteen and when I started reading today I was on chapter eight. The chapters are about twenty pages each. McGowan's a very methodical writer. He always keeps his chapters about the same length. I've timed myself before and it takes me about fifteen minutes per chapter--I'm a very brisk reader. I would have read that part about Harold sometime between 11:30 and 11:45 this morning."

The two detectives couldn't believe their good fortune. The woman had clocked Helen Sotheby's fatal fall, heard the killer exit the apartment, and had then continued reading chapter fourteen to find out what happened with Harold and the casket!

"Mrs. Turnbull, did you think about going over to Helen's apartment to find out for sure if she had gone out? Did you hear the dog bark or indicate any distress sounds from the apartment next door? Did you do anything to make sure your neighbor was all right?"

"I told you Sergeant that I distinctly heard the woman go out so I obviously thought that she was O.K."

"But in fact she wasn't O.K.," Burch pressed, "she was dead or dying while you sat and read in that chair."

"Really Detective I don't think I like that accusatory tone you're taking. I certainly didn't kill her and how was I to know what was going on?"

"Forgive Detective Burch but we are involved in a totally frustrating investigation with this case. By any chance did you hear anything else from the apartment next door?"

"Voices."

"Voices? What voices?"

"Before the thump I heard voices. People talking, you know."

"How many voices. Male or female? Did you recognize them?"

Once Upon a Murder

"At first I thought it was the television, but then I realized that there were no interruptions, no commercials, no music. I like to think of myself as a mystery buff so I try to be observant, figure things out without all the information. When I correctly guessed it wasn't the television my second thought was that she was talking to that creature. Then I heard another voice that was low and soft. I heard it twice and then I went back to my book; it was much more interesting than who was visiting old Mrs. Sotheby. Now I wish I had paid more attention. It could have been a man or a woman. I'm sorry but I just don't know."

"Is that it, all you remember? Did you ever hear anyone being let into the apartment?"

"I only heard the door just that once and I didn't associate it with a visitor leaving only with Mrs. Sotheby leaving. And the dog never made any unusual noise that I haven't been accustomed to hearing."

"Mrs. Turnbull, did you pick up your mail today?"

"Of course. But it wasn't 'til around noon. My mail has no surprises to offer, Sergeant, so I don't rush to pick it up."

"Over the last several months have you received a chain letter asking you to respond by sending a return letter to a name on a list?"

213

Once Upon a Murder

"Certainly not. I wouldn't have responded to that kind of nonsense anyway. Why do you ask?"

"Someone in the building received such a letter so I thought I'd ask you and the other tenants about it. It was probably from someone who got names off of a list. It's not important. Mrs. Turnbull, do you have any children?"

"Yes, Sergeant, I have two sons. They are law partners in New York."

"Sounds like they must be very close to have gone into business together."

The sergeant motioned to Burch and they both rose from the couch and made their way to the door.

"Thank you for your help, Mrs. Turnbull, and if you remember anything that you think might be helpful to us call myself or Detective Burch at police headquarters."

He handed her a business card and they backed out of the apartment leaving Clare Turnbull to continue reading the fictional mystery novel that had so engrossed her as to take precedence over a real murder that had been committed a mere thirty feet from her chair.

*   *   *   *

"Burch you handle this one. I'm getting a headache. It's brought on when I can foresee my

214

futile efforts being repeated over and over again or when I get unbelievable results like those from Clare Turnbull. I may jump in with a question or two, but you take the lead."

"I've got the same headache, Sarge."

"But mine has a higher rank."

"Right."

The two detectives stood in front of Maria Montoya's door far after the dinner hour and they were now regretting not having taken the stockpile of sandwiches that had been offered in the Brown apartment.

"Let's keep it short and to the point or we'll never get out of here."

"O.K., Sarge, I'll do my best not to make our brief questioning of an emotionally distraught widow and murder suspect appear to be exactly what it is."

"Thanks, Burch, I knew I could count on you."

After a light tapping by Burch, Mrs. Montoya opened the door for the two men.

"Come in gentlemen, I have been both expecting and dreading your visit."

"Mrs. Montoya, I am Detective Burch and this is Sergeant Savitch. Just a few more questions, ma'am, if you don't mind."

"Of course not, Detective, I remember you both from the last time. And where is the other

Once Upon a Murder

detective who was with you then? He had such a nice smile."

"You mean Ed, Detective Koslovsky, he's investigating another aspect of this case today but I'll tell him you asked about him."

"Thank you, Detective. Now how can I help you and the Sergeant? I want to help if I can, but more I want to know why this is happening. I came to this apartment to spend the remaining years God will give me in peace and serenity. Why these murders? The people here have done nothing to deserve this punishment. I came here to be happy and content and now I fear for my life. My children will demand for me to move."

"We want you to feel protected and taken care of until this thing is over. We will have twenty-four hour police protection on this apartment and its tenants from the outside and from the inside. I assure you, Mrs. Montoya, that you can rely on us to make it safe for you here."

"I want to believe you, Detective, but just today a woman was killed right down the hall from me and no one could protect her. This evil person is like a spirit or a ghost coming and going and doing these murders and then vanishing to safety. How can you catch such a thing as that?"

Mrs. Montoya, in her fear and nervousness, had automatically dropped her slow and deliberate manner of speaking and was talking faster with each sentence, her heavy Spanish accent disguising the sound of every word.

Savitch felt it was time to intervene.

"You went to the Cleaners today, didn't you? You went to help your daughter and son-in-law at your old place of business."

"Yes. I went because they had no tailor in the shop today. The work could have waited until he returned but I needed to keep myself busy. I sometimes go even when he is there. We work well together."

"What time did you leave and what time did you return?"

"They open at eight and there was one unfinished alteration to be ready by eight-thirty so I went there at seven-thirty with my Catherine to finish the job for the lady on time. I stayed until one o'clock and then Carlos, her husband, made me leave. My eyes they get tired with only a few hours of close work now. He drove me home then. We arrived here one twenty or one thirty I think."

"When you came home did you see anyone?"

"No. I don't remember...yes, I saw a man standing at Mrs. Gotjcik's door. He was facing away from us as we came from the garage."

"Carlos walked you to your apartment?"

"Yes. He insists always and now he will use his influence with Catherine to make me move

Once Upon a Murder

from here I know. I will be sorry to leave. I think this apartment suits me well. I have friends here."

"Mrs. Montoya, just two more questions. Have you received any letters in the mail over the last few weeks or maybe even before then that seemed odd to you? Letters asking you to send them back by mailing them to an address unfamiliar to you, an address from a list on the letter?"

"What kind of letter is that? You mean to buy something? To have something sent to my home?"

"No. Not a letter asking you to buy anything. Just a letter that said you should mail it back right away to another name and address that would be printed on a list. It is what is called a chain letter and by sending it back you keep up a kind of chain of communication between the names on the list."

"I think I see what you mean. It is a sort of letter game you describe. But no, I have received no such letter."

"This is the last question we will bother you with tonight. How many children do you have?"

"I have six, four boys and two girls."

"I know about your daughter, Catherine. Where is your other daughter?"

"Maria Marlena is a nun. She is called Sister Sarafina. She lives in South America in a convent."

Once Upon a Murder

"Thank you Mrs. Montoya. I see that we have tired you after an already full day of work. We will leave you to rest now. Please don't be uncomfortable or troubled about staying here. There will be no more incidents occurring here without my knowledge and that of the officers I will leave behind. No harm will come to any other tenants. You have my promise. Good night."

"Good night. I will try to believe you because I think you are a sincere man and will try to keep your promise."

* * * *

Savitch and Burch stood outside the Montoya apartment as Savitch lit a cigarette and leaned against the grill work of the upstairs railing. After only a few minutes outside the humidity had sufficiently dampened the men's shirts enough to make them wish themselves inside again if only for the relief that the living room window air conditioning units offered them.

"Burch, I need to take time out here and make a few calls: the coroner, Ed, and the station dispatcher to set up round-the-clock protection here. I want you to handle the rest of the tenant follow-up interviews. You know what I want, what we're looking for. Get back to me if there's anything that needs my personal attention. I'm going to ask Polly a few more questions and maybe get a cold drink with my conversation. Let the detectives downstairs know where I am, and Burch, don't go to the Gotjciks' apartment without me--save them for last."

Burch was wiping his forehead and patting his face dry with a well-used handkerchief he had pulled from his pants' pocket.

"I guess I will take the Sergeant's Exam after all. Sergeants get all the cushy jobs. I'd like to be sipping a cool drink across from the attractively endowed Ms. Sloan myself, if I had a choice that is."

"Ah, but you don't have a choice. My wish is your command. This is business not pleasure, although she has a hellova lot of charisma for brown and brown. You know my preference is blonde and blue."

"Yeah, I know. But why should you limit yourself, right?"

"Exactly."

FOURTEEN

Savitch left Burch at the bottom of the stairs after embedding what was left of his cigarette in the dirt of the accident prone potted palm on the first level. He walked to Sara Cornwall's apartment where Polly was staying by herself for a few days until Sara returned from New Orleans. He knocked, identified himself, and heard the door being unsecured on the other side. Polly invited him in. He noticed that she had changed into a chocolate-colored sleeveless sheath that came just above her knees. On Polly even brown was a striking color. He was sure that she was wearing the dress simply because it was cool and comfortable and that she had no idea or interest in the way her strength and composure affected him. Polly noticed him noticing her and felt in his look was a question that needed explanation.

"There was blood and perfume on my other clothes. I had to take a long shower to get the smell off my skin. I'll never be able to associate the smell of floral perfume with beautiful bouquets of fragrant flowers again. That poor unfortunate woman. When I was on the floor in that bedroom I felt the terror and pain that was on her face, what she must have felt in those last moments. She shouldn't have died like that. She should have passed away quietly while sleeping in her own bed. I want to do something to stop this craziness. Let me help you. I can find out things you can't. I'm here. I know you must have something that I can do. I'm warning you in advance that I won't stay uninvolved in this. If you won't give me permission to help, I'll do it on my own."

"Whoa!"

He'd let her go on, let her tell him how she was feeling, the toll the murders were taking in her head. He wanted to know her state of mind; how strong she was. He was judging her professionally and, he had to admit, personally as well. He was sure she wasn't part of this, in fact, couldn't have been part of this. She was on a plane during the commission of the first two murders and in his office during the second. It was dangerous to trust her, to tell her things about the case; yet he knew he would do both. What would she tell inadvertently to Frieda or someone else here at

Meadow Oaks, someone who might be writing another chain letter or planning another murder?

"Listen to me. I will not have another murder on my hands--namely yours. You will follow my orders or I'll bring you down to the station and handcuff you to my desk until this is over. Believe me, the most helpful you can be to me now is to give me your opinions and input as a woman and as a temporary tenant here. It's shaping up here as some kind of woman thing. Maybe there's a pattern. Maybe there's a reasonable way to sift out the extraneous clues and sidelights on this case or maybe this is really one directed murder in a muddle of evidence that disguises it as one in a series of random killings."

"You mean the killer only wanted one person dead all along and is leading you to think this is a serial crime with a totally different motive?"

"Precisely. That would mean all of our energy and time could be focusing on the wrong clues. We could end up following along after the carefully planted sequence of worthless evidence like jackasses following a dangling carrot. Meanwhile, the killer has gotten away with annihilating his initial murder victim and has left us buried in hypothetical supposition so far away from fact that he escapes unscathed."

Once Upon a Murder

"Does that kind of thing keep you awake nights? Fear that you're reading the case wrong, that is? Reading the killer wrong?"

"Yeah. It's hard to imagine yourself in the mind of a killer, but it's what I have to do on a case like this. But it's harder still when there seems to be no gain from the murder. No money collected. No wife out of the way so a man can marry his mistress. The closest to gain I can see in this case is that someone might have gained silence, closed the door forever on the revelation of some secret that might have ruined the killer's life."

"Let's get back to the woman thing. You don't think Stephen Jacobson was a murder target, do you? You think he just happened to be there or he surprised the killer in the act and had to be dealt with."

"No, I don't think the husband was a target unless, as I said before, he was the real victim and the killing of his wife and Helen Sotheby was to make it appear that women were the targets or that it was just elderly people our killer was after."

"You have to be going off in all directions at the same time, considering all the trails of evidence and continuously backtracking to reinforce your theories."

"It does require a lot of crosschecking and overlapping sources of information before a trail is

Once Upon a Murder

abandoned as not viable, no longer able to sustain the theory that originated it. But one trail that you tried to point out to me this morning, one that we should follow now, is the trail of the chain letters. There are fifteen apartments here and I am determined to find out by no later than tomorrow morning how many tenants received duplicate letters. On the off chance that more than just this apartment building is involved, I have placed a public service ad which will appear in the morning newspaper asking anyone who has received such a letter to call the police station with information. It's not the type of duty the officers will like, taking care of the volume of calls that will be generated by such an ad; but we should know in a day or two if we've got an epidemic on our hands or just a specialized lunatic with his sights set on only this building and its tenants."

"How many tenants have you canvassed already regarding the letters?"

"Most of the upstairs tenants and Burch is finishing up the remaining downstairs tenant statements for me now. Koslovsky was put on the chain letter angle after you left my office this morning. He should be letting me know how he did today by phone or in person when I leave here and return to the station. He went to the post office to check out the P.O. Box in the chain letters and to set up a stakeout there for any mail pickup. I also asked him to go through any mail that's being held for the three vacationing tenants while he's there to see if they received letters. When he's done at the post office and checks in at the station he'll receive my message that he's in charge of assigning officers to provide round-the-clock protection for the people here as well as calling in the extra staff we'll need in the office when the ad appears."

"I could help there. I could answer phones for you. I know the contents of both letters, what we're looking for....I mean what you're looking for. Actually I'd be better than most of the officers because I've been part of this from the beginning. I've seen the bodies. I've...I've felt the killer's presence. I can sense his kind of evil. I'd know him if I heard him on the phone. I'm sure of it."

"Don't be too sure. It happens to all of us who investigate criminals. This sense of closeness with the perpetrator. We're into a case; we live for it. We're the criminals and it's the victim and every one of us is out to snuff the life out of the case by finding the key to its solution. We've all felt at times tuned into a killer, certain we would know him if we met him on the street. It very rarely happens and then only when we have solid physical likenesses to work with or specific personality traits and habits or aberrant behavior that gives him away. A couple of times detectives have been so cocksure of themselves and their *intuitions* about killers they're chasing that they let their guard down. When confronted by the selfsame killers they're searching for no warning bells go off. Then they're dead. I don't want to see you that way. You're a novice, an inexperienced and vulnerable visitor here, and I assure you that to this murderer you're just as dispensable as the three who've died. Don't take chances with your life and don't ask me to either. Don't underestimate your danger here. The last letter had your name on it not Saras. The killer has identified you as a player in his game and the list of living letter-carrying players is narrowing."

"Don't you think I know that? That's why I want to help. How dare this creep single me out and blame me for something I'm not guilty of; classify me for murder as if I have no free choice in the matter and will simply allow him to eliminate me! I'm not going to hide here when there's a chance I can be used to lure him out. Use me to get him. Set me up. I'm ready. It's better than waiting. The best defense is taking the offense. Why not attack?"

"I'll think about it, but until I've had a chance to formalize a plan no independent action, okay?"

"I can't promise. I'm already a sitting duck here. How do you know that putting guards around this place won't chase him to another apartment building or frustrate him into stopping all together?"

"He's trying to make a point. If we don't know what it is yet, even if it's only a point being made in his mind, he's still trying to say something with these murders. We just have to interpret the psychological code. The fact that the murders are getting more brutal indicates he's madder than he originally thought about what's pissing him off or, what's worse, he feels justified now in inflicting pain to satisfy that anger."

"What do you think about the letters? You said you believed they are tied into this somehow. So do I, but I don't see them helping a lot in any direct way. I certainly don't think the killer is so stupid he would directly link himself to the murders by filling out a post office box address card with the right information."

"Maybe not, but we might get lucky with the follow-up. Loose ends always unravel. People who try to disguise their personal information sometimes keep parts of it the same: their initials, an old street they used to live on, et cetera. Identification is required for those boxes. Somewhere down the line this guy might have messed up and given us a clue. Ed's very good about details. That's why I sent him and not Burch. Koslovsky will have seen to every angle, every witness connection, every possible way to nail whoever set up the letters.

"So far we know about seven of the fifteen apartments. Apartments seven and nine, where the murders occurred, both got letters. They're also both upstairs apartments. Whether or not that is significant I don't know yet. The murderer's choice may only have had to do with opportunity and not preference. Apartments 6, 8, and 10C also upstairs, no letters received. Apartment one, the Manager, no letter. Apartment five, this apartment, both you and Sara received letters. Did you just take her place to keep things the same in the killer's scheme or did you actually do something to earn your chain letter? I'm sorry to say that I have to add that to a growing list of unanswerable questions at this point. So far all we've got to go on is coincidence and imagined similarities in this case. The letters are our first real connection. As I said before this thing could shape up with some female motivation given the recent discovery of Marilyn Henry and her background. Two of the three dead are woman and I want to exhaust this theory until I uncover information to the contrary. Another reason I'm pressing in this direction is the letters. Mrs. Jacobson and Helen Sotheby and Sara and you all got letters so far. The two dead women had daughters. According to Mrs. Goldman you also have a daughter, don't you Polly?"

"Yes Sergeant I have a daughter. But how could the killer know that? How could that be the common denominator here?"

"You can answer your own question by telling me something about your friend, by verifying for me some facts I'd rather not have verified. Sara was never married was she?"

"No. It was planned though after her first year in college. Then her fiancé quit school abruptly and went to Europe with some debutante. He subsequently went to work for her father's company and Sara never saw him again."

"Is that the way the relationship ended or is there more?"

"What do you mean more? Sara was rid of the selfish bastard when he left her."

"Polly, no secrets. This is too important and absolutely necessary for stopping this insanity. You didn't know Sara then, did you?"

"No."

Polly got up and went to the window not sure of her control on this subject. Sara hadn't told her about the baby girl until years into their relationship. It had always been hard for Sara to trust people and get close and revelatory. Polly on the other hand could meet someone casually and know immediately enough about their character to trust them completely with the most personal secrets. It was another difference between the two friends, another reason they shouldn't have gotten so close to each other and into each other's lives the way they had. Polly had taken the few minutes Savitch had given her to make a slow circle of the room and ultimately reclaimed her seat on the couch. Her thoughts had come full circle too around the events she knew concerning the birth over twenty years ago.

"You have to understand the way things were for her then. She was twenty, unattached, pregnant, broke, and Catholic. A deadly combination for a rational decision. Bryan, that was the selfish bastard's name, found out about the pregnancy from a mutual friend at college. He had married his debutante by then, a condition of his employment no doubt, and the idea of a baby appealed to the couple with one small catch. She wanted the baby, but not the hard way. She was afraid of ruining her figure and then there was all that pain. Bryan thought his rich wife was perfect when he met her and changing perfection was not what he had in mind. He pleaded with Sara over the phone and through letters to let him and Stephanie have the baby, raise it in a two parent home. Sara was thinking about adoption anyway since her religion made abortion out of the question. What was more logical, two completely

Once Upon a Murder

unknown people adopting her child or two people one of whom was the child's natural father? They pressed; she weakened. The adoption by Bryan and Stephanie made her feel better about giving up the child. The child's a debutante herself now and, knowing Sara, I doubt that the two of them would have a thing in common except genetics. That doesn't make the loss for her any easier, but the family stability she gave her daughter through adoption reinforced her decision. Can you believe that the rat and the debutante have stayed married all these years?"

"Where do the rat and family live now?"

"They live in Italy. Bryan's firm is a foreign conglomerate and they have no real ties here in the States. The girl is studying art in Paris the last I heard. What are you thinking?"

"Mrs. Jacobson had a daughter given up for adoption. Sara had a daughter given up for adoption. Both women received letters."

"So? Mrs. Sotheby had a daughter not given up for adoption and I have a daughter not given up for adoption. We both got letters. Also, Mrs. Montoya has two daughters, no letter. Frieda has a daughter and no letter and that woman on vacation, Mrs. whats-her-name, has daughters. Did she get a letter?"

"Don't know that yet. Tomorrow promises to be either full of revelations or dead ends. I should

232

know the results from the investigation into the post office box, the complete tally on the number of tenants here who received letters, the response to the ad in the newspaper, the copy of Stephen Jacobson's will....."

A loud knock on the door stopped his cataloguing of tomorrow's events and sent Polly to the door with an admonition from Savitch to ask who it was before opening it. Burch stepped into the room and panned back and forth between the two occupants trying to see the state of things between Polly and the sergeant before he spoke.

"What have you got for me, Burch?"

"I finished the tenant follow-up statements, except for the Gotjciks. I left them for last like you told me. It's getting late. We better finish up here. The officers downstairs want to leave--shift change--and we have to set up coverage here tonight before the officers go home, otherwise we'll have twice as many calls to make."

"I know. For a while I forgot I was still on duty"

He turned to Polly and thanked her for her ideas and conversation and instructed her again about the door and staying inside for the night. With regret as deep as the eider-soft cushions on Sara's sofa he reluctantly got up to leave.

*   *   *   *

Apartment ten's porch light was on. An orange bulb glowed from beneath a frosted globe. A shadowy impression of a female fortuneteller complete with crystal ball was etched into the globe of the outside light. The arriving detectives were splayed by orange light that seeped out of the cutouts in the globe where the fortuneteller's eyes should have been.

"I can tell this is going to be the highlight of my day. I feel an astronomical headache coming on--no pun intended--not to mention that everywhere I look I see orange spots."

"Yeah. It reminds me of my last hangover. It was before this case. Since these murders began you haven't given me time to drink."

"You should thank me for your sobriety not blame me for taking away your chance for a painful bender."

"Forgive me. I knew not what I said. I do thank you for mercifully protecting me from myself."

Pressing the doorbell elicited a loud grating buzzer sound which was followed by a mixture of excited voices from within. After about thirty seconds the front door was opened by the daughter who gestured them in by bowing and backing away from the opened door. Stepping over the threshold and into the apartment the two

Once Upon a Murder

men faced Flo Gotjcik in full regalia which included flowing robes and incandescent eye makeup that glowed in the dimly lit room. It was like entering a fortunetelling booth at a carnival. All that was missing was a sign with the prices and the time for the next seance.

It took Savitch a few minutes to adjust his eyes to the darkness before he could safely approach the chair near Mrs. Gotjcik, but as he moved closer to the woman so he could address her she started in.

"I could have told you there would be another murder. I predicted..."

"Then why didn't you? Why didn't you call me or one of my detectives if you had some key information, insight, or a word from the spirit world? I would love some help, would welcome it. If all you have to offer though is mumbo jumbo about star alignment or some vague premonition based on your infernal pessimism then please keep it to yourself. People are dying and I intend to find out exactly what you know, if anything, so let's not dance around our mutual hostility. I want direct answers to a few direct questions and we can end this interview on an upbeat note by both of us waving bye-bye as I leave this aromatic voodoo chamber."

He turned to speak to Burch who was still standing just inside the door. "Find the

Once Upon a Murder

goddamned light switch or open the curtains. I like to see a murder suspect when I talk to one," he instructed the officer while glaring at her through the darkness.

Flo was taken aback, offended and unsure how to respond to Savitch's attack on her personal and professional competence.

"This is my home. How dare you order people to do what you please here without my permission!"

"We can always go to Police Headquarters and you can be interrogated in complete discomfort. Let's go."

"Wait. Perhaps I was a little hasty. I am unaccustomed to having anyone give orders in my apartment besides me. You win, Sergeant, as you knew you would. I will submit to your questioning here rather than in the cold and unfriendly atmosphere of the police station."

"A wise choice on your part, but maybe your refusal to go to headquarters is more personal than you'd like me to believe. Does your distaste for my office surroundings have anything to do with your having spent more time in a police station than you'd like to admit?"

The curtains were open now and the lights from the courtyard filtered in. Burch had turned on two lamps which directly illuminated the sitting room scene between the two antagonists. The added light on Flo Gotjcik almost completely defused the powerful aura her costume and makeup had cast when the two officers had walked in. She was on the defensive on her own turf, something she hadn't anticipated. She closed her eyes as she visibly stiffened in her chair as if she physically felt the unpleasantness of his words or remembered something from the past that made her shiver with renewed abhorrence. Momentarily she regained her composure and was ready to control the conversation again, to see and be seen as the instrument of fate.

"Be careful what you accuse me of and how far your authority has power over me. I warn you I will not be used ill without radiating all the retaliation it is in my immense power to levy on you and yours."

"More threats?"

He thought he heard her hiss through her teeth at him before her daughter finally went to her mother's side and whispered something soothing into her mother's ear. Suddenly Flo was all smiles and cooperation as she indicated that he and his partner might be more comfortable in the large overstuffed chairs near her which she usually reserved for others who came to listen and appreciate her sage advice.

"I apologize for speaking so candidly before of my predictions. Not everyone is prepared to

Once Upon a Murder

have my forecasts reinforced when those forecasts threaten their own livelihood."

"I don't think an *I told you so* spouted tauntingly in the face of murder is a positive attention-getter. But let's try to leave your questionable talent as a soothsayer out of this interview. Where were you and your daughter earlier today, say between ten o'clock this morning and two o'clock this afternoon? And don't offer to vouch for each other. Whatever you may tell your customers about your reputation for cosmic divination is one thing; I assure you that I expect concrete facts substantiated by reliable witnesses."

Flo turned to her daughter and asked, "Where is my appointment book?" as if she wasn't totally aware of what she had done with every hour of her day.

"Ah yes, I see I had a seven o'clock appointment with Mrs. Smithson--bringing her husband back from the spirit world--she's a regular twice a week. On Mondays it's her mother that I have to resurrect. Not my specialty, but I try to offer a full spectrum of options to my clients. At eight I had a cancellation. Mrs. Harvey's sick cat. I could possibly bring back from the dead a lovely feline temptress who was a not so lovely human to deal with that beast if I wanted to. That's her second canceled appointment this month over that.....dear sweet kitty. I thought perhaps she

Once Upon a Murder

might show up after all so I waited twenty or thirty minutes. Regular and enthusiastic clients like her are, shall we say, hard to replace in the psychic/mystic/other world market. Then I went and had a nail repaired at Pamela's Natural Nails on Burlington. I had no appointment so I had to wait until she was free to do the repair personally. I was there until after ten. I stopped and picked up an early lunch from a Chinese takeout place around the corner from Pamela's Shop. I had to be back for an eleven o'clock appointment."

Flo Gotjcik hesitated at that point a little too long to match the pacing the woman had used in ticking off the events of the morning.

"With who Mrs. Gotjcik? Who was your eleven o'clock appointment?"

"Eh..er..well I'm sure he will speak up for me when asked. It was a rather long appointment, two hours or more as I recall."

"Whoever it was must have needed a powerful spiritual lift to take that long."

"Yes. He has had some recent misfortune."

"And his name?"

"Phil Jacobson."

Burch and Savitch couldn't stop the inevitable glance at each other and the silent accompanying telepathic sight wave that substituted for *and the plot thickens*.

"Phil Jacobson is one of your clients?"

Once Upon a Murder

"Yes. The dearly departed Mrs. Jacobson told him about me some time ago. I never realized how superstitious farmers were until I started to consult with him. He has what we call in my trade a dual fixation, with the land in his case. It's his blessing and his curse and he needed me, of course, to keep the balance that would prevent nature from overrunning his farm and wiping him out."

"Just how did you consult with him? He doesn't even live in this state."

"Originally I did his chart at Mrs. Jacobson's request. It's a great way to get new clients by offering something tangible at no cost. If you have the calling like I do the potential customer is amazed by what you know about them without ever having met them and very often the relationship starts from there. After he received my charting of his particular birth-moonphase-spatial limitations guide and how it related to his working the Jacobson Property, he began to ask for decisions from me about things at the farm. I sent him responses and suggestions of courses of action he should take along with further readings of his cycle. When I predicted several natural catastrophes and helped him protect himself from them he had to have my help on a regular basis, in fact, he never acted without it where his farm and the land were concerned."

Once Upon a Murder

"It pleases me that you told us about it. His being here was observed by one of the other tenants. Where did he go after he left you, Mrs. Gotjcik? Mrs. Gotjcik was he here until one o'clock? What time did he leave and where did he go?"

Flo Gotjcik looked directly at Sergeant Savitch, considering and then reconsidering the consequences of something, and then yelled out, "Phil, come on out here. We have company and your presence is requested."

Phil Jacobson lumbered out in the familiar gait he had demonstrated crossing the grass at his brother's funeral. It was obvious he felt uncomfortable being revealed to the detectives, but he moved forward to stand near Flo's chair as she had directed.

"Phil, the sergeant only wants to ask you a few questions and since you were with me during the murder of Helen Sotheby I can't imagine what additional information he hopes to learn from you."

"Thank you, Mrs. Gotjcik, for coaching him and trying to give the three of you an alibi at the time of the murder. If only my suspicions regarding the three of you could be so easily dismissed. Mr. Jacobson, apparently you are quite happy with Mrs. Gotjcik's professional advice.

Once Upon a Murder

How much do you know about her previous career?"

"Well, I never asked about that."

"Let me elucidate it for you, Phil."

"Sergeant, I don't think that will be necessary."

"Ahhh, but it will. I intended to ask you these questions before Mr. Jacobson appeared and now, since we are all here and so unexpectedly cozy, I see no reason to prolong the questions."

"What's he talkin' about, Flo?"

"This isn't your first involvement with the police is it, Mrs. Gotjcik?"

Her stare never wavered but a nervous tick pulled at the corner of her mouth.

"You left North Carolina in rather a hurry after you were released from jail."

"Jail! Flo you've been in jail? Not you. A pure spirit like yours?" Phil Jacobson spat at her from behind his spiritual purist beliefs.

"Mama was framed. She is a marvelous psychic and only wanted to help that man."

"She helped him all right. And then she helped herself to his $50,000 and then tried to help him into the grave when he disobeyed her warnings. Just how far will you go to make your predictions come true? All the way to murder?"

"I was innocent. I proved where I was."

"But where was your devoted daughter? Where was dear Sonia? Witnesses swore it was a young woman driving the car that hit Robert Clifton and then drove off."

"My daughter was cleared and I was sent to jail on a minor charge."

"...if you consider fraud a minor charge."

Phil Jacobson was astounded by what was going on between his psychic priestess and the sergeant. He tried to interject his disbelief but was motioned firmly by Burch to a chair while the two antagonists continued to debate.

"Sergeant, nonbelievers are never of interest to me. I assure you there are plenty of people who know my power and respect my ability to reach beyond the physical world. I need never convince them through violence."

"That had better be true. I'm building a lengthy file on your operations in Florida so don't think you've found a place here where you'll not have to watch your behavior. A few more entries in my computer should restrict your activities nicely in this state and any other you try to operate in. There had better not be any suspicion of any kind around you or your dealings with clientele. Any complaints and I'll pull you in just the way you seem to have pulled Jacobson and who knows how many more into your shady schemes."

Once Upon a Murder

With that comment Savitch retreated from his verbal attack on Mrs. Gotjcik and turned to Jacobson.

"Have you been here since eleven this morning?"

"Yessir. And I was here before eleven too."

"Before eleven?"

"I was here before my appointment talkin' with Sonia before Flo got home. I been here since around 9:30 waitin' for Flo to get here and talk to me about my farm and all. When she got here we three of us ate some Chinese food Flo brought home with her."

"Where were you before you came to this apartment today? Did you leave here for a short time and pay a visit earlier to Helen Sotheby's apartment and strangle her because of something put into your head by this self-professed astrological potentate?"

"NO. I didn't do anything to that woman before or after my appointment with Flo. I didn't even know her. I couldn't leave; I tried to but there were police everywhere by that time. I had to stay and Flo thought it best I stay until everything settled down."

"I'll just bet she did. You'd think, Phil, that she would have a little more control over what's happening in her own building wouldn't you? Somehow I don't think Mrs. Gotjcik dare risk claiming credit for this latest bit of misfortune telling. Don't bother to fume and pontificate; I've had enough for one day.

"Burch, I want you to drive Mr. Jacobson to his hotel. I think he's had enough spiritual exposure for one day as well. And Burch, first thing tomorrow check and make sure a license for Mrs. Gotjcik to conduct business out of her apartment is on file in this city. Make sure it hasn't expired and that all the t's are crossed and all the i's are dotted. And while you're at it Burch, maybe you ought to tell the clerk to check the paper it's printed on to see if it's legit."

As they left he turned away from Flo, walked to a wall socket overloaded with extension cords, and pulled the main plug leaving the Gotjciks alone in their darkened lair again.

FIFTEEN

Her feet approached but never quite touched the field; her movements slow and synchronized like the flowers swaying in the light wind. Lightness and drifting all she possessed when she wanted concreteness and control. Her legs were muscleless as they met the ground so that each step took her nowhere. She had to enter the field again and start over. This time she would make it; she willed it so.

First the hint of fragrance, pleasant yet insignificant. Okay to linger here. Then as she went on further into the field the assertive fragrance of several flowers thick around her legs threatened her advance. Now, where she should start to run, she couldn't get any traction. She made only one small step ahead for every dozen she took. And then the wind picked up ahead of her and wafted her face with the fragrance and strength of the significant flowers, powerfully strong and suffocating. No fresh air was reaching her at all; she was given only airborne pollen to breathe. Dizziness and sinking and roses gone mad assaulted her senses. The field ahead where it had been flat was now an incline, a hill of impossible blossoms. It had been like this last time, the field tilting up just as she had gained some ground. She couldn't go back. That wasn't allowed. *Press ahead you'll make it* a voice encouraged her, but a feeling of hopelessness dragged her down among the flowers. Maybe she could crawl and advance where walking had been useless. Yet every time she moved a hand to stretch ahead the distance widened. She cried in despair. It was just like the last time she'd been here. She had to scream so the flowers would feel sorry for her and help her get through them. They must feel something, some pity. They're alive and I know they hear me.

Then the humming started high and incessant- -torture of another kind. Aren't the flowers enough? Droning on and on worrying my head inside with noise while the flowers battle my outsides. I must not let it affect me. I must concentrate on the field of flowers. But the noise. The flowers are screaming back at me, punishing me for wanting them dead, wanting them to perish so that I can live. It seems too selfish to be me, but I am so desperate to be through the field before....before what?....before the flowers dissolve me. I am a spineless stalk with only weightless petals for a head. I am like a flower. I should be content among my kind sharing my life of beauty and fragrance. Too short; a flower's life is too short. I demand more than that! If I can escape the overwhelming fragrance I will be a flower no longer.

Every breath clogs my life with scent. I will try not to breathe through my nose....that's it! That's the answer! If I breathe without using my nose I will get safely away in just a few feet. It is the fragrance preventing my advance, my freedom, my release. Why didn't I know that before and all the other times I came to this same field? Exhilaration at finding the answer will help me to leap the flowers. I will soar now that I know I have solved the problem. I must get through now before the noise returns, while I have the answer to escaping the field. I know it now. The answer is that I must simply do....what? She heard the echo of her own scream as the answer was lost again.

Frustrated agony and paralyzed action alone must have awakened her. Lying on the bed, feeling herself one single loudly pounding pulse too rapid to survive, Polly fought back to reality from her dream. She forced her heart to return to its normal rhythm with her controlled breathing and her increasingly relaxed mental state. All she remembered from her dream was the painful smell of flowers and the futility she had felt for....how long? Looking at her watch she found she had been asleep only about an hour, but the dream had seemed to last an eternity.

The television was a frozen picture accompanied by a harsh tone that signaled the end of programming. That must have been the intermittent droning sound in her dream, the sound that had gradually dragged her back from the field and awakened her. She pressed the remote control and ended that misery and lay there thinking about the other. The dream she reasoned must have been a manifestation of her recent experience in Mrs. Sotheby's bedroom. The flowers and blood smell comingled in her subconscious the way it had in reality when she had carelessly found herself on the floor with the woman's body. Another shudder sped her heart again and forced her to seek another environment, somewhere she would not be tempted to drift off again and recreate the dreamed sequence she was trying to purge from her mind.

She flipped the light on in the bathroom and went to splash her face with water. She saw the reflection of her sweat-drenched clothing and her frantic expression, both of which gave visual testimony to the horror her mind had put her through. The water cooled the outside but couldn't reach where she sought to have relief. Think about something else she told herself. Get involved in doing something simple and mindless. Establish a routine of serenity to bring your senses back in line.

She went slowly through Sara's apartment turning on all the lights ending in the living room where earlier she had spoken with Savitch about the murders. He was competent and he swore no more would happen at Meadow Oaks. She wanted so to believe he could deliver. That would go a long way toward stopping dreams like the one she had just had. Then the questions replaced the dreams in her waking mind. Who wrote the letters? Why were the people in this building killed? Had Sara done anything unknowingly to instigate the trouble? And why had she, Polly Sloan, now received her own personal letter? There were inconsistencies forming unless it was the building itself and not its unwitting occupants that was the target. It seemed to her that a plan with some design had gotten out of hand and now the design was incident to a continuing murder spree.

Just how safe was she here she wondered. It was funny that she never worried about that in her own home; she only worried about it here while she was on vacation. She had no weapons in her house, no alarm system, no security measures of any kind. There were no contingency plans for the possibility of crime being perpetuated against her or her property. Yet there she felt safe. Perhaps in time she would have felt safe again here but not now, not when both her waking and sleeping thoughts doted on death and what she could do to prevent any more of it from happening.

She felt the mental energy and alertness moving through her body making her want to do something. Spying the dirty laundry she'd gathered and put by the door, she went to get her shoes in the bedroom and then the soap from out of the kitchen. She shoved the laundry into a plastic basket, picked up her keys, and left the apartment.

Outside the air's thick heat stopped her for a moment. She had almost forgotten how hot it had been today. Inside Sara's apartment the air conditioning artificialized the comfort of a Florida summer. She followed the walkway around to the back where the laundry room was. Everyone was asleep by now and she was confidant the laundry room would be empty and that the noise would disturb no one since the occupants of the two closest apartments to the utility room were on vacation.

The room was narrow and bare and the walls were dull gray stucco. The single unshielded light bulb hung from an electrical wire in the center of the ceiling. The room was constructed to follow the design of one of the temporarily vacant apartments next to it with a ten foot distance between floor and ceiling. The room's high single wooden-sashed window was crammed into a corner of the far wall so it was at walkway level in the courtyard and allowed for only minimum air circulation. It was unnervingly quiet in the laundry room, the only sound the burning gas flame under the water heater which had come on right after she entered. She quickly rotated the washer dial to the setting she wanted and pulled the control out which immediately started the tub filling with water. She dumped in some soap and sorted out a load of clothes and shoved them in and closed the lid. No chairs or place to sit so she hopped up on the still dryer and began again her musings on the situation at *the Oaks*.

Before long she heard the loud click that terminated the cycle of the rotating machine dial and hopped down to take her clothes out. She found it hard to believe that she had been lost in thought for over half an hour without even hearing the cyclic filling and unfilling of the machine. She pushed her load into the dryer and set the control which began the tub spinning. She sorted through the remaining laundry on the floor to make another load only to realize that she had forgotten a couple

Once Upon a Murder

of items she had meant to include in the wash. Sure that no one would disturb her mess on the floor, she grabbed her keys and left the laundry room to go back to the apartment.

While in the apartment she got the laundry items and also picked up a magazine to read that had come in the mail for Sara earlier in the week. An article title on the cover intrigued her and she paused momentarily to flip to the page specified. She had read two columns of the article before remembering she had been in the middle of doing laundry and she had to return to finish the job. She reluctantly closed the magazine and took it with her.

She noticed the heat again outside the apartment door and, as she walked across the courtyard, she was alerted to the sounds of a breezing wind that worked its way through the curling eaves of the building. The decorative pattern made a tunnel to trap the wind and as the wind fled the clutches of the roof's overhang it made the sound of wheezing laughter at its triumphant escape. The natural wind chimes followed her as she walked. No light came from outside to the balconies above her as a row of ancient palms and eucalyptus trees barricaded the moon's light from providing more than fingered branch shadows that danced along the walls.

Once Upon a Murder

Coming around the corner of the building she was startled by an officer who greeted her and asked where she was going. She told him and he was about to make her return to her apartment when he received a radio message to go to his car and call the station. He said that he would check on her in the laundry room and escort her back to her apartment when he returned from making the call. She thanked him and walked on. She had just entered the dark entryway that led to the back of the building when a shape stood out from the wall.

"I know. I'm not supposed to leave my apartment. The other detective already told me. He's making a call and will join me in the laundry room and walk me back to my apartment when he's done with the call. So, you see, it isn't necessary for you to worry about me. One city official is all that I require, I assure you. What's your name? I'll be sure and tell the sergeant that you were doing your duty anyway."

"Henderson. Good night ma'am."

"Good night, Henderson. I'll be O.K."

She walked into the room where the sound of the spinning dryer was eerier than she remembered and the darkness shadowing in from outside a little murkier in spite of the reassurances of the two officers. The smell of dampness, the hint of perfumed soap, and the stagnant heated air

254

persuaded her to finish up quickly. While putting her second load into the washing machine her increased perspiration registered as drops of sweat that stung her eyes. She closed the lid and automatically looked up and over at the window in the corner. It was closed. She thought it had been open before or maybe that was the last time she had been in here when she had washed several loads for Sara in preparation for her friend's trip.

With both the washer and the dryer spinning the noise was annoying so she flipped her magazine to the article she had been reading before and picked up where she had left off. A few more pages and the article took an unexpected and uninteresting direction to Polly and she was beginning to regret having decided to read it when the door to the outside suddenly swung shut interrupting any interest Polly had in finishing the article.

"Who's there? Is that you, officer? Henderson?"

She approached the door assertively, sure now that it must have closed from the wind in the outside hall. The door opened out and she was satisfied with her reasoned logic. She grabbed and turned the handle sure of its give under the movement and slammed into a solid object.

"Who's out there? Open this door immediately!"

Her heart rate was up to unpleasant dream pace again and this time there was no controlling it. Sweat ran off her face in response to her body's objection to the fear, the humidity, and the heat generated in a closed room where the two appliances had raised the temperature to intolerable levels. Polly stopped the washing machine and opened the door to the dryer, but it kept turning and pumping hot air into the stifling room. The dial broke off in her hand when she tried to force it to stop. She had to pull the plug in the back of the machine. The machine wouldn't budge. It was wedged in between the washer and the water heater and every time she tried to pull it out it wouldn't yield.

She went to the door again, sure that she hadn't tried hard enough to open it the first time. Twisting and turning the handle in combination with the push of her shoulder and body weight against the door did nothing. The door seemed to have expanded against the jam and wouldn't detach. She pounded on the door and yelled for a few minutes but no one came. Her strength was going since she needed to breath harder as no new air entered the room. The window. It was almost four feet above her and she had nothing to stand on. She threw her keys, the box of soap, and then her shoes; but they all deflected off the thick old glass without affect. The dryer continued to pump its heat into the room. She was extremely hot and needed air. Already her nose and mouth had become painfully dry and her lips were chapping. Her eyes burned and a dry crust sealed the corners. Her body temperature was getting dangerously high.

She went to the washer and flipped the water temperature to cold and spun the dial to fill. She drank handfuls of the water as it entered the tub and splashed her face to cool herself. She drenched a towel and wiped her arms and neck. It refreshed her only briefly; she still needed fresh air. She screamed at the door and was shocked by the pitiful sound she produced. Pounding the door and calling out tired her. She used the water again, but her efforts took so long and drained her strength to the point of wasting the relief she had gained.

She dragged herself to the door and fell to the floor to catch any air that might be seeping in. There was no air! She forced her swollen eyes to see why. Something was under the door! A desperate moan signalled her agony and her confirmation that someone had deliberately imprisoned her. Her finger under the door just touched something blocking the crack. She needed something else, something longer to dislodge the obstacle. She gagged on the hot air close to the dryer but managed to make it over to pick up the magazine she had dropped when the door slammed. Crawling back to the door, she pushed the magazine against the blockage. It wouldn't budge. Polly pushed the magazine along the length of the door and sobbed when one corner was cleared and a little fresh air reached her. She tried to clear more space under the door but it was hopeless. She had the strength of a newborn baby. She wanted to sleep. Dizziness and nausea fought her concentration.

Over the noise of the dryer, with her face on the floor next to the door, she could hear the sounds of something happening outside. It wasn't close to the laundry room but further away in the apartment courtyard. She could hear the muted sound of voices, of police radios, and of someone running. By now she had no energy to pursue her escape and could only smile weakly knowing that someone was close. She had a little vent of air. She had a wet towel which she dragged around her neck, sticking one wet corner in her mouth so she could suck the moisture. She curved her body into a fetal position so that she could continuously kick the door by using a minimal amount of effort.

How long she was able to keep that up she didn't know. She went into shock and passed out, awakening to the sound of the siren on the ambulance that was rushing her to the hospital.

SIXTEEN

"You could have stayed another night for your own health and safety and my peace of mind. God damn it! I've got enough going on with these murders."

"Well excuse me for being such a burden, but there's absolutely nothing wrong with me. Now I know how Sara felt when she blamed herself for her fall; I feel the same way she did--just plain stupid getting myself trapped like that. I won't be pampered and taken care of when I'm perfectly able to do everything for myself."

"It wasn't too many hours ago when we found you locked in the laundry room barely breathing, my dear."

"Don't call me *my dear* it makes me furious! I knew I would be all right. I had air. I was just a little overheated."

"A little! Do you want me to quote the doctor's diagnosis for you and tell you how close you came to dying last night?"

Polly backed off from her verbal engagement with Savitch. She was too shaky yet and easily exhausted by the least effort. She could have stayed another night. It would have meant a peaceful sleep under the protective eye of Nurse Krantz, but she just couldn't justify the luxury or the selfishness of the act to herself. She'd been raised to be self-reliant and back in action after an illness or injury in record time. That's just the way she was. And she thought it not a bad way to be either. It had been close for her and she knew it, but she didn't have to make that admission to anyone else.

The killer had been at *the Oaks* last night. He had eluded capture after disabling an officer, taking the officer's radio, and actually being in on the transmissions involved in his own pursuit. Nothing had happened. Well, no one had been murdered that is. The attempt--yes, that's what it had been--on her life was the only crime committed. And the sergeant and his men were still debating whether that was intentional or just a way to keep her out of the way while another murder plan was carried out.

Savitch had reported to her earlier today what they had found out after examining the laundry room. The window, which was usually left propped open, had been shut and the prop used to hold the window open had been used to secure it closed from the outside. The dial on the dryer had been forced the wrong way, broken off, and left to hang uselessly from its metal peg. A coat hanger that someone had left in the laundry room had been hastily wrapped around the pipe attached to the wall behind the dryer with the hook closed over the dryer hose preventing anyone from moving the unit away from the wall to disconnect it. One of her own towels had been rolled and jammed under the door.

She shivered at what the killer had been doing while she had briefly left the laundry room to return to Sara's apartment. He had fixed the window, the dryer, and very nearly fixed her. He had gone through her laundry and touched her things until he had found the towel needed to seal her in his manmade crypt. Last night gave new meaning to the phrase *feeling as if someone had walked on her grave.*

She risked a sidelong look at Savitch and observed him lighting his third or fourth cigarette since they'd left the hospital. Every time she argued him out of the point he was making he'd grind the current cigarette into the ashtray until only flakes of tobacco and paper were left. She imagined he'd much rather be doing that to her since his anger paralleled his cigarette-crushing motions. He hadn't told her much about last night. She wanted to know more. She wanted to drag the information out of him and she wasn't above any kind of respectable finagling. After what she'd been through he owed it to her. For all both of them knew she might even be the next real target and the trap she'd begged him to set using her as bait might be possible now. She'd push just the slightest bit to find out what he was thinking.

"Things may not have gone exactly as planned but you were able to prevent another murder--mine--and to protect everyone here including me. Any description from the officer who was disabled and robbed of his radio and his self-respect?"

"No. He was just tapped on the side of the head, went down on his knees, and fell forward hitting his forehead hard on the cement. The doctor's convinced the fall and subsequent injury to his head knocked him out, not the blow from the killer. The officer didn't see or hear anything. Transmission on his radio was scratchy so we couldn't even decipher whether the voice we later realized was not the officer's voice was from a man or a woman. Whoever it was took advantage of the confusion and interjected conflicting information into the communication system which directed the other officers involved in the pursuit away from the building so our killer could get away.

"The officer who got conked was Burch, I'm afraid, and he feels awful about last night. He feels he personally let you down. He was in charge of the protection detail here and he's too ashamed of what a fool the killer made of him to face you yet. It was him who carried you out into the air last night and insisted on riding with you to the hospital. He'll reason it out in a day or two that he didn't act in an unprofessional way and then he'll come around. It just takes time for him to forgive himself any lapse in proficiency on the job."

"I'll try to make it easy for him when I do see him. What about the other detective, the one you sent to the Post Office?"

"Detective Koslovsky has been busy ferreting out quite a bit of information from the postal system. Ed had one of our officers staked out at the P.O. boxes even before he spoke to the supervisor about the procedure involved in renting and collecting mail from the boxes. Before I go into that aspect of the investigation let me continue my tally of tenants and letters.

Two of the apartment tenants on vacation, the Kearneys in 10B and Chrystal Langford in 10A, both had their mail stopped and held for them at the Post Office. The single in 10A had no letter. The wife in 10B, Ruth Kearney, had the first letter addressed to her only in the couple's stack of mail. We also finished our checklist of the other tenants, polling them to see who got letters. Besides you and or Sara, Mrs. Sotheby, Mrs. Jacobson, and now Ruth Kearney, there was only one other tenant who received the first letter....."

"Tell me. Go ahead. Who was it?"

"Flo Gotjcik!"

"The harmless woman who tells fortunes and walks around like she knows something about everybody's business? Why her? What could the common denominator be between her and us, the others who got letters? I don't see how that fits. Are you sure?"

"She didn't want to admit it, but the letter's contents aren't common knowledge and she quoted almost word for word the language in the letter when she gave her original statement to the detective after the Jacobsons were murdered. We just didn't know then that it was important."

"Quoted? From her letter?"

"No. She burned the actual letter. She saw it as some kind of threat to her ability and power and burned it during some kind of evil-purging ceremony."

"Great. But you do believe she actually got one of the letters and couldn't have heard about it or seen someone else's letter?"

Once Upon a Murder

"Reasonably sure. No second letter though. So far only you and Mrs. Sotheby have that privilege."

"Some privilege. Since I'm the only one left alive, what do you think my chances are? Will one aborted attempt stop the killer or make him lose interest in continuing his agenda?"

"Not likely. We searched the apartments of the tenants again last night after you were safely hustled off to your comfy hospital bed. Alibis for everyone who wasn't home at the time of the crime check out and, for those who were home, all claimed to have some other tenant or spouse who vouched for them. No help there. It's hard not to think of this as a tenant conspiracy. Maybe they are protecting one of their own and I keep being used by a crafty bunch of senior citizens!"

"What else can you think until some real evidence surfaces? Go on about the Post Office. You were telling me what Ed learned."

"P.O. boxes require full name, address, proof that you are a local resident of South Blandford--a current bill showing your mailing address is accepted--as well as a driver's license or picture I.D. Our letter writer had a problem. How to rent one and keep his/her/their name out of the process. Ever heard of or heard Sara mention somebody named Hector Serrano?"

Once Upon a Murder

"I don't recall the name. Does she know him? Should I?"

"Not really. Just hoping for a break; but I didn't expect this to link up either. Nothing else has."

"Who is he? What's he got to do with the murders or the letters or...?"

"The box where the letters were to be returned was rented in his name. Let me explain. Koslovsky got the information from the Post Office Supervisor, Serrano's name and address that is, and he took a couple of cars over there late yesterday while you and I were engrossed in the Sotheby murder. Mr. Serrano lives alone in an apartment about six blocks from the Post Office. He's a janitor and sort of a maintenance man for the building where he has his apartment and lives on that income plus a small pension. He was forced to retire prematurely due to a leg injury. Walks with a limp, but still gets around well enough to do the job he has now. Mr. Serrano walks to the Post Office to pick up his pension checks. Doesn't trust the mail service. Afraid someone will break into his apartment box and steal his check. The Post Office Sup. knows the guy, feels sorry for him, so he lets the guy have a P.O. box for almost nothing--senior citizen rate only there isn't one. Serrano has his mail put into the box and then he walks over there every day to

Once Upon a Murder

see if he has anything. Real gregarious guy according to Ed. Everyone at the Post Office knows him. He talks to anyone who'll listen to him. One day he gets a different kind of letter in his box. The letter says the writer spoke to him one day and sympathized with his financial problems and wanted to help him. The letter was folded over a $50 bill and asked for a little favor in return. The sender wanted to use Serrano's box for a few letters that he would be receiving. That's all. Seemed like a simple request to Serrano and fifty bucks....well....fifty to Serrano is a lot of money. So he allowed his P.O. box to be used by the person who sent him the money anonymously."

"How did he answer the letter? Did he see the person? How was he contacted?"

"Hold on a minute. I'm getting to it. To sum it up and to not try your patience any further, Serrano was sent a second letter a few days after the first one, just enough time for Serrano to have spent the fifty and to have guaranteed the writer permission to use the box. The second message explained the need for Serrano's help by giving him some story about mail being stolen from the writer's box, something Serrano definitely identified with. The letter writer blamed his apartment manager, said she was a real witch and a snoop as well. So the writer, he pays Serrano not only to let the letters come to his box, but to walk them over to his apartment personally and slip them under the door for him being very careful not to let the landlady or anyone else see him doing it. The writer goes on to say that it would only be for about a month until our letter writer returned from *out of town*. And when he returned another $50 would miraculously appear in Serrano's box if the letters were delivered as requested."

"...and the address? What's the address? How many letters did he deliver? Wait. You don't look too thrilled about this development. Not like someone who has just had a breakthrough in a major murder case. Why not?"

"Because I haven't.....at least I don't want to get my hopes up. This clue, just like all the others, points us back in the same direction."

"What direction? You are maddening! Why aren't we going to the place Serrano took the letters? Do you know what's there? Did Koslovsky go already? What did he find?"

"We are. No. No. Nothing yet. I think I've answered all your questions, so far that is."

"Meaning?"

"We are going to where Serrano was asked to take the letters. I don't know what's there and Koslovsky hasn't been there yet. You and I, and I see Burch pulling in behind us, are going to be the ones to make any discoveries."

"I don't understand. Why are you turning here? This is *the Oaks*."

"Exactly."

SEVENTEEN

It stood there in the glare of the afternoon sun as a testament of indefatigable permanence and as a storehouse of secrets. The bright stucco exterior welcomed guests, tenants, and murderers alike. The fears of the night lay ahead and the fears of other nights past seemed too far away to awaken terror in those living there from a building whose every corner and hiding place was revealed in the piercing scrutiny of the sun. Last night's episode seemed comical and trivialized as things of the night appear against the light of day. It was easy to dismiss the night's pain against the backdrop of the day's rightness; to imagine the murders a mistake of shadows coalescing ingeniously to plague the lives of the innocent tenants of *the Oaks*. Nevertheless, there it was. The day made the madness remote, but night would soon fall and hopefully not take anyone with it.

Polly's thoughts about the building covered the surface of her mind refusing to move away and allow more probing and insightful ideas to break through. As her psychological procrastination paralleled her fixed position in the patrol car, Savitch's voice brought her through the fog so her mind came into focus with reality again. He was coaxing her out of the car, a concept she was mentally fighting very hard to accept and even harder to do.

"I was saying that Jacobson's will left everything free and clear to his brother Phil. How's that for a murder motive? He says he didn't know his brother's intentions about the farm-- thought the *old bastard* would leave it to the church. I checked. Stephen had a falling out with some of the officials at his church and had the will redone within the last year. Phil thinks that was Mrs. Jacobson's influence; swears his brother hated him. Are you with me? You wanted me to catch you up on the case and then you black out on me."

"I'm listening. Jacobson is off the hook for the murders--he gets the farm."

"You're only half listening. He gets the farm and improves his chance at being the murderer with or without our harmless fortuneteller pulling his strings. We did finally clear the seniors club and the church group of any participation or knowledge in the murders or with the writing of the letters. There were only about five or six alibis in doubt from both groups after the original statements were taken anyway. Then there are still two outside chances for possible implication in the killings: Marvin Henry, Marilyn's stepfather; and Larry Stone, tenant from apartment two. Henry was on another one of his business trips, sells outdoor furniture to hotels, and can't provide an alibi for the time of the Jacobson murders, but couldn't have killed Sotheby. Stone left for Hawaii late on the day of the murders and was not in touch with the tour leader of his group at all at the time of Sotheby's death so he could have done them both.

"Speaking of the letters, so far our ad has mainly drawn kooks--no legit copycat correspondence yet that can be verified. However, we are following up on some unusual accidents that have been reported which have similarities to the situation in this case.

"By the way Marilyn is leaving tomorrow. Nothing violent here can be connected to her directly. I'm more or less convinced that the timing of her finding out about her adoption and the Jacobsons' murders was strictly coincidence. She's angry about the deception, but not enough to wipe out her real mother, her supposed father, and another old lady just for the hell of it. And then what about you? She had nothing to gain by

Once Upon a Murder

imprisoning you in the laundry room, besides I thought the two of you kind of hit it off."

"I won't be inviting her to spend her vacations with me if that's what you mean, but I think she likes me. She realizes I'm not judgmental about her hostility and bewilderment, and I don't expect her to miraculously accept her life as it's become."

"....to continue. The tenants in 10B who were having a chain letter held at the Post Office for them are both on their second marriage. The wife has no kids, but the husband has two daughters by his first wife. The current wife tries to play the part of wonderful stepmother, but has difficulty with one of the girls. The daughter, the youngest girl, can't accept wife #2 as her father's choice. The daughter and the wife virtually ignore each other-- minimum tolerance on visits. According to the apartment renters who are closest to the couple here, the second wife has given up trying to reconcile and lets the daughter have her way. A few of the tenants say that's why the kid is such a spoiled brat and is messed up in the head.

"I also have some surprising developments regarding Helen Sotheby, but not now. Let's go. I can tell you later. Koslovsky's car just pulled up and I'm hoping we'll have much meatier news to occupy us ravenous crime seekers in a few minutes."

Once out of the car she became an insignificant part of an entourage that was forming and going somewhere that was still a mystery to her. Savitch, Koslovsky, and a third car with two uniformed officers as well as Burch, who gave her an almost imperceptible nod of his head, had gathered to form the group. Just inside the courtyard the group encountered a nervously pacing Frieda Goldman who was dangling a mass of keys from her hand as she walked back and forth. Savitch exchanged words with her, took the keys she proffered, walked past her, and left her to fall in with the insignificant part of the entourage.

Polly halted briefly when she saw their direction, but quickly caught up and joined them as they entered the small hallway that led past the infamous laundry room and to the back of the apartment building. She looked into the room as she passed to assure herself that it was unoccupied, and to free herself from last night's trauma when she visualized the room's interior this time. The room was empty but the memory was lasting. She very nearly knocked the 5'6" policewoman down as she plowed into the officer while coming around the corner with her head still glancing back toward the laundry room. She was being held back by a uniformed arm and had to be content with her view and no explanation of what was to happen as the policewoman gestured silence to her and Mrs. Goldman.

Burch was hugging the stucco wall just in front of the policewoman. His gun was drawn and ahead of him the others had their weapons out too, Koslovsky and Savitch cautiously outside the door and the other uniformed officer on the far side past the door. The sergeant knocked on the door of 10B, identified himself, waited only seconds and then inserted a single key he had removed from the ring Mrs. Goldman had given him. There was no noise of any kind as the door opened inward and everyone entered quickly except the policewoman, Frieda, and Polly. The impatience Polly felt while waiting to be notified of what or who was in the apartment was like a living thing, it built up and consumed any polite reserve she should have felt under the circumstances. She had already gathered a deep breath in her lungs to tell the officer how she felt at being restrained when Burch walked out the door and motioned for them to advance.

Nothing could have prepared her for the room that cried agony from every wall. She hadn't known what to expect, what the others had come to this apartment for, and as the entourage stood in the center of the room equidistant from the tortured walls she had time to see what had greeted the others when the door to 10B was first opened. Faces drawn in red, gaping mouths, empty eyes, sadness, pain, and despair was the prevailing expression. A kind of artistic horror permeated the room. The pictures, more than just faces, houses and swings and trees ran into and over each other in one continuous mural; a study in red. Not neat and organized and well thought out, but each subject unfinished and ending with a downward streak of red as if hope had run out before an image could be completed. As if for the artist recreating the painful pictures of the mind evoked too much reminiscence to endure.

The person who had spent time here and done this had left other signs of presence. The furniture had been moved away from the walls to allow the artist to use from floor to ceiling as his canvas. Whoever it was had taken sheets and towels from the linen closet to use as covers for the furniture and as rags to clean the brushes. There was red paint dripped everywhere as if the artist had interrupted work on the drawings and wandered around the room making corrections or responding to a new inspiration or simply admiring the work. The careful touch of the furniture coverings was completely lost in the careless way the painter had toured the room with brush in hand; the furniture and carpeting were ruined despite the attempts at neatness.

Once Upon a Murder

Polly tried to look away from the faces. They seemed to be pleading with her, asking her for something, asking her for help. That was why she couldn't stare any longer; the faces wanted assurances and answers and she had none. The painter with his crude attempt at art had made his plea felt more convincingly than he ever could have by getting the figures right or by finishing the scene he began again and again around the room. Just like the overlays of crayon on the three dead faces, the simplicity and innocence of the walled drawings froze something from the artist's world forever in a permanence that refused change.

Frieda's appalling disbelief and shrieks of fear about the defacement of her tenant's property were coupled with the same uneasiness Polly felt, an inescapable reality staring at them all--the reality that the murderer was deeply disturbed and that his mental menacings were for this specific building. While each individual tenant had presumed his or herself safely secure within the confines of their apartments, someone else was equally as surely plotting and fixating on another one of them for destruction within those same walls. There could be no doubt now. Confirmation from Savitch was unnecessary. This building and its tenants were the murderer's specific target. Polly felt that he had settled himself in here to do a lot of killing and if not caught would rid *the Oaks* of any inhabitants he chose.

Additional police personnel were entering the apartment and making similar adjustments to the interior before going about their assigned tasks. Polly never felt someone take her arm and gently move her over to one corner of the room and it didn't register that she had been moved. Savitch's words had to awaken her from her catatonic trance and he was mildly perturbed that he had to repeat himself over and over until she could hear and listen successfully to what he was saying.

"I said Serrano never delivered any letters and he's still expecting the second fifty bucks. He told Ed he had plans for the money and the old guy is actually trying to get it from us since we spoiled his setup."

"You don't think Serrano's the one, do you?"

"Nah. Not bright enough or agile enough mentally or physically to do this under everyone's nose and escape detection. But I'm convinced not getting any letters inflamed the murderer, made him do this. He waited. He threw down his challenge, his offer of repentance in the first chain letter and waited for his *victims* to fall in line with their responses. Who knows what might have happened here if he'd gotten letters back. Maybe nothing. But wishful thinking won't take us anywhere now.

"I want your feeling about something over here. What does this mean to you? Does it fit in with what we discussed about motivation, does it symbolize another direction all together, or is it evidence that another sicko who didn't adjust properly to potty training is on the rampage?"

Where Savitch had taken her in the room there was a single chair, a makeshift bed with pillows and blankets piled to overflowing. He gave her a few minutes to take in the scene and then handed her a plastic evidence bag and a pair of gloves.

"Don't take it out until you put the gloves on."

"Where did it come from?"

"We found it in the blankets. A little light reading material for our murderer."

Polly had an incredulous look on her face, a frown that queried the significance of the newly found evidence. She took the thin little book from its wrapper and stared at the cover. Slowly she read and turned the well-used pages until the story was over without evincing any expression change. He could see she was trying to make the book fit neatly with the drawings and the letters and the painted faces but her own face asked the same question he had asked her: *What does it mean?*

"Sergeant, I recognize the book. I used to read books from this series to my own daughter.

Once Upon a Murder

The *Little Red Writer Series* of fairy tales is popular even today, but I'm sure this one is very old, a collector's item. It may be as old as I am. Why did he leave it?"

"He? I'm still not convinced it's a he, but to answer your question I don't think it was meant to be found. I think the murderer was in here last night before the laundry room incident and then couldn't safely return with police officers all over the place so close to this apartment. I doubt that he or she would save the book for so many years and let it be taken without trying to preserve it. What about the story?"

"Once upon a time stuff that all kids read as children. *The Proud Princess* is a classic story, actually a copy of the story line from a lot of other original tales. Poor and frail little girl who has nothing but a generous heart discovers, after her mother dies, that she is a wealthy princess and lives happily ever after. To most kids the loss of the mother would have been too horrible to replace with money or a title. What does it mean here? The mother is replaceable by money or something else? The mother should be replaced by something else? The child and mother thing again. What is the right message? What are the right clues to why this is happening?"

"A real bitch isn't it? Only the correct interpretation may possibly help us; anything else

Once Upon a Murder

may just lead us in circles. Before you overload on this new glitch let me tell you about the *Sotheby surprise.*"

"I don't know if I want any more now. Can't it wait?"

"No. I've got to enlighten and run. We'll be here most of the day and then reports to do at the office. I want you escorted up to your apartment as soon as I've told you. And you're to stay there this time. I'll try to call later. Please try and have something new and different to add to my muddle on this case, will you?"

"I'll try, but this cop stuff's harder than I imagined."

"Yeah. I'm taking a bona fide vacation after this one's done. Sotheby. You know how she doted on her daughter and grand kids and made my sappy detective think she was his second and more perfect grandmother?"

"Yes, sooo....?"

"She never had any kids. No records of births, no papers, no will to anyone except the pooch. All the pictures were phonies, a rogues' gallery of magazine art she cut out to resemble a developing and aging family she didn't have. Coroner verified she had no natural children and the town she said her daughter and grandchildren lived in is small--all checks of records there for any children or anyone who knew her are negative.

Phone bills show no history of calls to anyone outside this city. Her whole life was a fabrication."

"Why did she do it? Why did she feel she had to do that? Why?"

"That very word will keep me awake again tonight trying to piece together a winning scenario for murder that I hope won't turn into another nightmare by morning. Ta ta."

EIGHTEEN

Polly flinched unknowingly as she drifted into another dream, trapped again in the laundry room only much worse. All her dreams were layered into one unpleasant nightmare. As she lay on the floor gasping what small amount of air she could inhale under the door, the room was alive with images. The red drawings dripped over the walls, the body of Helen Sotheby lay next to her on the floor, and the noxious smell of perfume permeated the little whiff of air she had fought so hard to survive on as it found its way under the door. The chain letters and the little red storybook mixed and mingled their words in her head until the frustration of her dream scene forced her awake.

Her heart thundered her awakening and she thought it never would again return to its rhythmic beat of normalcy. Long after her body signaled its release from the dream and its aftereffects she felt herself mentally coming to grips with her panic.

Once Upon a Murder

She lifted the curtain near the bed to convince herself the night was past, and she let the sun's light spread over her in bed to announce the sanity of a new day.

It was late for her to be getting up as the clock displayed a time past nine. Sara was coming back tomorrow and Polly was determined to thoroughly clean Sara's apartment before then. Polly never strived for nor would she ever achieve of her own free will being as neat a person as Sara. Polly felt that being organized and orderly in her mind was chore enough for her. Housework was a loathsome waste of time but, after all, she had been a guest of Saras for the last few days and it was Pollys doing that had let the apartment mess get out of hand. She should dust and vacuum and clean the kitchen and bathroom at least.

The mass of laundry still sat in the corner, a hodgepodge of clean and unclean clothing that had been hastily retrieved for her from the laundry room by one of the officers after she had been discovered and taken to the hospital. She hadn't wanted to touch it or return to the room to finish the job she had started. The clothes were unwearable. None had been folded and all were wrinkled together, the clean with the dirty. She needed something to wear the next few days. Jeans and a shirt were enough for today, but for tomorrow she would have to buy something new.

Most of the clothes she had brought for the cruise were unsuitable for every day wear here except for those she had tried to wash the previous evening. She wasn't ready for another trip to the laundry room and she wanted to avoid the sorting out of that awful pile by the front door which symbolized the jumbled thoughts that troubled her.

As her plans for the day further formulated in her head she experienced a burst of excitement and interest that had been absent since she had arrived in Florida. Today was going to be a better day for her, at least she was making mental plans to try and enjoy herself in spite of the circumstances. Maybe she could even coax Frieda to go out with her. Polly's recollection of the previous day in 10B and Frieda's unsettling reaction to what they had both seen and felt made Polly more determined than ever to get the woman away from Meadow Oaks for a few hours.

The promise of a good day was just outside her window. The birds were foraging in the freshly turned earth of the flower beds for bugs and worms. The gardener had been there earlier and left the smell of freshly cut grass in the air, and everywhere she looked the recently watered flowers dripped and sparkled in the sunlight. Two detectives were talking and drinking coffee in the courtyard and an old yellow cat was secretly

Once Upon a Murder

calculating odds in his favor of catching one of the distracted birds digging in the dirt.

She was inspired by her mood to make the most of the day and began a general cleanup of the apartment. She had dragged out the vacuum and some dusting rags and spray cleaner and was ready to attack the dirt with vigor when the phone rang. It was Savitch.

"Good morning. Can you hear the birds outside your office window?"

"What birds? Is this Polly Sloan?"

"Yes, of course it's me. I was just commenting on what a gloriously innocent day it appears to be."

"Nature can be deceptively deadly. Haven't you figured that out yet? I can't afford to get involved with frivolous sentimentality until this case is wrapped up. And speaking of the case....I just want to let you know that a hellova lot has happened, investigation wise that is, since I saw you yesterday. Don't ask. I can't fill you in now. I can only tell you that I am confident an arrest will be made today. Actually it may be two or three arrests, but that's all I can say for now."

"That's cruel to give me only half the information. Who is it? Who are they? Why? Etcetera, etcetera, etcetera."

"That's all I am at liberty to tell you--typical cop cliché--but sadly it's the truth. Will tell all later. Promise to stay close to the apartment for me will you so I'll have one less thing to worry about? You'll get your reward for good behavior, I swear. Got to go. I shouldn't even have taken the time to brief you but, well you know."

"Yeah, thanks. Don't worry about me. No dangerous plans just another boring day in *Flamingo City*. Bye."

Hanging up the phone had brought the curtain down on an otherwise sunny day. She felt a mixture of calm elation that the madness would end and yet a definite let down at not being there for the finale. She had to admit to herself that she had found some perverse pleasure at being in the midst of danger and excitement and a sort of high at being considered almost an insider in the investigation. Don't let his news depress you, stupid, no one else will be dying at *the Oaks* except from natural causes and that's the way it should be.

* * * *

It seemed as if she had been cleaning for days when she finally wheeled the vacuum cleaner back into its appointed closet. She had worked hard and diligently. She had cut corners in her pursuit

Once Upon a Murder

of cleanliness; but she had also rationalized that some slipshod jobs completed were good enough for today or excused her methods as efficient timesaving ways of handling unnecessarily tedious tasks. Having left the cleaning of the tub and shower for last, she stepped out of her work clothes on the bathroom floor and with cleanser, spray cleaner, a rag and a brush, she stepped into the tub and began cleaning the tile and shower in the nude with the intention of rinsing the enclosure at the same time she took her shower. Forty-five minutes later she backed out of the bathroom cleaning and wiping the floor as she exited. She threw the dirty towel and cleaning rags back in the tub from the doorway vowing to return later in the day to wash them.

She felt happier again since some of the guilt she felt about messing up Sara's apartment had been purged away with the dirt. After another peek outside to reinforce her happiness with a view of nature, she dressed and made up her face quickly, tied her full hair back with a scarf, and left the apartment. She pranced, yes it could only be termed pranced, as she confidently jaunted over to the manager's apartment. She nodded to the two officers and continued on her way after explaining where she would be. They didn't evince the slightest concern that she had left her apartment or that she was now ringing Frieda's doorbell. They must know about the arrests. Why else would they seem oblivious to her actions and continue their conversation and laughing as if they were not here on a serious case?

Frieda demanded to know who her visitor was from inside the closed and bolted door. After peeping through the side curtain to confirm Polly's presence the landlady unbolted the door and let her guest in. Thereafter proceeded several reassuring and pacifying phrases from Polly to calm Frieda and bolster her interest in venturing out to the mall on a shopping spree. Although Frieda Goldman found some comfort in Polly's reassurances of an impending criminal arrest, she begged off from participation in a pleasure trip claiming she was suffering a particularly painful day of arthritis. Polly sympathized immediately and went around behind Frieda to massage the shoulder Frieda had indicated was troubling her. Frieda winced and then moaned appreciation but assured Polly that only the doctor's pills would give her the relief she needed after having spent a sleepless and torturous night.

"Child, I just can't stand the pain any longer. I should have gone days ago to renew my prescription, but I dared not leave the protection I've had here to go out on my own even though I've badly needed the medication. And now I ache too much to do it myself. Can I impose on you to pick the pills up for me since you are going out anyway? I can call ahead and have them ready for you."

"Don't be concerned any longer, Frieda, I insist on going to get the medication for you. I'm very upset that you didn't ask me sooner or mention it to one of the officers here so he could have stopped by the doctor's office for you. You needn't have been so uncomfortable for even one day. It was very foolish of you not to ask me before this. Tell me where to go to get your medicine."

"Let me call first. Oh, look at the time and its Thursday; they close at three and its almost that time now......Hello, this is Mrs. Goldman. I need a refill today on both types of my pills--the pink for pain and the white capsule that makes the tightness relax. Can I have them today? I'm having so much discomfort....I know you close the office soon and I can't come myself but I'm sending a friend, Polly Sloan. Don't argue with me nurse. I'm in too much pain to put up with your nonsense. Then ask him. I'm sure he'll say it's okay." She put her hand over the mouthpiece and started to explain to Polly that a different nurse worked with the doctor on Thursdays, when the nurse returned to the line. "Yes, I thought so. Next time don't be so quick to make decisions for the doctor. Miss

Once Upon a Murder

Sloan will be there before you close. Please have the medication ready for her. Thank you."

Polly smiled at the way Frieda had dispatched the nurse. Frieda was a feisty character and had little patience with other people's agendas. She was direct and to the point when she wanted something, saving her intricate and drawnout storytelling style for afternoons at her leisure and for her pleasure.

"It's after two now and the nurse will have to wait for you after I made a fuss. I'm sure the medicine will be ready by the time you get to the doctor's office. Dr. Spellman is in the old South City Bank Building on Lemon Grove. You can't miss it. It's the only building with a blue door, old plaster, and ivy in the front. The address is 2310 just off Barkley Avenue. Barkley is the street that goes to the mall so you will be close to your stores for shopping when you leave the office."

"I'll find it. Let me go now. I don't want to get there too late. That nurse might just leave early to spite you for taking her to task."

"She'll be there. Dr. Spellman knows you're coming. He won't forget. He always tries to be so helpful to all of us and he really listens to my complaints. Remember how he came by the day Mrs. Sotheby died just because she didn't keep her appointment?"

"Yes. He was very kind to do that. I'll be back as soon as possible and don't worry, I'm not going to the mall. I'm coming straight back here to give you your medicine and be sure you take it. Until then please go lie down and try to relax and I'll be back before you know it."

*   *   *   *

Driving to the medical building she couldn't help but notice the differences in driving quirks and trends between Florida and Minneapolis. In Minneapolis they drove slow because of the predominantly bad weather and fast when the weather was good; if you didn't want to do likewise you stayed in the right lane. For the most part inherent rules of the road were observed. Here you could very easily be killed because you happened to be driving in the middle lane next to a driver whose car was in the right lane wanting to turn left across your lane in front of you without signaling. Decisions were made here and drivers went wherever they had a sudden urge to go. Rules of the road seemed to be made up as individual drivers went along. Watching the cars here was a matter of self-preservation, but she was gettting the hang of it. She complimented herself too soon as a blue compact ran a pickup truck off the road to change lanes suddenly right behind her.

She only had time to see a partial glimpse of the complete process behind her through her rearview mirror as she needed to concentrate her attention on other extemporaneous drivers around her.

The traffic was only getting part of her mind. What could be happening right now on the murder investigation had her pressing concentration. An arrest or arrests. One arrest could mean Jacobson or Marilyn or someone she didn't know about. More that one. The Gotjcik conspiracy with or without Jacobson. Or maybe the whole gang at *the Oaks* were in collusion. She hoped it was none of them. The tenants were an odd set of characters, almost caricatures like she had told Sara previously, but Polly wanted to believe them innocent. She hated to think of anything plottingly evil going on within the stuccoed walls of the quaint old two story she had reluctantly left behind her in order to venture out for Frieda's medicine.

It was humid and she fought her anger at the weather as she felt her clean clothes dripping with perspiration and clinging stickily to her skin. There was a single trickle from under her hair that remained isolated until it joined the mass of wetness on her back which molded her body into the car's seat. How could people live in such heat and humidity 99% of the time? She certainly wouldn't miss that part of her trip here to visit Sara at all.

Back on track with speculation about the impending arrests she felt left out of the best part as she was sure the culprit or culprits had already been apprehended. What if the murderer isn't related to anyone at *the Oaks*? What if he, she, or they were simply injured or slighted by one of the tenants: a salesman, a peddler, a paper boy or even a transient that had been asked to move on when he had sought the shelter of one of the apartment building's alcoves? What a massive group of suspects that could be!

There must be a high luck factor involved in solving criminal cases. Maybe that's what happened, Savitch got some help from an unexpected source and everything fell into place. But what about Mrs. Sotheby? Why the lies? Did she need someone to brag about with the other women, was it too painful for her to be alone without even a husband to sustain her? Was there a significance to the crayons used on the dead faces and the paint on the ruined walls of 10B other than as extensions of the anguish of a tortured mind? And the book, *The Proud Princess,* what the hell did that mean? Was it a sin to be proud, to act like a princess, or just love or hate children's books? Was that the killer's tender side and the harsh demands of the chain letters the other side of the killer's psyche?

And to be responsible, like Savitch was, to make sure it all fit. All the questions had to be answered; all the pieces had to fit some master plan. And oh the tendency he must constantly feel to reach for the quickest and easiest solution to pacify superiors, to release the tired and overworked detectives, and to have at least one case finally closed while others were stacked high and waiting. What finally interrupted her contemplation was her arrival at 2310 Lemon Grove, its neatly clipped ivy flanking a brick walkway that led to a blue door.

NINETEEN

Her last insecure thought about the case was how Savitch would feel if he knew she had conveniently waited until the guarding detectives' backs were turned before she had snuck out of *the Oaks*. What difference could it make now that he had probably completed his arrests? None whatsoever now that the danger surrounding her and the tenants had been diffused. Now she was into positive thinking and trying to make the most of what was left of her vacation. Sara would be home tomorrow and it was time for the two of them to return to a normal day to day existence for the balance of Polly's stay in Florida.

Polly turned into the building parking lot, a one level cement underground maze of columns and spaces, and pulled into the first spot that allowed easy access. Several sections in the underground lot were undergoing construction or renovation of some kind which blocked off areas and formed little mini lots separated by equipment and supplies. The lot appeared to be crowded but she didn't see any other vehicles.

Her door slam echoed and reverberated in the hollowness of the facility and it almost seemed as though half a dozen other people had exited their vehicles at the same time as she had. Near the elevator to the business floors she read a sign that announced that three of the five floors were under construction for a new firm that would not be in residence until fall. Another door slam echo started behind her as the parking garage elevator doors slowed to a close.

All the strangeness and apprehension she felt when visiting doctors' offices greeted her as the elevator doors uninvitingly opened on the second floor. The too clean smell of astringent and alcohol and antiseptic signaled someone was here for an unpleasant treatment and that made her edgy. Soothing and reassuring it had never been for her to walk medical building corridors. The silent alarms and defenses her being here triggered only added to the fear. Fear of what she didn't know this time. She wasn't *seeing the doctor* in the usual sense of the words. She was just here to pick up prescriptions for somebody else. This wasn't even her doctor. No doctor here was going to probe any deeper into medicine with her than to say the very benign words *How are you?* Old qualms she had about doctors' and dentists' offices died hard. She had never been able to rationalize them away, in fact, they had only gotten worse once she realized how fallible medical professionals were, not unlike any other professionals when scrutinized.

She didn't want to be here even if it wasn't for her, even though she was on an errand for Frieda. The feelings got worse when she saw that the office had frosted glass entrance doors from the hallway, similar to the ones she remembered from age four when she had been coaxed inside and bribed so her tonsils could be removed. All that was missing was the cloying smell of ether that made her want to hold her breath and stay awake. What a strange memory to awaken here and now. This was a harmless trip. That was a strange choice of words she thought as if harm were the intention here rather than help. She couldn't sort out or edit her thoughts today.

Frieda awaits and it's almost time for the office to close. This place is sure a downer from my earlier euphoria. Go get the pills! Stop daydreaming! The verbal assault on herself seemed to have worked since she found herself crossing the high low swirl carpeting that started just inside the door, and walking toward an open bar-type counter that was brightly lit from inside.

Once Upon a Murder

It appeared to be the opening into an in office pharmacy and Polly was looking for a button or bell to summon any occupants when she heard a woman's voice yell out challengingly, "Well, who's out there?"

"Polly Sloan to pick up prescriptions for Frieda Goldman."

The officious woman who appeared fit Frieda's description of her perfectly and Polly dared not risk the hysterical laughter she felt ready to overtake her.

"As it turns out," the nurse began, "we were out of one of the capsules doctor prescribed for Mrs. Goldman, but I was able to reach our salesman and he will be here any minute to deliver. So you can sit and wait for him or go with only the one kind; it's of no consequence to me. It's past my leave time as it is, but doctor insisted I wait."

Having made the declaration she put the single bottle of pills on the counter and went back into the recesses of the shelves leaving Polly alone in the dimly lit waiting room.

As Polly turned to find a chair in which to wait, Dr. Spellman materialized from the shadows of the hall as if he had been listening to his nurse's diatribe and had advisedly kept out of it.

"How are you today, Miss Sloan?" he greeted her in his perfectly practiced doctorese.

Once Upon a Murder

"Since this morning I am starting to feel almost normal. I'm even beginning to enjoy your Florida weather thanks to Sergeant Savitch. He is going to be making arrests today and taking the unexpected danger out of my life."

"Oh? I hadn't heard. You know who's guilty then?"

"No, not me. The police couldn't jeopardize their case by telling anyone, but I have my sources and I'm sure that by the time I leave here and return to *the Oaks* it will all be cleared up. At any rate by the end of today I'm sure."

"How interesting. I've never been privy to gossip about a murder before. Do come into my office and let's see if we can out guess the police, shall we?"

"I really couldn't take the time. I promised Frieda to have her medicine back as soon as possible. I can't allow myself to indulge in conversational speculation while she's waiting for me and the medicine that will stop her pain."

"But the man hasn't come yet with the other medication. I heard Berniece tell you so herself. Come along. You can go as soon as he delivers."

"I really haven't anything to tell you. My guess is as good as yours about the murders."

With this said she still found herself being escorted and cajoled into a large corner office where she sank into the softest and deepest

Once Upon a Murder

burgundy leather chair imaginable. What a smooth bedside manner. He had gotten her to go exactly where she didn't want to go and she hadn't felt a thing; hadn't noticed she was being manipulated until she was looking at him across a huge glass-topped desk. No wonder Frieda raved about him. He was good! Now I know what people mean when they say someone has a hypnotic personality. Maybe he doesn't even use anesthetic, he just convinces his patients they don't feel pain.

"Now you tell me who you think murdered those people at Frieda Goldman's apartment building and I'll see if I can add any new ideas."

"I'm not even sure if it's one person or two or maybe more, although I would tend to think it's one."

"Male or female? Is it someone who lives there?"

"I don't know, but my gut or my heart or something somewhere in my head won't let me believe any of those dear crazy people who live there did it."

"Are you then a student of human nature? And if not those people, then who? Who is it?"

"I told you I really don't know who it is; it's more a sense of who didn't do it. This is really a beautiful office. I can see you must love to work here. You've arranged everything so neatly and elegantly in here and the view is spectacular."

Once Upon a Murder

"Yes. I surround myself with mementos and presents to myself that make my time here seem less like work and more like time with family and friends, especially in this room."

The room was a perfectly balanced combination of the precise and the meticulous blended with personal keepsakes and trivia to look warmly cluttered and comfortable. That was definitely the effect. She felt incredibly comfortable.

"You probably wonder why I still stay in this old building. I have this entire floor due to a special arrangement I have with the owner. I don't occupy all the office space--he simply doesn't rent out the rest. Did you know I'm the only physician in this building?"

"No. But I couldn't help notice that there is hardly anyone here today."

"Actually, the offices on the first floor are occupied, but the employees and visitors use the lot on the side of the building during construction. They don't need the elevator access from the garage and the parking is limited in there now so the employees are requested to use the side door during the renovation."

Polly hoped the medicine was ready by now. She moved to the edge of her chair and regretfully would have forced herself up and out of it but was anticipated by the doctor.

"Please relax. Berniece will let us know. I assure you it's only been minutes since we left her."

"All right. Why do you stay here then, Dr. Spellman?"

"Because I hate change and cling to the good things of the past. But then don't we all?"

"When we cling to the past then it's hard to grow and get past some of the barriers we are meant to remove when moving forward. And isn't change necessary to make life interesting and give our existence variety and challenge?"

"Sounds remotely like a graduation speech to a group of wayward adolescents, Ms. Sloan."

"I didn't mean it to. I like old and familiar things around me too so I can remember the pleasant memories I've made, but I intend to keep making them so I always leave plenty of room in my life for growth and change."

"Touché Ms. Sloan. I must sound like an old stick in the mud to you."

"Not at all. The person who created this room could never be that."

Those words seemed to soften the effects of the lectural tone Polly had taken with the doctor and she even saw the hint of a smile developing on his face. Just a hint though, it was as if he just couldn't give in to it.

The care that had gone into this room was deliberate. It was almost as if he could survive here without outside sustenance, as if he could live in this one room and be completely happy. She didn't mean to stare around the room and spread her glances between the doctor and the things that drew her eyes away, but each new thing she saw demanded her attention. It was the culmination of a classic doctor's office: the furniture, the wood wainscoting and wallpaper, and the thick carpet reinforcing the intimacy and the importance of what transpired here.

What cemented the room, made it familiar and held its occupant's attention, was a collection of lifelike china-faced dolls that peeked and smiled and welcomed from cases and shelves and counters around the room. They were surely expensive collectibles but in here they were more, in here they appeared also to be conspiratorial, as if when Polly looked away they sneaked a wink between them. On the credenza behind his desk were more dolls and framed pictures of all sizes depicting a series of adults and children--family? friends? patients?--she could only guess. In the forefront of the other larger and more colorful photos was a small black and white picture of a child, a little girl about eight or nine. Polly squinted to make out the features but could only see the slightly built child sitting in a chair a little

Once Upon a Murder

better by squinting than with her eyes completely open. The photo belonged. Its placement dictated that it alone was in command here.

Polly moved her eyes back to the doctor's face and had missed something because he was waiting for her answer to some unheard inquiry.

"I'm sorry. I missed what you were saying because I'm fascinated by the collection of dolls in here. They are so lifelike in their stillness."

"They are exquisite, aren't they? Their faces were painted with expert hands that never failed to create even the smallest detail of expression. Penelope for instance, a tinge of the softest lilac at the corner of her eyes makes them appear to get larger as you stare at her. You don't seem surprised that I've named them and memorized their finest features."

"No, I'm not surprised. I have a habit of doing that with animals, anthropomorphizing them, but that's because they all have different personalities to me which are based on their actions and responses, just like similar responses define the psychology of humans. But then I'm a little weird, doctor, but I understand just the same what you mean about the dolls."

At that moment the doctor's nurse reappeared after a brief yet loud knock. She entered and didn't even glance at Polly but continued directly to the doctor. He scrawled something large and

Once Upon a Murder

quick with a red pen over the paper she offered him and started to leave the office with it when he asked her about the medicine.

"It's on the counter of the pharmacy. She can pick it up on her way out." The nurse had only imperceptively broken stride to offer these curt words and then the door was closed.

"You never answered my question before, Ms. Sloan."

"I don't remember you asking me anything and now the medicine is ready and I really must go."

"Very well if you insist, but I had counted on talking a little longer. Let me see you out so I can lock the door behind you. I still have all these files to update from the patients I've seen today and now I'll need to add Mrs. Goldmans to the pile as well."

Polly rose from the embracing comfort of the chair and had just turned to walk to the door when the doctor lightly touched her back guiding her forward.

"I knew you'd agree with me about your daughter when I saw how sympathetic and attentive you were to my girls in here."

His voice behind her touched a memory she couldn't grasp but she let that slide in lieu of a response to the doctor's unusual comment.

"I don't remember agreeing to any statements of yours or even mentioning my daughter. I'm afraid I've missed a key part of this conversation."

"We were talking......I was talking about girls, how troublesome they can be and you seemed to agree or perhaps I took your silence for assent."

They had reached the counter and two bottles of pills were back-lit from the pharmacy shelves. All the other lights were out. Polly moved to pick up the medication and leave the doctor to ponder his strange conversation with himself as she was sure she would have remembered entering a discussion that in any way concerned her daughter.

His reach, longer than hers, captured both bottles at once and enclosed them in a fist. Moving in between her and the door he shocked her into standing there open-mouthed with his next statement.

"So you really didn't want your daughter?"

After seconds of slow motion reasoning the only astounded response she could make didn't begin to answer his comment with the total disbelief she was feeling.

"You have totally misunderstood something I didn't even say and something I would never have implied even with silence. I adore my child and always have through everything we have endured together, the good and the bad. She is a strength I have to call on and a friend and confidante whose

Once Upon a Murder

advice I value and respect as I never will anyone elses."

".....but you would have left her on a bad day if she'd done something that made her a baggage you didn't need and couldn't tolerate."

"NEVER! The idea never entered my head, only the thought occasionally that I was failing her somehow, but never that she had failed me."

While she watched his face change its expression subtly several times until he finally decided upon a placid facial exterior, the hand she held out for the medicine received the two bottles as he opened his fist above her fingers and let the bottles roll and fall. While his look of catatonic quiet purpose froze him there thinking, she edged by him to open the door and slip out.

The strangeness of the meeting with Dr. Spellman twisted and intermingled with her previous apprehension about visiting doctors' offices and another rung of unpleasantness was added to the ladder she would have to climb before she went on her next professional visit. But it was more than that. Something didn't make sense and she was confusing it with the doctor fear thing. The voice and the dog and the dolls and the picture were flashing and spinning in her head. The voice spoke but the dog didn't. Why didn't the dog bark when Spellman came to Mrs. Sotheby's apartment for the first time, and why

Once Upon a Murder

was the doctor's voice in her head insisting that she remember something?

Around the corner and facing the elevator waiting for the car to answer its yellow light she heard a door with a loose glass panel in the center open and close. A frosted glass door. Her visit to the doctor was not over yet and suddenly Polly knew why. The dolls had told her but she hadn't been listening. The little girl's picture had told her but it didn't connect in her head then as it did now. Her concentration had been on the ever professional Dr. Spellman and making conversation that made sense even when he didn't. It was the room: like an inquisition, a sentencing chamber. Mrs. Sotheby and Mrs. Jacobson had sat there and he hadn't heard them either. Where was the doctor's compassion? They had trusted him with their secrets and he had betrayed them with his punishment. And the voice....Henderson....he was Henderson the night of the laundry trap!

Polly swore at the elevator and at herself for being caught on the second floor with no exit. The sign and arrow for the stairs were the other way, past the office. The steel facade of the ancient elevator opened haltingly and she slid in and around to the button panel using both hands to hold down first the *door close* button and then the button that read *garage*. As the elevator closed its last few inches Dr. Spellman's face looked in at her

Once Upon a Murder

but he made no attempt to stop the elevator. His eyes were questioning. He looked for a conciliatory *Good-bye Doc, thanks for your professional services.* He got *Go to hell you bastard!* He knew she knew.

If she'd gotten it figured out before she left the office she could have gone the other way down the stairs that must open out onto the street. Now she had to try for the car. The medicine bottles fell and rolled as the elevator creaked and swayed in its descent. Dumping her purse out on the floor she found she had nothing to use as a weapon, not even a mirror to break and conceal in her hand. Her ring of keys was all she had to defend herself with against the man who had taken the lives of three people with cold deliberation and intent and absolutely no remorse.

The elevator came to rest uneasily at the garage level, bouncing and jarring before it stopped, taking up precious seconds she needed. The doors opened and she moved out ready to fight; ready to take on Dr. Spellman, at least draw blood and maybe gouge an eye or take a bite out of his smug, self-satisfied, judgmental face. She saw the car across the garage from the elevator. And then she saw him moving between her and the car in such a way that the stairway was blocked to her as well. He had all the advantage. Polly didn't want to get backed into the elevator or pinned in a

Once Upon a Murder

corner so she moved forward along the brick wall. Her only hope was to make him commit to a tactic and a direction and then try and slip by him to escape up the stairs or to go for the car. He still had all the advantage, but determination was an advantage too and she had plenty of that.

On the way down she had decided against reusing the elevator. The buttons for the upper floors had been removed and could not be used by anyone other then the construction crews who had a special key. If she tried to return to the doctor's floor he might be waiting for her when she arrived. The elevator door took too long to close. She was sure he would overtake her before she could escape this time. She was extremely claustrophobic and didn't need that to add to her problems now anyway. If he wanted her it would be in the open, kicking and screaming and fighting him, not at his convenience and by his plan. She wasn't an elderly and physically weak person like the others and he would find out that she wouldn't trustingly let him kill her as his three victims had.

He had no weapon, but his mood and stance signaled his readiness for anything and his preparation for physical violence.

Surprisingly she wasn't afraid, just angry. She moved forward hoping to throw him off with her own aggression and determination. As she moved along the wall an unexpected source of aid

Once Upon a Murder

appeared to her out of the corner of her eye. One opportunity before a physical confrontation. She walked ahead slowly close to the wall gaging his movements and trying to anticipate which avenue of exit he would favor cutting off to her. No chance yet to escape but one chance to startle him and throw him off balance. Less that ten feet now to her goal and dreading the inevitable struggle of wills and limbs for her life if her attempt failed. Polly's fingers singled out the two biggest and heaviest of the keys and she grasped them tightly together as one final defense in her right hand. Now was her shot. With her left hand she feinted a movement at him with her handbag while bringing her right hand up to lunge at the small glass plate with the firmly clasped keys. Stabbing quickly again and again the plate finally broke and the fire alarm reverberated deafeningly throughout the garage. The doctor, a very cautious and reasoning man, was frozen as he queried and sought to react from the duel action of the handbag and the keys. His stunning passed and he advanced to cover the ground between them as Polly took a fighting stance ready to wield her purse, the keys, and herself at the good doctor. The doctor suddenly reconsidered his options and his chances against her and ran back to the stairway from which he had come.

Once Upon a Murder

The stairway door banged against the wall of the garage with the full force of the doctor's anger and frustration while Polly continued to pound robotically on the alarm through the fragmented glass long after the action could have caused any additional help. Realization of her unexpected safety finally registered and she risked a glance at her wounded and bloody hand. It looked unfamiliar and odd, the rapidly swelling fingers unable to feel the wet redness of the keys any longer. The need to escape came back to her and mobilized her across the few remaining yards to her car. Get out of here! Get out into the stifling Florida humidity. Find people. There's safety in numbers. Find a telephone to call Savitch. And eventually find a well-balanced doctor to treat the bloated hand that rested uselessly on the steering wheel; the hand that was causing an all too familiar pool of blood to form in her lap.

TWENTY

"I refuse to be treated like an invalid, Sara. I have a simple cast on my hand; my body I assure you is in no way injured and I don't need to be completely immobilized."

"Poll, I saw the x-rays. The mess you made of those three fingers....why the pictures looked as if each finger had two or three extra joints. And the doctor said..."

"Fuck the doctor! He just wanted to lecture me about what a stupid thing I had done. He wasn't there. I'm lucky that my hand was all that was mangled. Why must doctors be so damned patronizing and then inflict pain on top of that as a punishment for a patient's supposed lack of common sense? I had to hold myself back from wrapping that gauze shit around his head."

"You are the worst pain in the ass when you can't get control of a situation."

Once Upon a Murder

"That's right. It's one of my best qualities and has taken a lifetime to perfect. But I am relieved that my episodes with doctors are over for now. And I am glad that you're back even though you missed everything--the excitement--and especially seeing Dr. Spellman turn from friendly G.P. to frenzied fanatic."

"I still can't believe it was him. You know Frieda talked me into going to see him once for some female problem I was having. Just my luck that he got the flu and canceled my appointment; my problem cleared up and I never met him. But I'm sorry to say that didn't stop Frieda from imparting to him my complete personal history which got me on his mailing list."

"Sara, he was the coldest warm person you'd ever like to meet. You didn't feel it with other people around, only one on one with the doctor. When he appeared at Mrs. Sothebys the day she died I thought him charming and genuinely concerned. But alone he used a deft verbal scalpel on you to elicit the response he wanted and then, wap, he nailed you with your own words or the words he thought you implied. He's a master manipulator, but with what motivation? Why did he have to kill? Savitch said it was all tied up with his childhood and his mother and his sister. He's coming over soon, Savitch I mean, and he's promised to lay it all out for me, for us if you want to hear the whole gruesome story."

"I don't really think I do, but I'm not leaving you alone to reinjure yourself with your stubbornness so I guess I'm in for the complete story. Shit. The bell again. I swear everyone here has come to see the resident maniac who's staying with me. Don't you dare get off that couch! The last visitor nearly closed the door on your hand. I'll handle this."

In a few quick strides Sara reached to open the door and then the outside screen which she had locked after the last unwanted and uninvited well-wisher.

"Hello, Olivia and Miles. Yes, she's here but I'm afraid not up to any more visitors. Doctor's orders. She's on medication and is not supposed to have too much excitement, although she's had more than enough the last few days; enough of that kind of excitement for any lifetime."

"Miles and I don't want to intrude, but we know it might have been me or him next. Who knows? We didn't get a letter, but still who knows? We owe her something the way we figure. Isn't that right, Miles?"

"Yes. Why we haven't been ourselves since this started. Can't hardly eat even, well, not like we ought to."

Once Upon a Murder

"That's right. And we were sure Polly might be feeling a little off her feed too, you know, so we brought her some things. There are some sandwiches and potato salad in here and a cake and some other snacks and things for both of you. Just our way of saying thanks for ending the terror here at *the Oaks*."

"Well, thank you both. I'm sure Polly will appreciate your kindness and thanks for stopping by. It's not likely you'll be seeing her before she goes. Her flight leaves very early tomorrow morning. Thanks again."

After opening the screen and taking the heavy bag from the Browns Sara returned to the sofa and plopped down next to Polly.

"Ugh. I don't even like the smell of that. What's in there?"

"Didn't you hear? Sandwiches, salad, cake, and sundry snacks."

"No doubt only a small sample of what the two of them consume daily, but they were nice to bring the food nevertheless. When you weigh the relative value of the items to the couple's attachment to them it turns out to be quite a priceless gift."

"If we add this to the other get well loot from earlier today we have enough to feed several needy families."

Once Upon a Murder

"Let's do it! There is a kind of shelter close to here. I noticed it before my encounter with the murderous doctor. We can't possibly make a dent in all that food and I'll be gone tomorrow. You won't want to deal with it and will simply throw it away. Let's call the shelter and we can load up the car after dark and drive over there. I want something good to come from all this misery."

"I'll do it if you insist, but alone. I don't want you lifting anything and straining that hand like the doctor told you to avoid. As it is you are going to have to take a leave of absence from the University when you get home."

"Like hell I will! I intend to be on campus bright and early Monday morning milking this injury for all the sympathy I can get. I have an assistant who thinks he's indispensable and for the first time I intend to let him prove it to me. If I start dragging before my last lecture I've learned numerous ways over the years to let the students' participation fill the hour. I also have some taped lectures I did earlier this year with breaks for discussion which I use for just such occasions as this."

"O. K. I give up. I'll load the food. I'll drive."

"You drive soooo slow."

Once Upon a Murder

"I'm driving nevertheless. That's the end of the discussion, besides you're the one with a curse hanging over your head not me."

"Do you think I believe for one minute in Flo Gotjcik's powers or curses or any other of that bull?"

"She seemed serious enough when she visited earlier today."

Sara couldn't suppress her laughter at recalling Flo's visit. Flo had been so relieved to be cleared of suspicion in the murders and to finally have Savitch out of her face that she had practiced being *back in business* with Polly as a perspective client. Flo had liberally sprinkled her acceptance of and relief at the actual murderer with warnings and innuendo to Polly regarding the danger of novices treading into the unknown where evildoers can only be sentenced before a tribunal imposed by the spirit world.

"All in all it has been one hellatious week. The one sad aftereffect of this mess is the state of mind of dear harmless Frieda. She takes so much blame for everything. I really don't think she'll ever be the same and if she doesn't return from California, if she sends her son-in-law to sell the place like she threatened--that is if she can with its now infamous history--I don't know where that will leave all the tenants. She protected us from rent increases and tried to be a friend to us all. Oh

Once Upon a Murder

sure, I'll manage, I'm one of the few here who are actually employed. But what about the others? I'm afraid they will be lost and I intend to call Frieda and press my case for her return until I convince her to come back and be our landlady again."

"You could go another way; you could buy *the Oaks*. Let her stay in California. Her nerves are shot. It will take more than your ministerings to bring her back after she saw the unfavorable press she got from the local paper."

"I can't buy this place!"

"You always say can't. Overextend yourself. I do it all the time. Live on the edge financially like I do. If I waited around until I had the purchase price of something I'd never own anything. Our economy is based on credit and I feel it my responsibility to perpetuate that foundation. Take a lesson from the queen of deficit spending--me."

"I can't talk my way around a bluff like you do. It's that imposing face that does it. They're afraid not to let you win."

"That and creative reasoning and making the credit manager's feel like they just might be discriminating against a woman on the move."

"A woman on the move! I've seen you turn the most stalwart of oppositions into psychological paste when you're through."

"You have to wear them down; show them the errors in their thinking; and use their own words against them. And then you stroll through the wreckage, pick up the spoils, and move on."

"You and your verbal battles."

Polly held her bandaged hand up for Sara. "This one wasn't verbal but I won it just the same."

"The face again. You bluffed him with it. And maybe, just maybe, any opposition was what he wanted from the others, any sign that would have stopped him short of murder."

"You think it was the face? I don't. Just guessing, but I think it was my not admitting to him willingly and confidentially things about my relationship with my daughter simply because he was *the doctor*. It had worked with Frieda, Mrs. Jacobson, and Mrs. Sotheby, and with others I'm sure. Maybe he needed that affirmation to proceed and when he didn't get it a link was left out, a necessary piece was missing to finalize and excuse the murders in his mind. In essence he simply couldn't overcome this missing link or fill the gap without his victim's acquiescence to guilt and therefore couldn't carry out the crime without it. Sick people are meticulous. They dwell on detail, organization, and planning. Reasons and justifications interlaced in the psychotic mind may appear messy and unnecessary to us, but may be inescapable and absolutely mandatory to a murderer with an elaborate M.O. He couldn't bypass the missing incentive for the crime. Maybe it was what fed his anger, what fueled his kill instinct."

"It's nice to sit here and objectively probe his sick perverted mind, but don't expect any sympathy from me for what he did and that includes my fall down the stairs before you got here. That man is evil personified and no amount of rationalization will convince me that an educated healer has any less guilt than any other mass murderer."

"Maybe Savitch will change your mind; change both our minds, because even if I'm not an absolutist about good and evil like you are, I can't forgive him either. I can only try to detach his mind from his deeds and analyze the reasons for his horrendous behavior."

Before any further speculation was possibly into the reasons or motivations behind the doctor's actions, Savitch knocked on the apartment screen door and interrupted their debate. Polly was off the couch with Sara's warnings falling futilely in the background, barely audible over the greetings being exchanged by the two conspiratorial crime fighters.

Savitch looked haggard. His preppy police look sagged miserably having lost its panache and snap days ago. Debriefing the doctor--Dr.

Once Upon a Murder

Spellman still refused to consider himself under arrest and subject to interrogation like other criminals--had been a lengthy business for Savitch. The sergeant explained to them that the main barrier to getting a statement from the doctor was Spellman's insistence that he had merely been an instrument for the correction of societal blemishes, that he had been society's plastic surgeon.

"I hoped to have been here sooner but initially when we picked up Spellman we thought his grasp on reality was tenuous at best and our psychiatrist advised us to get a statement quick before he shut down altogether and refused to tell us anything. The bravado stage, or something like that according to our expert, doesn't last long before a kind of paranoia closes the mental gates, possibly forever in extreme cases. I know its been two days since your ordeal in his building but well....you did get my flowers....didn't you?"

"They were wonderful. How did you know how much I adore fresh gardenias, not a bottled fragrance, but the real thing? And look at them; they're still gorgeous."

"I took a chance. It was something you said about flowers after Mrs. Sotheby's perfumes broke."

"I don't remember anything I said then. I was in shock and flowers were the last thing on my mind after her floral scented perfumes mingled with the smell of blood and made me barf. Thanks again for your thoughtfulness."

"Speaking of being thoughtful, I hope you don't mind but I brought the tape from the expert's combined sessions with Spellman. It's not exactly how I envisioned spending an evening with you, but somehow I didn't think you'd be happy with less than a firsthand confession from our murderer."

"You were right. Sara and I were speculating about the reasons behind the murders. All we can agree on is that his position in life doesn't make his crimes any less heinous than if he were a common criminal off the street."

"I disagree to some extent. His reasons required a lot of linking up with background, family, location, and opportunity. A common criminal sees something he wants and more or less makes a direct beeline for it obliterating anything and anyone in his way. For Dr. Spellman a game of sit and wait and bide your time for the one opportunity actually backfired on him. He started too late, waited too long, and opportunity eluded him."

"I hope you've come to clarify this case and not leave us even more frustrated and baffled than with our own hypothesizing."

"Forgive me Sara. The real object of Dr. Spellman's revenge was out of reach before he could exact his vengeance. He might never have put his plan into action if he hadn't become Frieda Goldman's doctor."

"Oh no!" Polly and Sara moaned in unison.

"Frieda's suspicions were true."

"She was more responsible for being the impetus for violence than I wanted to believe."

"I won't tell her if you don't, besides the police doc said Spellman's desire for revenge was far too strong to have lain submerged for long. It was a case of fermenting anger looking for an outlet and *the Oaks* got the full treatment."

With this last puzzling statement Savitch began to set up a tape recorder he had left near the door. It was a small reel to reel unit with tape storage in the lid. As he busied himself finding the plug and then slipping one of the several tapes he had laid on the table into the machine, Polly felt uneasy and edgy about what she was going to hear. Sara, on the other hand, sat quietly after having gone to the kitchen and returned with drink requests for the three of them. Polly could never relax that completely. She had to prepare herself for the worst that could happen in any given situation and then, as the worst failed to happen, she could gradually let go of her reservations knowing that the fear would lessen as the situation unfolded.

Once Upon a Murder

"I wrote down the number that starts each section that I want to play for you on the tapes. There are three that are relevant. He repeats himself, digresses into old memories, and just talks about life--philosophizing on everything from childhood discipline to the way a woman should live her life. I'll cut out most of that for you. I feel sorry for the psychiatrist who has about twenty tapes of his own to go through and sort out. He isn't even sure of Spellman's clinical malady. The last time we talked the only thing he said was 'I'm definite about this not being a classical case.' He thinks it's a combination of severe mental illness, psychoneuroses, and phobias. Our psychiatrist is going to have several weeks to make up his mind one way or the other, and he'll only be one of a panel of doctors who will evaluate and classify Spellman's mental condition.

"Understand that what you will be hearing--and I will have to fill in the gaps for you if you don't get the transitions--are the ramblings of a grown man who has created his own unique reality out of just a few fragments of memory from his childhood. At least that's the quicky layman explanation according to the doc."

"Shall we begin?"

TWENTY--ONE

I took over. I had to. There was no one else you see. She left us. I was the oldest. I set the schedule, the routine for both of us..I had to think-don't interrupt-where was I? I know, I was thinking. This is the way I thought it out. She left us some money, not enough I figured out later, but to a kid of eleven it looked like a lot. Mama tried to tell me about bills, but I didn't want to understand. Later I understood when the mail piled up and all of them wanted money and I had so little of it. Bills from the hospital, the electric company, the telephone, and bills that she ran up for her clothes and stuff...those I burned as if to....

My princess didn't go to school. That was okay; but I had to go to school or they'd know. But I skipped on bad days and wrote notes to cover. By then I could write her name as good as mama did. After school I'd play games. I got so

Once Upon a Murder

good at after school games. The stores weren't always the same. I had to move around, hit them smart. I didn't want to do it at first; then I loved the danger. She called that day--damn her ugly heart--she upset the princess and I could have killed her. Just let her walk in I begged in my dreams. I could do it, after all I had destroyed everything that was hers by then, everything that had her smell on it. I made the house mine. It belonged to me and my princess.

Me and the princess didn't need her, we were doin' okay. At home I did everything for her. She said I was strong and so I made her lean on me. I didn't let her do nothing, that way her strength would last until....until the books and the stories of once upon a time that made her lay quiet and sleep.

I couldn't go back to the hospital after the last time. They wanted to talk to mama. No more treatments without mama. Princess said she didn't care. She just wanted me and the books and our house. Mama hated the hospital and she fought with the doctors and nurses all the time so they didn't think that us missing the treatments was funny. Then they wanted us back so I rode the bus with the princess. Two more times and that was it. She got too tired and the money ran out.

Once Upon a Murder

Savitch fast forwarded to another place on the first tape, not needing to glance up to know the impact of the doctor's childhood story on his listeners' faces.

...food was easy, finding the telephone numbers on the bills and begging for time was easy....but then it got bad. I told the princess not to answer the phone or the door when I was at school. And then I couldn't go to school any more. The school sent letters and stuff but mama had told those people at the school to 'go to hell' before so they just expelled me. By then we had lost the telephone and the lights. The gas was last, but it went too. The princess loved the books and the candles and pretending to be in our own castle. We did that for a long time. Sometimes neighbors would knock and try to get in but we were hidden behind barricades of furniture that I had piled against the doors.

At night I had to go out and scrounge around for stuff...and to cry. By then my princess would only drink juice and eat a little cereal. She was like a rag doll and never got up from her chair. We had medicine though from that last time at the hospital. I asked the nurse all kinds of questions and she showed me the bottles the princess needed and I got some. I was clever and careful. I knocked over one of those carts in the wing with other people who had the same diseases and took some of that kind of medicine. All the bottles and little paper cups scattered and made a mess. I pretended to help and got the kinds of pills the nurse told me about, the ones with the funny shape and the ones with two colors on the same pill. And then I was the doctor, giving my princess something for the pain and for when she threw up, doing everything I could for her at home.

Savitch pulled the tape out and was about to put in the next one.

"Not yet. I'm still reeling from how horrifying his life must have been. His voice. It's as if he's eleven again. And the princess--his sister?"

"Yes. She was eight when the mother, Teri Schumacher, walked out on them."

"Schumacher, not Spellman?" Sara asked quietly as her opinion of the doctor had softened considerably since the tape had begun. Now she was merely trying to grasp the immensity of the pain and anger and hatred that must have motivated the doctor's actions.

"He changed his name when he was eighteen. He came right out of an orphanage on his birthday and went to court trying to rid himself of any trace of his mother. By then he had turned his anger and hatred into the positive output of study. He received a special hardship grant to go to an out of state university and later worked his way through medical school. I know this is brutal but the worst part is almost over."

They got in. I fought them and begged but the policeman held me and I screamed and kicked and bit him when they took the princess away in an ambulance. She was so sick. In the dark I couldn't see, but she was like a skeleton in the light and reached out for me to do something more for her as they took her from the house. Maybe I shoulda called someone, asked for help sooner, but I didn't want them to find mama and bring her back. She woulda run away again. I was gonna find her; not anybody else, just me. Shit. I could do it. I had kept everybody away from my princess for six months, had got the food, kept her warm, read to her, been our mama for a long time. I knew I could do anything after that.

They never let me see her again. She died after about a week and all I had left was the books and the bright red crayons she used to color with and a picture of my proud princess.

"There's more of the same, but you've heard the gist of it. Spellman, or Shumacher at the time, was hostile and violent when they put him in an orphanage. No adoption for him for the obvious reasons. Even the staff at Hill Haven Orphanage were afraid of an eleven year old boy. They had a psychologist in attendance, but the kid needed outpatient psychiatric care two or three times a week. He set the pattern for the sessions. Every time he had a session he would walk in and ask, 'Have you found her yet?' After the doctor said no, he would say 'Good. If you found her I'd have to kill her.' Then the session would begin.

"They made very little headway with him the first year. The only reason he was kept at the orphanage and not sent to a hospital was that he stayed to himself and didn't cause any trouble if he was left alone. Shortly after the psychiatrist began coming to treat him, Spellman wanted to know more about his sister's illness. After that the psychiatrist started lending him medical books as a kind of therapy. Once the kid was hooked on medicine he went to the sessions to talk medicine not to be treated himself. After a while the doctor and the staff were convinced he was on his way toward being completely rehabilitated away from violence and hostility and toward a productive life. He didn't even ask the question any more.

The authorities had stopped looking for the mother by then. There was an outstanding child negligence warrant for her but it got lost among so many similar warrants and the desire to bring the kid and his mother together in the same room with all their bad history slowly dwindled in the light of his progress. The kid hadn't forgotten though. He had a debt to pay so he hired his own private investigators when he was in college. Had his own *find mama fund.* They tracked her to Florida where the trail died. That's why he came here after med school. He got so wound up in studying and working he had to let his interest in finding her go until he graduated.

Actually it was five or six years later that he tried to pick up her trail. He lived at the hospital and spent his money on another series of investigators, always dissatisfied with their progress reports and angry at their feeble attempts to close in on her. He even beat up one of the guys and it was hushed up by hospital administrators on the condition that he undergo extensive psychiatric evaluation or be dropped from the staff. By then he was an expert at his own mental illness and fooled the doctors who were treating him. He dropped the search for a while, not wanting to arouse suspicion about his personal life. He's pushing thirty by now. No girls or women can get close to him and he refuses to be interested; instead he busies himself with the kids in the Childrens Ward and their illnesses.

"Let's pick it up here on the tape. This is right before he severs ties with the Northern Baytide Hospital a year or two later. You'll notice a change in his voice here. This tape is as an adult and he talks as such; little Arty is gone now and we begin to hear from grownup Arthur."

Once Upon a Murder

I did it. Not those worthless bullshit artists who called themselves P.I.'s. It was really very clever of me to find her. I had a righteous reason! I had the desire! I began to smell her; the faint smell coming unwantedly back to me through the years. Then I knew I had her. Her smell, her rotten smell was on everything I touched.

I confined my search to trailer parks. Even though the places she'd lived at were mostly apartments, there was one trailer park she had lived at for two years when she first moved to Florida and it seemed to suit her lifestyle. She had her privacy and could be away from people and no one could get close enough to see her evil side.

Once when she still lived with us I went through a magazine she had been reading and there was this big trailer ad in there and she had drawn a circle around it and put a stick figure of her in the door. After I remembered that the evil smell of her got stronger every trailer park I went to. I had the hounddog scent of her then. Every night I asked the question 'Did you find her yet?' and I screamed 'No, but I can smell her!' She went South and I went South working in clinics and big city hospitals where I could lose myself when I needed to and where they begged for help from anyone because they were so short staffed.

Once Upon a Murder

The third tape was slipped in the machine. "I'm going to put this one in and play it through without stopping. It's better than any summary explanation I can give you."

I found her after too many years, too much failure and frustration. The princess whispered to me now whenever the smell tried to drown me. Her voice would calm me and remind me of my errand, keep me on track.

It was muggy and the air settled on my shirt in sheets. I wanted to go back to my place and take a shower, but I had two more parks on the list for that day. I had been driving in a remote area, two or three miles onto an unpaved road, when a dirty unlit sign caught my eye--Trails End Trailer Park. Rundown and fairly hopeless as a lead I thought.

I had two pictures of her, both I got from the P.I. that I had beaten the shit out of. One was an old out of state drivers license photo and the other was her sitting on some asshole's lap--that one the P.I. had gotten from one of her old boyfriends-- and now I had them both.

Some toothless old man was sitting in a chair out in the dirt and he motioned for me to come over to him. I showed him the pictures and he couldn't say one way or the other even after he put his glasses on. Then some kid comes up and sticks his nose in my business and grabs one of

Once Upon a Murder

the pictures and before I can get it back he knows her, he offers to take me to her trailer. All the time I'm walking I'm smelling her. Not the smell of the old gutted-out cars alongside the trailers. Not the smell of the swamp water nearby or the smell of my own excitement as it turns to sweat on my clothes. Her smell--pure and evil.

I'm there. Time is irrelevant. It's as if she just left me and the princess and I'm there to find out when she's coming home, when she's coming back for us. I have the chance to ask her this time. She can't get away. I can turn back time and make the necessary corrections. I can make her make it up to us. The princess is with me. It's me and her against the smell.

The kid's pulling at me and yelling something. What's that, you say she's not home? Where in the hell is she? I'll find her. 'It's Saturday, mister, she won't come home tonight. Come back tomorra, she sleeps on Sundays. She'll be back tomorra like I telled ya'. I know her.' ..... I know her too, boy, I'll wait.

Me and my princess go back to the car, the smell of mama dispelling in the thick air. I pull farther into the park to a point where I can watch the trailer and I settle in for the night. Forgotten is any wish to take a shower or go for something to eat. All I want is to taste the vengeance that

Once Upon a Murder

will overpower and stifle the smell once and for all.

It seems only minutes that I've been asleep when I waken frantically to the red flashing light that pierces my eyelids. A police car has gotten past my staked out position and between me and her trailer. People have come outside to snoop and see what's going on and the kid finds me and wants to let me know what he knows. 'It's about the lady, mister, the one you was lookin' for. The police man has come to tell Barker--the one you was talkin' to in the chair--to tell Barker she done been killed. She dead. The lady in the picture.'

Surely a dream brought on by my mind doing its bizarre trickery has come to plague me when it knows, it damn well knows, I allow no loose thinking on this subject. I must believe in only the realities I see or that are told to me by my princess, her reasoning is infallible. Where is the proud princess? Why doesn't she come to me now when I am in need of her? It must be a dream. Oh God don't steal this chance from me; she will be yours soon enough. Fiendish Bitch your smell is gone! Someone else has taken what was mine, what was only mine to take. No-o-o-o. No-o-o-o-o.

The click of the tape released Polly, Sara, and Savitch from the agony of his screams.

Once Upon a Murder

"No more. I've had enough. It wasn't a dream, was it? She was dead and he lost out on his revenge, against her that is."

"Yeah. Mama and apparently a sometime boyfriend were drunk and went off the road, flipped over and were crushed under the car. Spellman dropped out of sight for a while. He explained it on his resume as a personal medical sabbatical for further study. He spent some time in a small sanitorium in Europe and resurfaced with a professional doctor veneer having sealed away in the past his childhood torments. He opened his own office here with the help of some foreign benefactor. He repaid the loan and cut off the benefactor. So much for friendship.

"A few quiet years and enter Mrs. Goldman who liberally sprinkled her visits with tales of her tenants and their personal lives. He listened and expertly probed for pertinent details and voilà, Mrs. Jacobson's secret daughter, rekindling his hatred and bringing his need for revenge close to the surface again. After her it was Sotheby or you Sara, I don't know which came first. Maybe the opportunity for scaring you didn't turn into murder by plan or maybe he thought better of further attacking you. He could have thought you might be a match for him or he could have felt your situation didn't effect him as personally as Mrs. Sothebys did. After all, she took credit for something she wasn't entitled to, granted it didn't hurt anyone, but it hit a nerve with him--her dishonesty was the epitome of womanhood to him and she became guilty of all kinds of things in his eyes."

"Why Mr. Jacobson?"

"The way he tells it, Jacobson accused Spellman, indirectly through his wife, of having an affair with her. I know this sounds ridiculous but Jacobson was very insecure and somewhat possessive. Mrs. Jacobson's revelation to Frieda and the subsequent threat of appearance by her daughter had caused an edge to the Jacobsons' relationship. Jacobson never left his wife alone except on her doctor's appointments so he made a giant leap that worked for him.

"The doctor had to kill Mrs. Jacobson. Her crime of desertion was staring him in the face. His conscience wouldn't allow him to hold back. He had been given a reprieve to enact his vengeance . He confronted her in the apartment thinking she was alone. Mr. Jacobson was asleep in the bedroom. He didn't even wake up. But when Spellman went to put her on the bed he saw the husband and gave him a whack on the head for good measure."

"But why the letters? What did he hope to accomplish?"

"It was a last ditch effort to get him off the hook. The way I understand it from the psychiatrist is that one reason the doctor flipped out about not doing a face to face confrontation with his mother was that he needed her to apologize, to explain that she planned to come back. He needed closure on the desertion question and never got the chance for it with his own mother. The psych said it was merely a formality, Dr. Spellman was never of a mind to grant absolution to mama or the victims at *the Oaks* in any case."

"...and me, why did he latch onto me, just because Sara went out of the picture?"

"Maybe at first, the guilt by association clause in his thinking. Believe it or not he liked you. But remember he only had one category for women. They were all guilty strictly because he saw them as such; the level of guilt was the only thing ever in question. The women tenants who received letters all had unsavory histories as mothers according to Spellman. I suspect his plan lost logic somewhere along the way. He couldn't guarantee to find victims who would fall within his stringent parameters for guilt so he manufactured their guilt by imposing it on them or convincing them of it in *the room*. That's what his office was for. He wouldn't have hurt you if you hadn't come for Mrs. Goldman's pills."

"Knowing my luck, I never should have volunteered to help her."

"It was during your conversation that he discovered you had a daughter. After that he saw red and lumped you with all the others and you became fair game to him."

"What's on the balance of the tape, not that I want to hear it, but is there anything else to enlighten us further?"

"Not really. A lot of digressing into why he had to carry out his plan at *the Oaks* and, oh yeah, he talks about staying in the Kearneys' apartment, but swears he doesn't remember anything about painting the walls. Something the specialists call *favorable selective memory*. They also threw in a lot more clinical terminology that I'm simplifying for you and probably getting wrong. Everything from Spellman being a split ego for both him and his sister; a healer who can't heal himself; and an unconditionally unforgiving person. I guess for the specialists he's a real find. He's theirs now. There's no doubt he's guilty but one thing none of us will ever know is whether as a kid he was psycho before his mother even left."

"Of course he wasn't," Sara chimed in, "how could you even suggest it?"

"Corny, we only heard his side and saw the way his mind and life went according to him. What if he was a freak before she split; maybe he was even the main reason she took off. Consider this. What if she was, just say, an average mom with a daughter dying of some blood disease. This mom also had a son who had already taken over for his mother, already rejected her because he blamed her for the sister's illness. Do we have any proof of neglect prior to the break in the family? How do we know she didn't try to get help, aid of some kind, someone to help her out. Where's the father? What about his responsibility? I'm not sticking up for her, leaving the kids was totally reprehensible, but what if we don't know everything?"

"Funny you should take this position, Polly. I got some background on the father by fax just before I came over. Father died in a mental institution at the age of twenty-nine. Kids were never even told about the father. As for the mother's negligence, according to one of the neighbors, everyone was constantly giving her advice and criticizing her but no one offered to help her. She had been working two jobs to support the kids before she left and, although everyone agreed she had a chip on her shoulder and a short fuse, she had been doing okay for eight years before she split. And the kid, little Arty Schumacher, we traced school problems with him all the way back to kindergarten--seems he *didn't*

Once Upon a Murder

play well with others and *had trouble adjusting to anyone in authority."*

"So he could have been a psycho in training and latched on to the situation to go full-blown?"

"That still doesn't excuse her." Sara offered as an attempt to fall back to the black and white decision she had already made about the doctor's mother.

"We'll never know her side. He's killed three people and of that we're absolutely sure. During the arraignment he doodled on his lawyer's pad. The drawings are replicas of the ones on the Kearneys' walls."

"On the lighter side, please, there's got to be one."

"There are two romantic footnotes to this case. Lilly Stangely met Phil Jacobson at a Group Psychic Meeting in Flo's apartment and now he wants to marry her and take her back to Kansas with him. That will leave Herbert Norwich with only one sister to court and he's really going to have to be careful he doesn't end up the same way. And the mysterious comings and goings of Marilyn Henry have been explained away by one of the officers on the case, Jerry Honig, asking for some emergency leave to go and meet his future wife's step-father, Marvin Henry."

"That makes me feel much better. Now I can fly home on an up note. Still I'd like to have

Once Upon a Murder

something pleasant to remember about this trip. Right now all I have is a battered hand and a lot of nightmares. Sorry, Savitch, it isn't your fault or anybodys really. Had I showed up a week earlier or a week later I would have collected oodles of frivolous memories about Florida," Polly gushed in an unbelievably sweet voice. "I feel cheated in some way. We haven't even tasted the night life and this is my last night here. Sara and I are going to drop off some care packages to the Shelter on Barkley Street later. I guess I'll settle for a good deed as my last memory of Florida."

"I told you that I can do that tomorrow after you've gone. You and I can spend a much deserved quiet evening here. You haven't packed yet anyway. I'll pack for you and you can complain about it as you watch. You'll love it."

"I have a much better idea. Why don't I take you both out to *Antonios* for a little vino, a little Italian music, and lots of pasta?"

"No thanks for me, Sargeant. I still have to pack for Polly and get all my notes from my trip into the computer, but you two go ahead."

"Are you sure, Sara? You need a break as much as I do."

"I'm sure. Go ahead and enjoy."

"Hartley Savitch, one question before I let you escort me out for the evening. When you go to the market and you're wandering around aimlessly in the produce department--how do you feel about the melons?"

##

TO REQUEST ADDITIONAL COPIES OF:

ONCE UPON A MURDER

AVAILABLE AT YOUR LOCAL BOOKSTORE, OR
SEND $6.95 PLUS $2.00 POSTAGE AND HANDLING
(CHECK OR MONEY ORDERS ONLY) TO:

**AMPERSAND PRESS
P.O. BOX 91445
CITY OF INDUSTRY, CA 91715-1445**

PLEASE INDICATE COMPLETE SHIPPING ADDRESS TO AVOID DELAYS

ALL ORDERS ARE SUBJECT TO AVAILABILITY. VALID IN U.S. ONLY
PRICES MAY INCREASE DUE TO CHANGES IN SALES TAX AND POSTAGE
EXPECTED DELIVERY WITHIN THREE WEEKS.

##